Thugs Cry 2

**Lock Down Publications
Presents
Thugs Cry 2
A Novel by *CA$H***

Lock Down Publications

P.O. Box 1482
Pine Lake, Ga 30072-1482

Lock Down Publications
Email: ldp.cash@gmail.com
Facebook: Cassius Alexander
Like our page on Facebook: Lock Down Publications @
www.facebook.com/lockdownpublications.ldp
Follow me on Twitter: https://twitter.com/cashshtreetlit
Cover design and layout by: **Marion Designs**
Book interior design by: **Shawn Walker**
Edited by: **Shawn Walker**

Ca$h

ONE

CJ

"Tamika, answer your muhfuckin' phone, ma! Fa real, baby girl. I hope you're not on no grimy shit!" That's the message I left on love's cell phone after being sent to voicemail for the third straight time.

Something didn't feel right. I had this mad crazy ass feeling in the pit of my stomach as I drove down Clinton Avenue in my black 2011 Maybach 62S, observing the traffic going in and out of my trap in the Stratford Apartments.

The line of *uncs* and *aunties* waiting to get served some Yack, Xanax or Percocet was wrapped around the building. It didn't matter that these apartments were only six blocks away from the Fifth Precinct because I paid *them boys* to look the other way. Niggaz couldn't fuck with my hustle. I had the hottest name in Newark since Akbar Pray. Bitches were sprung on my dark skin tone, my perpetual scowl, and my turnt up swag. I had mad honies tryna cuff a nigga, but only one mattered to me. Nah mean?

This was my favorite time of the year. The nostalgia of summer was fading to black and the days were cooler, making it perfect chill weather. I was looking forward to swooping up lil' mama and doing just that. I dialed her number for the fourth time but again I was sent to voicemail. "Fuck you at, ma?" I mumbled, tossing my iPhone on the console between the front seats then turning down the music so I could hear myself think.

"Everything a'ight, big bruh?" asked Eric from the passenger seat.

"I don't know, fam," I replied, stopping at the red light on Clinton and Bergen.

Glancing over at Mama Kim's Deli, I ran a hand down my face as worry rose up in my chest. I hadn't spoken with Tamika since

5

earlier today. What had me concerned was we had just gotten back together a week ago after months of doing our own thing. The green laces, the street fame, and the groupie hos had gone to my head for a minute, causing mad conflict between me and my girl. I had fucked Tamika's cousin Nee Nee—a violation that had broken Tamika's heart but baby girl had forgiven me for all that dumb shit.

On the flip side, I had to swallow my pride to get back with her. While we were beefin', Tamika hooked up with this young boy named Nard, who was from Little Bricks as well. It fucked with my pride every time I heard that she was seen somewhere with him. It shouldn't have mattered what the fuck I did in the streets, Tamika was supposed to have kept it tight. But I guess she got tired of me shittin' on her with the next bitch and decided that we both could play that game.

For years I had taken her for granted, figuring that because I kept her laced she would never leave me. When she finally bounced, a nigga was fucked up. Around my mans I fronted like it was nothin', but that shit had me sick. That's why I went and snatched Tamika right off Nard's arm. I had to let the streets know that Cam'ron Jeffries is still that muhfuckin' nigga in The Bricks.

I fell up in The Atmosphere with my goons to reclaim my bitch, straight G-style. We surrounded VIP ready to put some niggaz on their asses if Nard's team didn't bow down. For a minute shit got real tense up in that piece until Nard realized that fuckin' with me would be like pissing in the wind, I was going to be all over that ass. He quickly got his people to fall back.

I walked out of the club that night with Tamika back on my arm where she belonged. Fuck that nigga think?

I got my girl back but I was still crushed inside because Tamika was bunned up with that young boy's seed. I had taken her to have an abortion ASAP. At the clinic, she looked at me with tears brimming her pretty brown doe eyes.

6

"CJ, do I have to do this? Can't I have the baby and give it to Nard?" she asked.

The question almost made me snap her neck. I bared my teeth and gritted, "Fuck no, ma! You're not having the next niggaz' child. Fuck I look like? You either go in there and do what the fuck you gotta do or I'm done. Straight up!"

Tamika dropped her head and began fidgeting with her hands. I put my hands on the steering wheel and stared out the window, breathing fire out of my nose. We sat in the parking lot with nothin' else being said as she weighed her decision. I was becoming more heated by the second, her hesitancy made a nigga feel some kind of way. I was seconds away from pulling off and taking her right back to that nigga since she seemed to have such a difficult time deciding what she wanted. Fuck I look like?

"CJ, do you really love me?" she asked on the verge of breaking down. The hurt in her voice calmed me down.

"Of course I love you, Mika. A nigga was sick without you, ma. I know I've been fuckin' up, but I promise you I'm gonna change." I reached over and pulled her into my arms. Her tears erupted and she sobbed loudly against my chest. "It's gonna be okay, ma," I soothed, rubbing her back.

"You promise?"

"Yeah, Love, I promise."

She looked up at me with tears still running down her face. "CJ, I love you so much," she whimpered.

"I love you too, baby girl. And I always have. I promise I'ma get on my square, a'ight?" I replied sincerely.

Whether she believed me or not didn't matter, I meant that shit from my heart. Fuck all the thirsty bitches that were on my dick now that I was gettin' more green laces than the U.S. Treasury. Tamika had held me down when I was nothin' but a block hugger with boss nigga dreams.

I gently took her face between my hands and wiped her tears with my thumbs then I leaned in and kissed her lips. "Ma, let's go and get this over with, a'ight?"

"Can you just hold me a little while longer, please?" she pleaded.

I pulled her further into my arms and told her how sorry I was for all of the bullshit I had ever done to hurt her. "From now on it's just you and me, ma," I promised. I lifted her chin so that her wet eyes locked with mine. "You still belong to me? Mind, body and soul?" I asked.

Looking deeper into my eyes, she replied, "Yes. I've always belonged to you CJ, and I always will. I'm sorry too, Papi. I should have never gotten myself into this predicament." Sincerity dripped from her every word like blood drops from a punctured heart.

"It's a'ight, Love. I forgive you. Let's go take care of this."

Tamika took a deep breath. "I'm ready, baby."

We got out of the car and walked in the clinic hand in hand. After the procedure was performed, we went back to Tamika's house. I could tell that the abortion remained heavy on her heart because sadness was etched across her face and she hadn't said two words since we left the clinic.

"You having regrets about that shit?" I asked with an undisguised attitude.

"No, I'm good, baby," she said but I didn't believed her. I called her Mom Dukes over to sit with her while I went out to handle my business. I needed to get out of her presence before I mistook her sorrow for remorse.

I heard a horn honking behind me. I had been so deep in thought I hadn't realized the light was now green. Eric hopped out of the whip in broad daylight waving his fo-fifth at the impatient fools behind us. "Just wait, muhfucka!" barked my fourteen year old brother. I smiled proudly because he was a young beast in the making.

"Fuck them clown ass niggaz, they don't want it," I called out to him and he got back in the ride.

As we pulled off, I picked up my cell phone and tried Tamika's number one last time, gettin' the same result as before. She knew that I hated it when she didn't answer her phone, and this had been going on for hours.

Maybe she went back to Nard, I considered for a second. Nah, she would never do no retarded shit like that. I was the air she breathed. It had to be some other reason she wasn't answering her phone.

Eric looked over and saw the worried look on my face. "Sup, fam?" he asked.

"Somethin' ain't right. Shorty wouldn't just ignore my call." I thought of every explanation but none made sense. Was I trippin' for no reason? "It's probably nothin'," I said.

"Maybe not, but let's go check it out." He click-clacked one in the chamber as I pressed down on the gas pedal.

Ca$h

TWO

CJ

As soon as we pulled up at Tamika's house I saw the cherry red 2011 BMW that I had copped for her the other day sittin' in the driveway next to her mother's silver Altima. A white Yukon, which I knew belonged to Tamika's cousin Danyelle, was parked at the curb. They were probably inside running their mouths.

I parked at the curb and mobbed up on the front porch with Eric close on my heels. I knocked on the door and waited for someone to answer, but no one came to the door. "Mika! Fuck y'all doing in there?" I pounded.

Still no muhfuckin' answer.

Eric pressed his ear against the door. "Bruh, it's mad quiet up in that piece, they must be asleep," he said.

I shook my head. "Not this time of day." I had a premonition that shit just wasn't right.

I reached down and tried the doorknob and to my surprise it was unlocked. I looked over my shoulder at Eric, his tool was out and down at his side. "This ain't good, yo," I uttered.

I eased my Nine off my waist and stepped inside. I was ready to blast at the first sign of trouble. "Mika where you at ma?" My eyes darted around as I cautiously walked through the living room. The house was as quiet as a tomb.

"Lil bruh, I'm going to check upstairs. You check shit out down here. If anything is wrong, don't hesitate to air this bitch out," I instructed. "Stay on point."

A feeling of dread came over me like fever as I climbed the staircase and entered Tamika's bedroom. Her canopy bed was neatly made and nothin' appeared to be out of place. I could smell the scent of her perfume in the air, but where the fuck was she at?

11

Did she go back to that young boy? I asked myself again. I couldn't see Tamika playing me like that. I looked around the bedroom for signs that something was wrong. Her dresser was lined with bottles of perfume that hadn't been disturbed and the clothes in her walk-in closet we're neatly arranged as usual, but an eeriness seemed to hang in the air as thick as city fog.

"CJ! Come down here quick, yo!" Eric called up to me excited-ly.

I hurried out of the bedroom and bounded down the stairs. Eric was waiting for me at the bottom of the staircase wearing a look that I had only seen on his face once before; that had been after our Mom Dukes and little sister got killed.

I looked at him and when his eyes wouldn't meet mine I knew what it meant. "No, bruh, don't tell me..."

I couldn't even finish the sentence.

"Yeah, bruh, I found 'em. They're in the den, all three of 'em." Eric's voice was so heavy with grief it left no doubt, but I didn't wanna accept it.

"Man, don't tell me no shit like that, yo. My girl ain't dead!" I shoved him against the wall.

"I'm sorry big bruh." He casted his eyes down to the floor.

"Where are they?"

"In the den. It's bad my nigga. Somebody did them real dirty," he mumbled.

My heart pounded as I walked to the back of the house where the den was located, praying that Eric was wrong. When I stepped in the room blood was all over the walls, floor, and the furniture. I stopped right there in the doorway as suddenly my airways felt constricted. My breath felt short and my pulse quickened. For the first time in my life my hands trembled.

On weighted legs I stepped further into the den. Tamika's mother's half-naked body was sprawled on the side of the couch.

Her head rested in a puddle of drying blood that had turned the beige carpet a dark brown beneath it.

"Nah, man. Nah!" I shook my head in disbelief. Not Ms. Jerkins. Things hadn't always been good between us because she hadn't held her tongue whenever I shitted on her daughter, but I cared for her. To see her like that fucked me up.

I turned my head away from the sight but that spared me nothing. To my left Danyelle's body was slumped on the sofa. I stepped closer and leaned down to see if she was still breathing because her eyes were open. But if she could see anything it was on the other side where angels rested. A streak of dried blood ran from a bullet hole in the center of her forehead down her face. In death she wore a grimace on her face that was an insult to the beautiful smile that she had worn in life.

Danyelle had loved everyone. Even when I did trifling shit behind Tamika's back and it became known, Danyelle never spoke against me. She was the type of good-hearted person that always saw the good in people and I had loved her for that.

"Is shorty done with me for real this time?" I had asked *Danyelle after Tamika found out that I fucked Nee Nee.*

"Love prevails CJ, but you have to stop taking her for granted or the love will die," she had once advised.

Danyelle had been wrong about that. Tamika's love for me had never perished, but the advice had been given with heartfelt concern that defined who she was.

"Damn, your heart was too good for you to die like this," I said, shaking my head.

I closed my eyes and tried to block out what I knew was next. I had slayed entire families in this same cold, heartless fashion. Now karma had come back to serve me the same pain that I had dished others.

I sucked in my breath and manned up to face what I knew would crush my heart. "Where my baby at?" I asked in a tone hoarse with impending grief.

"She's behind the couch," informed Eric.

I took another deep breath before I opened my eyes and prepared myself to see what I knew awaited me. Eric put a hand on my elbow. "Don't go look at her, big bruh. You don't want to remember her like that," he said, sounding like the man-child that the streets of Newark had bred him to be.

"I'm good," I said.

I stepped over Ms. Jerkin's body and wearily walked behind the couch. I saw her feet first; her toenails were painted in a rainbow of purple, pink, and blue just like they had been the other night when I massaged her feet. As my eyes slowly traveled from her feet, up her legs, and to her body, I saw that her entire midsection was covered with blood. My legs wobbled and I stumbled back into the wall, squeezing my eyes shut to block out a reality too painful to accept.

I knew I had no right to call on Him because I lived in direct opposition to everything that I had ever been taught about God, but with all other hope gone I did the only thing that was left to do—I prayed. For the very first time in my life. I didn't know how to pray so I just talked to Him in my own way.

"God," I said quickly. "I know that I've done a lot of foul things yo. So you probably don't fuck wit' me. But I'll make you a deal. Just don't let her be dead, and I promise to walk away from the streets. I'll stop hustlin', killin', er'thing. I'll leave this gutter life alone and pick up The Good Book and spread your word all over the same hoods that I helped destroy. Just don't let my girl be dead. Do me that one good and I'll turn my life over to You."

I stood there for a moment before I opened my eyes to see if He had heard my prayer. The answer was *Hell no!* My girl was curled up on her side with her knees drawn up to her chest.

"I knew you didn't muhfuckin' exist," I gritted bitterly. "And if you do, you never have answered a hood niggaz' prayer."

I reached up and wiped the tears that were running down my face. And with the strength of a warrior I faced the death of my baby girl without His assistance.

A bullet hole was in the center of her left cheek and the collar of her baby blue silk top was sticky with blood. Her hair was splayed all over her head and it was matted with blood. One of her eyes was open and the other was shut tight, as if she had winced right before being shot. The image of the terror that she must've felt flashed through my mind vividly.

"Mika, I'm sorry, baby."

There was no question, baby girl was dead. I had taken many lives myself, up close and personal, so I knew death when I saw it. I sat down with my legs spread out and placed my banger on the floor right beside me, then I gently lifted Mika's head and rested it in my lap. Blood soaked my jeans but I didn't give a fuck.

"Baby—baby—baby," I broke down. "This is all my fault ma. If I hadn't let my ego take control this wouldn't have happened."

"You want me to call 911, yo?" asked Eric.

"For what, lil' bruh? She's gone. My girl is gone away."

I leaned my forehead against Tamika's and my tears mixed with the blood on her face. I kissed her lips and whispered, "Shorty, I'm sorry. I should have never made you do it like that. You shouldn't have had to prove a muhfuckin' thing to me. Damn baby girl, I wish you would've told me no. Fuck my pride and all the other shit that don't really matter. Shorty, I would give anything to undo this shit right here. Fa real, lil' mama, you know nothin' will ever be the same without you."

I hugged my boo tight and thought about all the ridiculous things I had put her through. Fuck was my problem? Why hadn't I been able to appreciate her love before things became so tragic?

15

Guilt pushed the tears from my eyes in floods. Eric looked down at me with sorrow all over his face. The only other time that he had ever seen me shed tears was when enemies of mine had murdered our Mom Dukes and our baby sister. I had gone on a killing spree after that as surely as I would go on one now.

"You a'ight, fam?" he asked.

"Nah, lil' souljah, I'm not a'ight. I'm not even gonna lie to you. Shorty was my heart. This shit right here has me fucked up, nah mean?" I fought back more tears for Eric's sake. I didn't want to destroy his image of me.

"Bruh, we gotta call 911," he said, displaying the calm that he had learned by watching me come up in the game, eliminating one rival after the other.

"I'll make the call. Take our tools outside and put them in the stash box inside the car. Once them boys get here they're gonna be all over us."

"A'ight." He bent down and picked up my strap. "I got it."

When he was gone I rocked Tamika in my arms and whispered, "I love you, ma. I always did, and I always will. I cost you your life shorty. I'm sorry for that. But I know who did this shit to you. On er'thing, I'ma kill that bitch ass nigga and everyone that he loves."

I held my baby girl tenderly as memories of her and I ran through my mind. Back when I was pitchin' stones she used to be out there with me watching out for the rollers so I wouldn't get cased up. I thought about the time when I had planned a birthday party at the club for Tamika and everything had gone crazy.

I was at the club with her Mom, Danyelle, and Tamika's bestie Star, tryna trick Tamika to come so that we could catch her off guard right as she walked through the door. The club was packed with people waiting to scream surprise!

Tamika had been at home moping because she thought that I was out with some other broad and that I had forgotten her birthday. Star had called her and tried to get her to come to the club without telling her I was throwing her a B-Day party, but Tamika was on some other shit. Star passed me the phone.

"*Tamika! What you doing, yo?*" *I questioned.*

"*Fuck you, CJ,*" *she cried. Then I heard the commode. "Did you hear that, muthafucka? I just flushed a kilo of your shit down the toilet.*"

"*Tamika! Don't do that shit, yo!*" *I barked.*

"*Fuck you, black bastard! You can be with your other ho. I'm flushing all of your shit down the muthafuckin' toilet!*" *She hung up the phone and refused to answer when I called back. By the time I got there she had flushed seventeen bricks!*

"Damn, Mika. This some hard shit to cope wit', yo!" I wept. Our relationship had been an inferno at times and at other times it was the epitome of hood love. Arguing, breaking up, making up, fighting, fuckin', ballin', shopping, jealousy. We couldn't live with or without each other. So much craziness but so much love. Muthafuckaz might not have understood why we just couldn't walk away from each other and stay away but we understood it.

"I stashed the guns, bruh. Now we gotta call 911," Eric's voice came from behind me.

"You make the call. I'ma just hold my girl," I muttered.

Eric dialed 911 while I held Tamika's body in my arms and plotted my revenge on the nigga that had taken her away from me. Nard had cut my heart out, so I made a vow to myself to literally do the same thing to him.

"Call the goons and tell 'em to get strapped. I want everybody in killa mode. Call Rah and tell him I need him."

The Bricks was about to see vengeance in biblical proportions.

Ca$h

THREE

RAHEEM

R&B SONGSTRESS SPARKLE DEAD AT AGE 25 screamed the headline that ran across the top of the Star- Ledger in big, boldface print.

I stared down at the headline in disbelief. Kayundra's dead? No matter how many times I read it or heard it broadcasted on the radio, it just didn't register. I sucked in air to help calm the emotions that swelled up inside of my chest threatening to fold me over in grief. My head felt dizzy from the shock of the tragic news, though hours had passed since I first learned of her death.

My sister, LaKeesha, had called in the middle of the night, crying, "Rah, turn on your television. It's all over the news; Kayundra is dead!"

It had felt like a bad dream, but the reality was worse. I had woke up and flicked the television on. The station was already programmed to *BET* where I had left it last night when I turned it off.

"It is being reported that R&B singer Sparkle is dead," said a somber sounding newscaster.

After hearing those words, I rushed out the house and caught an overnight flight out of my Atlanta home to Newark. I needed to be around fam and friends just to keep my sanity because Sparkle's death rocked me to the core.

I sat on the flower-printed sofa in Big Ma's apartment in Georgia King, in a daze. My eyes watered as I read the article that accompanied the screaming headline. The word *suicide* hit me like a bullet to the center of my heart. I bowed my head, fighting back tears. She had said many times that she would rather die than live without me but I hadn't taken her threat seriously. I knew that she was a fragile bird with wings that were easily broken, but I had always believed that she would soar with or without me.

How wrong I had been.

A single tear broke from the dam that was holding them back. It trickled down my face, hot on my skin, plopping onto the article and smearing the ink in the very spot where her name appeared in the first sentence.

Sparkle. I had given her that pet name before she became known to the world. I had called her that because even when she was down and out—before the music and the fame—there was this glint in her eyes; a sparkle when she talked about her musical dreams.

I sniffled back more tears as fond memories of the only girl that I had ever loved came rushing to the forefront of my thoughts. *Our first tongue kiss as adolescents. Sharing burgers at White Castles on Elizabeth Ave. The first time, as teenagers, that we made love. We had been each other's first. She had bitten down on her bottom lip as I patiently pushed inside of her, breaking her hymen. Afterwards, we had vowed to always be in love. I'd held her in my arms and listened to her sing in a whisper.*

"Her voice was so beautiful," I said, burying my face in my hands.

Big Ma sat on one side of me rubbing my back consolingly. On the other side of me LaKeesha wept openly.

"I let her down," I said.

"No, Raheem, you didn't. You did everything in your power to save her from her from destruction. There's only so much you could do. That life was way too fast for her," imparted Big Ma, sagely. But I shook off her wisdom.

"Big Ma, I was supposed to protect her. I knew that she was weak without me. And even though she betrayed my trust I still loved her. I allowed foolish pride to stand in the way of us getting back together. I was supposed to set all of that aside and love her unconditionally."

I rose up off the sofa and walked over to the window with my hands shoved down in my pockets and my shoulders slumped. Guilt and shock had me in a torturous headlock that the streets of Newark hadn't ever been able to put me in. I felt trapped within my own torment, like residents of the projects who saw no way out of their misery. I had never succumbed to that type of despair but this was something altogether different. One minute I was applauding Sparkle's courage, and the next minute I was feeling responsible for her tragic demise.

Just last night I had watched her perform live on BET. The whole world had held its collective breath waiting to hear her belt out that first beautiful note after returning from a drug addiction that had pulled her down so low that many had given up on her. But not me. Her transgressions had cut me too deep to take her back as my woman, but I had continued to love and support her during her recovery.

I had tuned in last night to hear her debut the first single to be released off her new CD. We were surprised when she took the stage and announced, "I was supposed to sing something from my new CD for y'all tonight, but there's been a change of plans. By now I'm sure everybody has heard about what I've been going through."

The television cameras zoomed in for a close up, catching the tears as they welled up in her eyes.

"I've lost a lot of things this past year. But none of it matters as much as the man I lost. How many of you ladies out there know what it is to lose the man you love?" Sparkle asked the live audience.

The women in attendance roared and urged her to go on.

"Well, I lost the man I love and it doesn't feel good. So, tonight I want to sing a song by the late, great Minnie Riperton, and I want

to dedicate it to the man I lost. Raheem, if you're out there watching, this is for you baby."

I had known which song she was going to sing before the first melody came across the airwaves. It was the same song that she had sung to win the talent show in junior high school.

"I stumbled on this photograph/ it kind of made me laugh/ it took me way back/ back down memory lane..."

The close-up camera shot showed the pain in her eyes as the lyrics came out with the sincerity found in a woman's diary.

"The way you held me/ no one could tell me that love would dieee..."

Sparkle belted out the high note from deep down in her soul where her many regrets resided. What came out was beautiful but heart wrenching.

The hurt in her heart had risen up like a tidal wave and washed over her so completely that she sunk to her knees in tears. The microphone clattered down on the stage, highlighting her pain. She had to be lifted up and helped backstage. The dramatic scene sent the ratings rocketing through the roof as many cried in their homes right along with her.

Big Ma had called to say, "That poor child. She misses you so much."

Surely there were some people watching that were cynical and suspected that the whole thing had been a publicity stunt to help rejuvenate Sparkle's meteoric rise to R&B superstardom. But when they turned on their television sets or read their newspapers this morning they would see proof that Sparkle's last performance was not a stunt. Nothing was more evident of that than her body lying up in a morgue.

I stared out of the window of Big Ma's 4th floor apartment into the slight drizzle of rain that fell from gray clouds that appeared to be low enough to reach up and touch. My mood matched the dreary weather.

"I should have given her one more chance," I said somberly as I brought my cell phone out of my pocket and stared at her face, which I had kept as my screen saver.

I dialed her number for the tenth time since learning of her suicide. I just didn't want to accept that she was gone.

I'm sorry I can't answer your call at the moment but please leave your name and number and I'll return your call at my earliest convenience. If this is Raheem, baby I love and miss and need you so much. Please come back to me. I am nothing without you.

My knees buckled. I dropped the cell phone and put my hands against both sides of the windowpane to hold myself up. Big Ma and LaKeesha rushed over to me.

"I'm good," I said.

I leaned my head against the window and listened to the melody of the raindrops drum against it. I could hear her singing softly to the rhythm of the rain. Allah knows I would've given anything to hear that angelic voice live again.

"LaKeesha, hand me my phone please," I spoke without making eye contact. I had to hit my nigga up, even though it was no secret that CJ hadn't cared for Kayundra.

To the rest of the world she was Sparkle, the R&B songstress with the most soulful voice in the industry. But to CJ she was nothing more than just another crack fiend.

"That bitch was nothin' until you came back home and pulled her up out of the gutters, yo. The only "sparkle" muhfuckaz associated with her was the one that flashed when she was hittin' the crack pipe. Then as soon as you rescued her ratchet ass and helped her bubble, the ungrateful ho betrayed you for the next nigga," CJ had spat venomously the last time that we had talked about Kayundra.

I hadn't ever traded words with my man about his deep dislike for Kayundra. CJ hadn't been hatin' on her come-up. That was just the way he expressed his love for me.

"It's all good, fam. As long as she's good, I'm good," I had assured him.

"Fuck that yo! I wanna see her reward you for all that you did for her. Because before you came back in her life she was a ratchet ass mess."

Recalling his bitter words now, my mind flashed back to what he was referring to. It was several years ago, and I had returned home from school on spring vacation.

I got out of the Tahoe with my fitted pulled down low, carrying the Gucci garment bag and a suitcase. I chirped the alarm and walked toward the front of the building. Suddenly, I was accosted by a fiend that looked like a skeleton with big bulging eyes about to pop out of her head.

"Sup, man? I'll suck your dick for five, take you around the world for ten. I got the tightest pussy ya dick has ever been in." *The fiend made her pitch as she reached out and grabbed my crotch.*

I smacked her hand away and stared into her face horrified.

"C'mon, man, just ten fuckin' dollars, and I'll fuck and suck you so good. C'mon, man."

"Kayundra! What the fuck happened to you yo?" *I shouted in disgust.*

"I'm good, baby. I'm tryin' to make you good too," *she replied, not recognizing me in the darkness.*

I sat my luggage down and removed my fitted. Then I grabbed her face with both hands. "Ma, this is Raheem you're talkin' to!" I grilled her.

Kayundra's eyes got even bigger as she recognized my face and my voice. She dropped her head in embarrassment and *fidgeted with her hands. I reached out to hug her, wanting to rescue her from the demons that had claimed her but she broke away from me and bolted off.*

That was the Kayundra that CJ forever judged her to be, but I had seen the gem that was buried deep underneath the ravages of her addiction.

After that night, it had become my mission to get her some help while I was home on vacation.

With my encouragement, Kayundra had entered a drug recovery program for the first time. With my love as her support, she had made it through and gained the strength to pursue her life-long dream to break into the music industry. The day she signed her very first professional contract, she had called me screaming with excitement. *"Baby, I got signed to a record deal! I love you so much for helping me do this."*

There was a pang in my heart as I remembered that now. The world seemed to be at our fingertips. And just a few months later when her first single soared to the top of the charts, Newark residents applauded the success of one of our own. I was mad proud of her.

Soon after that, Sparkle was scheduled to go on tour. Everyone expected her to be excited, but she was frightened to death. *"Please come with me, Rah,"* she had begged me.

"You'll be fine," I tried to reassure her.

But she hadn't been fine at all, and that was the beginning of a plummet that would take her way down. It destroyed a love between us that had once seemed epic.

"I failed her," I said as I dialed CJ's number. His phone rang and rang until his voicemail picked up. I waited until I heard the beep then I left him a short message. *"Fam, get at me."*

I hung up and stared out the window chastising myself for all the things I should've done but would never get the chance to do.

Ca$h

FOUR

CJ

I stood alone in the corner of the waiting room at the city morgue pounding my fists against the wall in a combination of burden and frustration.

"Damn, Mika, I fucked up." I leaned my head against the wall and tried to pull myself together.

Ten feet away my goons were huddled together tryna figure out what to do. No one knew what to say; they had never witnessed me this distraught before. I knew that they were watching to see how I handled this. I had already proven to them that I was not to be tested. They knew my get-down, but the streets will make a man prove himself over and over again. When adversity struck a boss nigga couldn't afford to appear weakened by it.

I straightened my shoulders and rejoined my team. I walked into the middle of the semi-circle that they formed, commanding their attention with my steady tone. "We're murking Nard and anybody associated with him," I said at a low decibel because several detectives hovered around.

I spotted my connect, Cujo, who was a narc with the city of Newark. He was talking to one of the detectives that had questioned me. Our eyes met briefly.

Cujo motioned with his head for me to walk outside. I frowned because I didn't feel like hearing his bullshit. He would plead with me to let the police handle what had happened, but I wasn't tryna hear that. Nah mean?

Tamika was dead. Danyelle was dead. Ms. Jerkins was dead! There was no muhfuckin' way I would just sit back and let the po po handle mines. "I'ma walk outside and clear my head yo," I told my niggaz.

27

"Let me go wit' you, fam, just in case that nigga is out there lurking," said Premo.

"Nah, I'm good, son. That nigga ain't built to come at me right here."

I strolled outside with a scowl on my face. A moment later Cujo joined me. He fired up a cigarette and blew smoke rings in the air. The sun was beginning to fade behind the clouds. Soon the sky would be as dark as my soul.

"What the hell happened?" inquired Cujo, leaning against the hood of his unmarked police vehicle. I didn't respond. I was devising Nard's death in my mind. "CJ, talk to me."

"There's nothin' to talk about. You already know what's about to happen so what the fuck do I need to say."

"Okay, I see where this is headed. I'm warning you not to take it there. We have a sweet arrangement, let's not fuck it up. If you know who did this, tell me and I'll have them dealt with any way you want. You don't have to run around killing recklessly. You have killers with badges on your team, let us do what we do," he urged.

I looked up at the cracker like he was retarded. "Nah man, this one is very personal. Don't even come at me with no alternatives. Right now I don't give a fuck about no coke, no money, or none of that shit. My shorty is in there laid out on a cold steel slab with her insides on the outside, and best believe a bitch is gonna pay for dat. You better tell your brethren to get the body bags ready, 'cause the streets are about to feel my pain," I decreed.

"I told you once before that murders bring heat. And heat is bad for business," Cujo whispered harshly as his beady eyes darted around. He dropped the cigarette on the ground and smashed it out with the heel of his patent leather shoe. The thought ran through my mind that that's how I was gonna crush Nard's punk ass.

Cujo shoved his hands down in his pockets and glared at me. I ⌐ded my arms across my chest and glared back. I could read his mind like an open book. I was a nigga that he couldn't control, and he detested that. The only reason he continued to fuck with me was because I was sick with my hustle and we made each other rich.

"I won't let you bring me down," he warned.

"You threatening me, cracker?" I unfolded my arms and balled up my fist. I didn't give a fuck about nothin'. If the wrong thing came out of his mouth I was gonna punch him in his shit.

"I don't make threats, CJ," he stated.

"Good, because I don't take 'em lightly and I never forgive 'em," I snarled, looking him in the eye. He could get it right there in the parking lot.

Cujo saw that I was ready to unleash my fury on whomever got in my way. He lowered his eyes just a second; long enough to let me know that he didn't wanna take it there. I turned and went back inside.

"CJ?" he called out, but I didn't turn around. Fuck that shit he was saying.

"You a'ight, fam?" asked Snoop when I rejoined them.

"Yeah, I'm good, B. Y'all can go on home now. It's business as usual. Don't nothin' stop the grind. I'll let y'all know when it's time to ride. I wanna bury my girl first."

As my goons headed out the door, I walked over to the water fountain to wet my throat before leaving. My cell phone vibrated in my pocket as I bent over the fountain and let the cold water splash over my dry lips. I took a swallow, and then rose up.

I felt someone wrap their arms around me from behind, in a feminine embrace. Their perfume wafted up my nose. I whirled around and was looking into Nee Nee's tear-stained face.

"Oh, my God. CJ, what happened?" She laid her head against my chest and wept uncontrollably.

"I don't know."

"Are they all dead for real?"

"Yeah, ma."

The sobs that came from Nee Nee echoed off the walls. I held her up so that she wouldn't collapse under her pain. Just then Star came running through the door. She looked ghetto fabulous in spite of the situation. She rushed up to us crying. "I just heard. Please tell me it's not true."

I removed my arms from around Nee Nee and gave Star a consoling hug. "It's true. My shorty is dead. Her mother and Danyelle too."

"This is too much!" She burst out in sobs.

We'd had our battles in the past because Star was loose with the goodies and I always worried that she was tryna hook Tamika up with other niggaz, but there was no doubt that she was a true friend to Tamika. She had never come at me sideways behind Mika's back, and they were there for each other in times of need.

"CJ, do you think Nard had something to do with this?" asked Star in a low tone.

I nodded *yeah*.

"You better make him pay!" she replied tersely.

I nodded again.

The fire in Star's eyes matched my own. Since contracting the HIV virus, she had given her life to God, but obviously she adhered to the adage "an eye for an eye" as opposed to "turning the other cheek."

"I want to see her," she said.

"Nah, I don't want you to remember her like that."

All of a sudden she looked at Nee Nee, breathing flames as if she had just noticed her standing there. "Why is your ratchet ass here?" she hissed.

"Because they're my family, bitch! What!" Nee Nee snapped.

"You didn't think about that when you were fuckin' my girl's man. Ol' thirsty ass ho."

Nee Nee kicked off her shoes and began removing her hoop earrings. "Bitch, you want some of this? Coming at me with that silly shit while my sister, cousin and auntie lie up in there dead."

"It should've been your grimy ass," spat Star, stepping toward her with her fist balled up.

I leaned in and pulled Nee Nee back. "Y'all not doing that shit up in here," I said, straining to keep her from going ham. "Star, chill the fuck out yo."

"Let me go, CJ! I'll fuck that bitch up. Who does she think she is? Bitch you fucked for a living and that's why your nasty ass have HIV."

Star charged at her throwing fists. A few punches connected with Nee Nee's jaw and she broke free of my grasp and her and Star started throwing down hood style, grabbing each other's hair and ripping each other's clothes. A couple of detectives came over and pulled them apart.

"Muthafucka, don't touch me!" Nee Nee raged.

"Ma'am if you don't calm down you're going to jail," one of the DT's warned.

"I don't give a fuuuccckkk!" she screamed, tryna come after Star again.

I grabbed Star around the waist and pulled her toward the door. "Chill the fuck out," I said.

Star followed my command but she stared at Nee Nee with contempt. "I want that ass bitch," she hurled one last insult.

"You can get it!" Nee Nee retorted, tryna break free.

"Man, sit your ass down," I shouted and carried Star outside.

"I'ma get that bitch," she huffed.

"Girl, cover your titties up and act like you got some damn sense. Out here acting ghetto as hell. I thought you're supposed to be saved. Turn the other cheek—you ever heard of that?"

Star fixed her clothes. "I can't stand that bitch," she seethed. "I wanna snatch that cheap ass weave outta her head. Ol' backstabbing trick. Eww! I swear CJ if you fuck with that bitch again I'll hate you; that would be spitting on my girl's grave."

"Chill, I'm not thinking about Nee Nee like that. My mind is on murder."

"It better be."

I looked at her curiously. "I thought you was all saved and shit?"

"An eye for an eye, nigga," she confirmed.

I nodded. "You know how I do. That nigga and everything he loves is gonna suffer for what he did to my baby."

"Damn, this is too sad. I was just talking to her earlier today. Man, I can't believe this." Tears began streaming down her face.

I wrapped my arms around her and let her cry in my arms. "Man, everybody is dying. I can't take this."

"What you mean 'everybody'? Who else died?" I asked.

"Didn't you hear about Sparkle?"

"Who?"

"Kayundra."

"Nah. What about her?" I asked.

"She committed suicide last night," reported Star.

"Dayum yo!" I remarked, knowing that my nigga Rah would be fucked up over it.

I unwrapped my arms from around Star and whipped out my cell phone to hit my people up. The light on my phone came on and I saw that I had several missed calls from Rah. I immediately hit him back.

"Sup, fam?" he answered in a dour tone. I could hear mad stress in his voice.

"I heard about your girl, and I'm real sorry to hear that. If you need me to come to the 'A', I'm there—ASAP."

"Nah, son, I'm in Newark. I flew in today. I'm over at Big Ma's," he said.

"A'ight, fam, I'ma come through in a minute. But I have some more bad news to tell you." I paused. "Tamika is dead and so is her mother and her cousin Danyelle." My voice almost cracked.

"Nah, son. Don't tell me that."

"Yeah, man, I'm fucked up over it."

"What happened? Were they in a car accident?" questioned Rah.

I walked off before answering because I didn't wanna put Star in the middle of men's business like dat. I had already said too much.

When I was out of earshot, I said, "Nah, fam, it wasn't a car accident. Nard and 'em ran up in Tamika's house and laid 'em down. They killed my boo and her peeps execution-style. They did my baby real foul."

"Damn," he replied with incredulity.

"Yeah, son. I know it was Nard because wasn't nothin' taken. That was retaliation for me making Tamika clown him. So I'm about to show him that when he touch mine, I touch back twice as hard."

"I feel you. Where you at?"

"At the morgue, but I'm about to head home."

"To your spot out New Haven?"

"Yeah. I gotta get my mind right. It's about to get turnt up, nah mean?"

"Don't do nothing yet. I'm gonna get Big Ma's car and meet you at your house, a'ight?"

"I appreciate you dawg, but you're over there dealing with your own loss. I'm good my nigga. I got a team full of goons to help me handle this," I assured him.

"Just chill, yo. I'm on my way." He hung up before I could object. That's how it was with us. Love was love and nothin' would ever change it.

Hours later, I was at the crib that I had up in New Haven, Connecticut. I was sitting in my refurnished basement, leaned back in my Italian leather recliner, blowing Kush and thinking about Tamika. Eric sat quietly on the couch, looking up at me occasionally.

"Sup, lil' souljah?" I broke the silence.

"Nothin'. I'm just thinkin," he replied with a look on his baby face that conveyed that he was worried about me.

I looked at him with the same confidence that had propelled me to made-man status in the muthafuckin' game. "Don't sweat it yo. You know your big bruh is a beast. This shit right here can't bring me down. What I look like lettin' a peon take my throne? That nigga ain't no threat to what I put together—he's not no killa. He laid three women down and killed 'em. That don't make him no beast. Real killaz murk other killaz," I said.

"I'm not worried," said Eric, but the tone of his voice wasn't convincing.

Eric wasn't afraid; he epitomized the 90's babies. Smashing a nigga was part of those youngin's pedigree. They came out the womb laying bitch niggaz down and opening up their backs. Nard didn't have my lil' brother shook; it was more like Eric was worried about my state of mind. He knew how much this shit hurt me because he had seen me break down when we found Tamika and 'ems bodies. Until that moment he had not witnessed me showing anything but a firm hand. I needed him to understand that my tears weren't a sign of weakness, they were proof that street niggaz weren't immune to heartache.

I held his stare. "Nothin' will ever break me. You can write that in blood. But that don't mean a nigga don't hurt. Thugs cry too," I told him.

"And we make niggaz cry," he replied, G'd up as always.

"Yeah, we muthafuckin' do," I consigned.

A text from Rah came in on my phone lettin' me know that he was about to pull up in my driveway.

A'ight. I texted him back then went to let him in.

Upstairs I turned the motion sensor alarm off in the driveway and stood in the door waiting for Rah to arrive. He pulled up a few seconds later, parked behind my ride and strolled up to the door. He stepped inside and we embraced each other with a brotherly hug.

I stepped back and looked at my nigga; he looked weary and tired. "I'm sorry about Kayundra, dawg. Believe me, I feel your pain."

"I know you do. Thanks," he said. "And I feel yours, too. Tamika was your other half, It's sad about her and her people. I loved all three of them."

I closed and locked the door behind him, and then he followed me down to the basement.

Eric greeted Rah with dap and a chest bump. I sat back down in the recliner and stared at my reflection in the mirrored ceiling. The sorrow that I felt had me looking old. I ran a hand down my face and let out a weary sigh.

Rah sat on the padded stool at the bar. His elbow rested on the counter and his hands were steepled under his chin. He reminded me of a young Malcolm X. He was clean cut and serious, a deep thinker. In contrast, I was hot-tempered. Our personalities never clashed though, because the love that we had for each other was real.

"Just give me the game plan my brotha. You know I'm gonna ride," he said.

"Nah, fam, I'ma handle it myself. The streets aren't your life anymore. You're doing your legit thing in the ATL. I'm not about to ask you to risk that. You're one of the few that made it out of The Bricks and this fucked up state of mind that it breeds in us.

I'm not lettin' you return to the very shit you moved away to escape," I declined.

"CJ, this ain't about the game. This ain't about The Bricks either. You're my brotha from a different mother, and what hurts you hurts me. When you bleed, I bleed. I'm saying yo—those nightclubs that I have in the 'A' don't mean nothing compared to you fam. You know my get down; I can rock a kufi or a ski mask. It's whatever the situation calls for. How many times have you rode for me?"

"I feel you my nigga, but you don't owe me for dat. I rode for the love."

"And that's the same reason I'm gonna ride," he proclaimed, unsteepling his hands and sittin' up straight.

I argued for him to stay out of it. This was *my* lifestyle, not his. I didn't want my nigga to get caught up in my troubles. He had made it out of the streets and this would pull him back in. Real love is wanting to see ya man living good, and not having to look over his shoulder 24/7. I did that shit because that's the nigga I was born to be, but Rah was born to be much better.

"Fam, I can't let you do it," I stood firm.

"And you can't stop me either," he shot back.

"Bruh, its one love—one blood, but I would never forgive myself if I let you rock with me on this and somethin' foul happened to you," I tried to explain. A lump rose up in my throat at the mere thought of that.

"Dawg, it's from the cradle to the grave," he vowed, talking about our bond. "I'm not just from these streets; I'm *about* 'em, especially when they touch the people I love."

"I hear you, my nigga."

"I know you do, but do you overstand? Because if you do then you know I'd rather die side by side than sit back and let you ride without me."

I couldn't do nothin' but respect that.

I rose up and walked over to Rah. He hopped off the bar stool and we hugged again, G-style. We we're two niggaz from The Bricks with heavy hearts, indomitable wills, and loyalty to each other that was unmatched. We sat at the bar in my basement for hours, reminiscing about the loves that we had tragically lost. We both shed a tear or two for our shorties.

I felt at ease with my nigga there. Eric, who had fallen asleep on the couch, seemed less stressed too. Another tear slid down my face as Rah spoke of the love that Tamika had for me.

"Fam, our tears won't be in vain," I promised. 'Cause when thugs cry, muhfuckaz die.

That became my motto and I was about to show muhfuckaz that I lived that shit.

I grabbed my pistol grip pump off the bar top and clacked it for war. "I'm not waiting. Somebody is dying tonight," I decided in my anger.

Rah just nodded his head.

I went behind the bar and tossed him a fo-fo and a black scarf. On the way upstairs I woke Eric up. "Let's roll. It's chalk line time."

At the mention of murder, Eric popped up like a Jack-in-the-box. He reached under the sofa for his strap and put it on his waist. "This is for Tamika," he said as he moved quickly toward the door.

FIVE

RAHEEM

We drove aimlessly around the city in search of members of Nard's team to cut loose on. But every spot of Nard's that we drove by and cased out was shut down. He had correctly anticipated CJ's response.

CJ's anger was unbridled. "A muhfucka is getting their chest opened up *tonight*!" he reemphasized.

I wanted to tell him that we should fall back and plot because anger bred recklessness, but my dawg wasn't leaving out of the streets tonight until somebody's blood ran down in the gutters.

"Eric, did that nigga Makhi from Hawthorne ever pay us those ten bands he owed?" asked CJ. He was searching to find a victim.

"No. He keeps coming up with excuses. Me and Premo was gonna get at him before all of this happened. His ass is on borrowed time."

"And it just ran out," replied CJ.

I sat quietly in the back of the car as we headed over to Hawthorne to collect what CJ was owed in blood. The thought occurred to me that after tonight there would be no turning back, I would officially be back in the streets.

Eric parked in front of Makhi's house and the three of us got out of the car. It was past midnight and drizzling rain so the block was relatively quiet as we moved in unison with scarves tied over the lower halves of our faces and our guns carried down at our sides.

The light from a television illuminated the living room of the two-story house. We crept around the back and surveyed the back door; it was a cheap wooden one that wouldn't take much effort to kick in. "When we come out of here we're not leaving nothin' breathing," instructed CJ.

This was the moment of truth. I blocked out the reservation that urged me not to take that leap into a darkness that encompasses a man's soul when he kills indiscriminately. I convinced myself that this was not unlike a jihad; maybe not a Muslim holy war but a war of principle and duty still. The duty to ride with my brotha.

I gripped the fo-fo tighter in my hand and became someone else as CJ used two powerful kicks to break down the door. We ran straight to the living room where the light came from. Two men were scrabbling up off the couch where they had been playing video games before the door came crashing in. A third one was reaching for something on the mantel. *Kaboom!* The pump in CJ's hand opened up his back before he could grab whatever he was after. His body lurched forward and his head banged hard against the lacquered wood shelf, knocking over framed pictures and sending them crashing to the floor alongside of him.

His body twitched and his legs thrashed out. CJ lowered the pump and sent his back flying out the front. Blood flew out of his body and splashed up on the wall in a spray of red.

I stepped to a tall, red haired, freckled face dude and stuck my burner in his face. "Sit the fuck down."

He threw his hands up in the air and sat back down on the sofa, looking up into my eyes. "Go ahead, make me put the back of your head on the ceiling," I warned.

"What the fuck is this about, man?" he cried.

"You know what this is about nigga. I told you to get my money," gritted Eric. He stood next to us with his banger trained on the third man.

CJ walked over with the pump braced against his side. He stopped right in front of freckled face and lowered his bandanna. When the boy saw CJ's face his eyes widened and his lips quivered. The sight of Newark's most notorious crack king all up in his spot with a shotgun in hand had to be like staring at the devil. I could smell the scent of fear emanating from his body and I wondered if he had lost control of his bowels.

"Makhi, didn't you know I was the wrong muhfucka to play with?" said CJ.

"Man, I got y'all money right here." The words came out in a high soprano.

"Why did you make me come collect it? Get my shit!" CJ raised the pump to Makhi's chest.

Beside us Eric ordered Makhi's boy to lay face down on the floor. "Make love to the carpet, nigga. And do that shit real fast," he barked.

While they handled the downstairs I crept upstairs, walking as lightly as a ballerina. I didn't know who or what I would encounter. My nerves jumped but I moved with stealth-like purpose. The first bedroom that I reached was empty so I moved on to the next. My heart thumped as I kicked the door open and pointed the fo-fo into the darkened room. The light from the hallway where I stood casted shadows on the wall. I almost squeezed the trigger and murdered some paint.

I felt up and down the wall by the door, located the light switch, and flipped it on. With my gun ready to pop hot I checked under the bed and in the closet. No one was there. I moved on to the third bedroom and found no one there either.

Proceeding across the narrow hall to the bathroom, I stood to the side as I eased the door open and peered inside. Roaches crawled across the porcelain sink and water dripped from the faucet. Clothes hung out of a laundry basket. I stepped further inside and saw a shadow crouched behind the shower curtain over the tub.

I kept my tool aimed at the shadow and my finger poised on the trigger as I approached ever so cautiously. My heart threatened to leap out of my chest as I reached up and snatched the shower curtain back. I was a nose hair away from squeezing the trigger when I realized that it was a young sistah, not much older than LaKeesha, and her arms were wrapped around a small child protectively.

She looked up at me pleadingly.

A succession of gunshots rang out from downstairs, muffling her scream. "Sshhh!" I quieted her.

"Please don't kill my baby," she begged.

No witnesses. No mercy. Those were the laws in the streets. But fuck that, I was not bound by another man's code. There was no way I was murking a young girl and her child. I could not have lived with that shit on my conscious.

I put my finger to my lips again. "Be quiet, shorty. I'm not gonna hurt you or your baby. Everybody downstairs is dead. If you make a sound there are people with me who will come up here and murder you without a second thought. Stay here until you're sure we're gone."

"Thank you."

I nodded my head, backed out of the bathroom and closed the door. When I turned around I bumped dead in to CJ.

"Sup, fam?" Blood was all over his clothes and his eyes looked wild, like one kill had him thirsting for another.

"Everything is good," I replied calmly.

"You sure?" He looked at me curiously.

I responded with a nod of my head.

CJ looked down at my hand on the door knob. I could see in his eyes that he sensed that someone was in the bathroom. He looked back up at me and asked, "You sure about this, fam? I'll do it if you can't."

"Nah, son, it's just a young girl and her baby. She hasn't seen any of our faces so there's no need to hurt her. Let's bounce, yo," I said.

CJ hesitated and then his respect for me kicked in and over-ruled his adherence to the code of the streets.

"You soft, nigga," he teased. He knew better but I made no apology for having compassion for women and children.

As we descended the stairs, Eric waited for us at the bottom. We made our way out of the back door and to the car. As we rode back to CJ's in the rain I thought about the young girl and her baby. I wondered what would become of them.

I closed my eyes and my thoughts drifted to the beautiful woman whose life I couldn't save.

SIX

RAHEEM

Riding in the passenger seat of CJ's Maybach, I looked out the window through the downpour. It had been a constant cascade in Newark almost non-stop for a week now, just as long as it had been raining in my heart.

Dark Gucci shades covered my eyes, hiding evidence of the torment that had consumed my every waking moment since I'd heard the news of Sparkle's suicide. My heart ached with indescribable pain. Nothing or no one could take away that hurt because there was no love that I would ever know that could replace the love that I had lost.

CJ placed a consoling hand on my shoulder while steering the car with his other hand. "And this too shall pass my nigga," he stated confidently.

"I can't even wrap my mind around that fam. It seems like it was just yesterday when I was holding her in my arms, telling her that together we could conquer the world," I reminisced as I continued to stare out into the streaming rainfall.

"You gave it your best Rah, and it would've happened but shorty couldn't handle the fame and the fast life. It ain't your fault, my nigga," said CJ.

"Yeah, bruh, it *is* my fault. See, I peeped muhfuckaz pulling her this way and that way. I saw her becoming weak to all the vultures and the temptations of that lifestyle before she relapsed. I tried not to say too much because I didn't want it to seem like I was blocking her shine, but I knew she was headed for destruction, fam. As her man—even as her friend—it was my duty to step in and protect her. Even from herself."

"You did what any real nigga would do. You held her down until she started creepin' wit' that clown ass rap nigga—you couldn't turn your head to that. A man has to have principles that he stands on, otherwise, he's nothing. Shorty violated, you had to let her go. That shit was on her, not you," CJ contested.

"Did I? I mean, why couldn't I just forgive her and try to get things back like they were? Why the fuck did I let pride get in the way?"

"Because pride is what separates niggaz like us from the average man."

"I feel you, but sometimes pride can be like fire. When we let it grow out of control it burns down everything around us."

"Rah, that may be some real shit you're spittin' but your pride wasn't out of control, Kayundra was."

I knew that what he was saying was Street Gospel 101. Because a man that stands on nothing ain't much of a man. But matters of the heart tested a man's principles. I had held fast to mine because my pride had been my shield. Had I surrendered a bit of my arrogance though, maybe Kayundra would still be alive? I couldn't help but wonder.

"Rah, I know what you're feelin'. My own shorty is gone too because of a decision I made," CJ went on. "Every night I question myself. Why the fuck did I make her do that? But no matter how many times I ask myself that question, I keep comin' up with the same answer: I made her do it because that's the nigga that I am yo. That's how I rock, for better or for worse. The same thing applies to you Rah. We're real niggaz, so we're not afraid to make real choices. Most times we win, but when we lose the consequences are severe because it's all or nothin' with us. Nah mean?"

I couldn't dispute CJ's logic, it was as real as the words of Allah, but so was my woe.

We arrived at the funeral flanked by CJ's squad who had trailed us in separate rides. We parked and dashed into the church to get out of the rain. At the door, the funeral director, a husky, gray-haired gentleman stuck his arm out to stop me from going any further. He held a large photo of me in his hand. The picture was a year or two old, but I still looked the same.

"I'm sorry," he said glancing back and forth at me and my picture, "but the mother of the deceased has politely asked that you not be allowed to attend. Please be respectful of her wishes in this time of grief young brother," he politely asked.

I guess it shouldn't have been a big shocker because Kayundra's mother, Miss Freeda, was something special. I brushed raindrops off the sleeves of my black Armani suit and looked the funeral director in the eye. I cleared my throat before speaking but my words still came out scratchy and harsh. The permanent rasp in my voice was the result of a gunshot wound to the throat that I had suffered one night when niggaz had tried to slay me. But the *harshness* of my tone was all about now.

"Overstand this, Ol' Skool," I said, keeping my voice respect-fully low, in consideration of the mourners. "I didn't come here to disrespect anyone. I came to say goodbye to the only girl that I've ever loved. No matter what you've been told, I loved that girl whose body is up there in that casket, and I loved her just as much as anybody in here today loved her—maybe more."

The old man was looking at me like it didn't matter; he was not letting me in. I didn't want to start a confrontation, but if he didn't hurry up and step to the side I was going to put something in his side. *Don't let him take you there,* I told myself.

I suppressed the beast within and continued to speak with a modicum of humbleness. "What I'm saying is that I'm here to pay my respect, one way or the other," I said. "You can't stop me from going in there. Do you comprehend what I'm telling you?"

"I'm sorry but we have to honor the mother's wishes." He stood firm.

"Really?" I sighed, trying to use the proper restraint. I furrowed my brow and said, "I'm gonna give you a second to rethink that. Get your thoughts right or prepare your will."

Beside me CJ bristled. I could feel the heat coming off of him. At that moment he was the wrong nigga to fuck with. He stepped around me, confronting the man with aggression. "Yo, Pop," he gritted. "You heard my mans. He's goin' inside to pay his last respects to his shorty. Ain't no ifs, ands or buts about it. You can step your ass aside and let him pass or you can try to be a hero, and next week your whole congregation will be here to mourn *your* muthafuckin' ass. "He opened the jacket of his black Hugo Boss suit, flashing the banger on his waistline. "The Lord can't protect you from this."

The sight of CJ's banger put some understanding in the director's life real fast. He looked at me and uttered, "Please don't make a scene."

"I won't," I promised as he stepped out of the way.

"Gon' pay your respects, fam. We gonna wait right here," said CJ.

Walking down the carpeted aisle, I surveyed each row of the pews as I passed by. The church was filled to capacity. Many people from the music industry were present. Amongst those in attendance was Jay-Z and BK. J. Cole, Keyshia Coles, Nicki Minaj, Rihanna, Lil Wayne, Drake, the homegirl Faith, and many others. Newark residents occupied most of the seats; they had shown up in droves to say goodbye to one of their very own.

When I reached the front of the church I saw Big Ma and LaKeesha seated in the third row. Our eyes met as I removed the dark shades and slid them in the inside pocket of the suit.

I briefly stopped in my tracks as the sad cry of the organ sucked the air out of me. I breathed in deeply then proceeded on. In the very first row sat Miss Freeda. She was visibly shaken, rocking back and forth and dabbing her eyes with a white handkerchief. Preston and Scare Me sat on opposite sides of her, trying in vain to console her. Her sobs rang out and echoed off the walls. I knew that her torment was real, yet I couldn't help despising her. She had pressured her daughter to abort my child without telling me. In all honesty, that was what began Kayundra's plummet.

Preston, the CEO of Platinum Entertainment, the record label that launched Sparkle's career, was not without blame. He had been in Freeda's ear the whole time, using her to drive a wedge between me and shorty because he wanted Sparkle to be with someone in the industry so that it would enhance her image.

I looked at them with a visage that couldn't be cracked. *Y'all thirsty muhfuckaz were only concerned with the riches. Y'all didn't care about what was best for her.*

Scare Me looked up and I was mean mugging him. He wilted under my gaze. Then, just as quickly, he regained his psuedo-gangsta. He inflated his chest and sneered back at me, frontin' like he was built for real beefs.

"You a studio gangsta. You murk niggaz on wax. I'll get at that ass fa real!" I mouthed.

I didn't like his bitch ass, and it wasn't because Kayundra had crept with him. It takes two to tango so that was on her, but he had used drugs, Kayundra's biggest weakness, to get her in bed. Then when their casual drug use led to her relapsing into a full blown addiction, he tossed her aside like yesterday's trash.

He gonna pay for that!

The stare-down intensified as I passed directly by his fake ass. I wanted to knock that platinum and diamond grill out of his mouth. I stopped right in front of him. "Your time is coming," I gritted.

"Get at me, Black. I bet I bust back," he said, reciting a bar from one of his rap songs.

"This ain't the studio yo. We gon' take this to the streets where shit is real," I uttered just loud enough for him to hear me over the organ.

"I'ma get at you, nigga," he shot back.

"Please do," I baited before continuing up on the stage where Kayundra's body was laid out for view in a powder blue casket with dove white bedding.

Although my heart was heavy and my soul wept, I steadied myself as I placed my hands on the sides of the casket and looked down at my Sparkle. She looked beautiful and serene, almost like she was taking an evening nap. The long sleeved blue and white Versace dress that she had been laid to rest in covered the marks of her slashed wrists, but everyone knew.

I looked down in her face and tried to conjure up only the good memories. I wanted to hold on to those and let go of everything else. "We held the world in the palms of our hands for a minute baby. For a while we were as happy as two people can be. Those are the memories that I'll forever cherish. And that is the way I'll always remember you. I love you Sparkle. Rest in paradise baby girl," I said in closure.

I leaned inside the casket and placed a soft kiss on her cheek.

"Noooo! Don't you dare put your lips on her!" screamed Miss Freeda, flying toward me like a witch on a broom. Her eyes were wild. She flailed her fists at me, screaming, "It's your fault she's dead!"

I raised up and blocked her harmless blows. Scare Me rushed up and moved Miss Freeda to the side. He got up in my face and jawed, "Nigga, if you know what's best for you, you better push on."

"You threatening me, pussy boy?" I said as my hand went inside my suit jacket. I had anticipated some acrimony so I was strapped.

The last thing I wanted to do was disrespect Kayundra's funeral, but if Scare Me wanted to pop shit off we could do that! I wrapped my hand around the Glock that was on my waistline and dared the nigga to test my G. I had already put the hands on his punk ass a few months back when I had caught him gettin' Kayundra high, this time I was gon' put some hot shit in his life.

Over his shoulder I saw Big Ma stand up. She glared at me reproachfully. Out of respect for her I let my hand fall down to my side. Scare Me misinterpreted the move and immediately tried to flex. "Where your heart at, Black?" he spat.

Before I could respond, CJ appeared out of nowhere. His voice was on the back of Scare Me's neck. "Sup, bitch ass nigga? Let's get to it." He called son's bluff.

Scare Me peeped that CJ's gangsta was street certified and he folded under its threat. "I'm good," he muttered.

"Fuck around and get your face blown off," warned CJ.

"I want them out of here!" Miss Freeda yelled, pointing at CJ, his goons, and me.

Big Ma got my attention through the sheer intensity of her gaze. When I looked at her she pointed toward the door.

I nodded my head respectfully.

While order was being restored, I stepped back up to the casket. The organist began playing I'm *Going Home to Be with Jesus*, and a heavy set, middle aged looking woman sang the words beautifully.

I looked down inside the casket and felt a tear slide down my face. "You see all of this drama you caused ma?" I said jokingly. "I can't do nothin' but shake my head. I apologize for any disrespect, but I had to come and say goodbye. Just know that you will forever dwell in my heart. Rest peacefully baby."

I kissed two fingers, and then touched them against her cheek.

"Forever and always," I said.

Ca$h

SEVEN

CJ

Again it was pouring down out this bitch. But the pelting thunder showers of yesterday had been replaced by thrashing rain and lightning that cracked the gray sky wide open like an old woman's worn out pussy. Thunder clapped louder than the sound of a thousand AK-47's bustin' off in the hood. It was as if God was angry at me for the death and destruction that would come in the wake of me having to bury my boo.

I looked up in the sky defiantly; I didn't fear His wrath no more than I feared a nigga'z gangsta on the streets. It was too late to stop the bloodshed now. I had murdered a different nigga every day since Tamika was killed. Any slight to me, real or imagined, got a bitch nigga an autopsy.

I ducked under the umbrella that Premo held open over my head as we led a procession of mourners to the plots at the cemetery where Tamika and her people were being laid to rest side by side.

The triple funeral hadn't drawn half the mourners that attended Kayundra's funeral yesterday, but the service had been just as sad.

In spite of the ache in my heart, I had maintained a face of stone. Rah had sat on one side of me in the front pew, and Nee Nee sat on the other, weeping on my shoulder as we all stared at the three closed caskets on the stage. Danyelle's husband and their small children sat down from us in the front row. I couldn't even look that man in the eye because I felt responsible for his wife's death. Behind us Star sobbed loudly.

Tamika rested in a metallic pink casket. A large portrait of her sat atop the closed lid. Her Moms was laid to rest in a mahogany casket surrounded by dozens of wreaths and other flower arrangements. A photo collage depicting her journey in life sat on

53

an easel next to her coffin. Danyelle rested eternally in a peach-colored casket placed to the right of Tamika's. A life-sized portrait captured her friendly smile. *If anyone deserved to live forever, it was her,* I thought every time I looked up at the portrait.

The pastor had risen up and delivered a sermon that still rang in my ears as we walked briskly in the rain to the gravesite.

"We must be thankful for the times that we had with them. Now that our Father has called them home, let our minds not question and our hearts not be bitter. For it is He alone that giveth life, and it is He alone that taketh. He has called his children home."

I was still seething inside over that lame ass shit. God hadn't called Tamika no muthafuckin' where. Nard had killed her and wasn't no sugar-coating it. I hadn't been able to stomach another key of the organist's sad songs. *Oh Precious Lord my ass!* I said to myself as we carried the caskets down a neat path and sat them on their respective stands.

From there everything went blank. I never would've thought that I would be burying my girl. As her casket was being lowered into the earth, the preacher announced, "Ashes to ashes and dust to dust."

Boc! Boc! Boc! Boc! Boc! Boc! Blocka! Blocka! Blocka! Blocka!

A burst of gunfire crackled from nearby. Loud screams erupted all around me as mourners dove behind headstones and trees. Some reacted too late and went down bloody and twisted. I dropped to the ground, pulling Nee Nee down with me. Bullets tattered the caskets and pelted the ground all around me.

In the distance, ski masked henchmen continued to unleash terror with weapons that sounded like choppers. They were mowing people down like paper targets. Frantic screams filled the air and all-out panic ensued.

My breathing became heavy as my street instincts kicked in. I rolled over on my back, snatched my banger off my waist and aired that bitch out, blasting back at the niggaz that were now fleeing. One of them stopped, turned around, and ripped off his mask. Even with the distance between us I knew who it was.

"Come see me, yo!" yelled Nard. He aimed his assault rifle back up at us and fired off more shots.

Beside me, my mans were poppin' off too. It was mad pandemonium in the cemetery as shots flew back and forth with no regard for the innocent.

As our attackers further retreated, I hurriedly looked around to make sure that all of my mans were a'ight. Rah was on the ground covering two small kids with his body. Eric and 'em looked to be good. I hopped to my feet and chased after Nard and his masked gunners, firing shots at their backs.

"Is this what you pussies want?" I yelled out as my Nine went crazy in my hand.

Boc! Boc! Boc! Boc!

"Bitch ass niggaz!" screamed Eric, setting it off at my side.

Premo, Snoop, and Quent's bangers joined in the gun battle but our bullets missed our targets as those bitch ass niggaz hopped in awaiting cars and peeled off.

Seconds after our guns grew quiet, the sound of screaming police sirens filled the air. A middle-aged man came running down the path; the front of his suit was soaked in blood and he was crying and screaming. "Somebody please help me! My son has been shot and he's dying."

I looked at the child in his arms and shook my head. There was a hole the size of a baseball in the little boy's chest. "Call an ambulance!" screamed the father. But he was gonna need the coroner.

More chaos poured down into the cemetery's parking lot as everyone ran for their cars. People were yelling for help that was already too late. Thunder roared and lightning struck like the crack of a whip. Rain drenched my clothes and blurred my vision. I looked up and saw Rah and Nee Nee running toward me. Nee Nee was crying and muttering. Rah was calm but decisive.

"Fam, you gotta get out of here before *one-time* arrives," he said. I could hear their sirens getting closer.

"Come on, CJ, let me get you away from here," said Nee Nee, taking a hold of my arm.

"A'ight."

I took one last look at the dead child in his father's arms. I looked up from the little boy's chubby face and into the man's eyes. Tears ran down his dark brown cheeks, clearly standing out from the rain that soaked him. His eyes slowly traveled from my face down to the banger that I held at my side. He lifted his eyes back up and scowled at me like I was nothin' but scum.

"I rebuke you Satan," he growled.

I gritted my teeth and tightened my grip on my Nine. "Fuck you say old man?" I raised my arm and pointed the banger dead between his eyes.

Just when I was about to squeeze the trigger, Rah placed a hand on my shoulder. "CJ, let it go. You gotta get out of here," he warned.

"Yeah, baby," chimed Nee Nee.

I kept my eyes fixed on the man a second longer then I let my arm fall back down to my side.

As I led my goons away from the cemetery, the anger inside of me bubbled up like lava. Nard was gonna pay the ultimate price for not allowing me to lay my girl to rest in peace.

EIGHT

NARD

Niggaz in The Bricks must've thought CJ was invincible. They talked about the nigga like he walked on water or something. But just because others bowed down to his gangsta didn't mean I was afraid to take his ass to war. This time he had violated the wrong youngin' and for that he was gonna die.

The triple funeral was just the beginning. Fuck what he had done in the streets, none of those war stories impressed me. In fact, I was tired of listening to muhfuckaz glorify the nigga. For several months I had listened to Tamika speak of CJ like he was a hood Messiah and I should revere his name. I hadn't said much, I just listened and ate the meat and spat out the bones. CJ might've been a boss, but I was destined to be the fiercest nigga to ever come out of Newark.

It was time for me to show the streets that CJ bleeds just like anyone else.

I had been laying low since me and my niggaz shot up the funeral two weeks ago. Four people had been killed and seven others had been injured in the attack. The streets were hot because a two-year-old child had been one of the casualties. I didn't give a fuck, my message had been received loud and clear. Any and everybody around CJ could get it.

I was on Central Avenue at this barbershop owned by an esteemed old head named Jamaican Black who sold weed out of the back of his establishment. The dread was well respected because it was said that he had put in work with the infamous Shower Posse in New York back in the day.

Besides selling the best loud in the city, Jamaican Black was known to have connections to some major suppliers of yay. He was also looked up to for having mediated a serious beef between the Irvington Bloods and a band of his Jamaican homeboys.

I wasn't at the barber shop for a haircut or a mediator. My negotiator was on my waist, cocked and locked.

"Whatchu need, rude boy?" asked Jamaican Black, greeting me with a fist lock and a light touch of shoulders.

No one else was in the shop so I spoke freely. "Let me get a pound of that Diesel."

He led me to a room in the back and put the weed on a scale so that I could see that its weight was on point.

After serving me, Jamaican Black steered the conversation to my beef with CJ. "What you gon' do 'bout it, rude boy?" he asked, looking at me with concern on his face.

"I'm taking it to the streets, Dread," I replied without hesitation.

"My youth, you don't wanna test da mon gun."

I smiled but discounted the mild warning. "I hear you, Dread. But CJ put his pants on the same way I do. I bleed, he bleeds. Either one of us can die."

He rested a hand on my shoulder. "Walk easy, my youth. Nuff man a run but no coward. Nah catti worth a man fortune," he cautioned.

"It's not about the bitch—it was never about her bum ass. It's about my unborn that CJ made her kill. If my seed didn't deserve to live, neither does CJ, yo," I explained my anger.

"Respect my youth, mon a mon overstand nah scared mon business 'em a deal 'wit. Nuff man walk into lion's den and not walk out. Be easy, brethren."

I respected his wisdom but his warning fell upon deaf ears because I feared no man.

"Jamaican Black, I'm that nigga that's gonna knock CJ off his throne," I said, placing the weed inside a shoe bag and tucking it under my arm as I prepared to leave.

"Walk easy, rude boy," he repeated his warning.

"Tell CJ that," I said, meaning no disrespect.

As I stepped out of the barbershop and moved toward the car that sat waiting for me at the curb, my eyes scanned the block for the slightest sign of trouble. My number one goon, Big Nasty, hopped out of the car with a Mac 11 down by his side just in case CJ popped up out of nowhere. He opened the passenger door for me then hurried back around to the driver's side and we moved out.

When we got back to my brother Man Dog's spot out in Ivy Hill where we all had been lounging the past few days, Man Dog and 'em had a party going on. Music was thumpin', they were taking bottles of Ciroc to the head and passing blunts around. Shorties were wall to wall up in that piece.

Man Dog sat on the couch with his girl Lemora on his lap with her arms around his neck. Quent and Zakee were playing the wall with drinks in their hands and a couple of broads all over them. A couple of my other mans were seated around the living room entertaining one hood rat or the other.

I got Man Dog's attention and gestured for him to follow me into the kitchen. I sat the pound of Diesel on the table and turned to face him, scowling. "What y'all got going on up in here?"

"We just celebrating a little, that's all."

I tilted my head to the side, looking at him through squinted eyes. "Celebrating? What the fuck we got to celebrate? CJ still walking around this bitch, ain't he? We can't sleep on him. Any one of those bitches out there besides Lemora could work for the other side. Get rid of 'em yo."

Without protest, Man Dog returned to the living room and abruptly turned off the music. "If you're not fam, get the fuck out," he announced.

I stood silently in the doorway of the kitchen and watched Man Dog and Big Nasty clear the house. When no others remained but my team, I walked out in the living room and surveyed the niggaz whose hands I had chosen to put my life in.

Big Nasty was a certified killa whose loyalty to me was canine-like. I recalled looking up to him when I was knee high and he had the hood shook. He had gone to serve a bid, when I was nine years old, for beating a nigga to death with a lead pipe. By the time he touched down, twelve years later, I was a young boss.

Word, niggaz wanted to smash Big Nasty as soon as his feet hit the pavement because they feared his strong-arm game. I didn't fear him, I respected him. I recalled how he single-handedly ran these Philly niggaz off the block. Somehow they had maneuvered their way into Little Bricks behind a relative of theirs who was from the hood.

I was ear hustling from the window of the apartment where I lived. I heard Big Nasty warn those Philly cats. "Y'all bama ass niggaz better get off the block. If you're not from The Bricks, you can't eat down here."

He walked off without saying anything else. Hours later the Philly boys were still out there hustlin'. Two of them got murked that night. Another one of them caught it the next day. After that, the others hopped back on the turnpike and never returned.

That had cemented Big Nasty's gangsta in my mind.

A lot of niggaz ate after Big Nasty cleared the block of out of state cats. But nobody fed him once he caught that bid for bludgeoning a nigga to death outside the movie theater on Bergen.

I didn't forget him though. As soon as I started gettin' my weight up I had given his mom's some mula to send to him. Since I was just a lil' knucklehead when he went in, he didn't remember me. But by the time he came home I had earned his loyalty.

I looked from Big Nasty around the room at my crew. In their own way each of them were as street certified as Big Nasty. Man Dog, Quent and Zakee had been down with me from the start. Talib and Show, who were both lounging on the couch, had joined the team a few months ago. I had recruited them because their reps for gunplay preceded them.

Lemora moved around the room clearing empty Ciroc bottles off of the tables. She wasn't part of the team, but she was official. I could speak freely in her company.

I took a seat on an end chair, commanding everyone's full attention as I prepared my words carefully. "When niggaz fall in love with the spotlight, the bitches, and the partying, that's how they blow their come up," I lectured.

Then I recoiled from my own words. I realized that Tamika had preached that very same thing to me. At the time I soaked up the jewels she dropped as if they were scriptures from the game. But time had revealed that she was more fraudulent than the rats she had constantly warned me about.

Just thinking about her ratchet ass caused my face to ball up. Moms had tried to tell me that Tamika didn't love me for me.

"She's trying to make you into who she wants you to be. Baby, can't you see that she's still in love with CJ? As soon as he comes calling, she'll run back to him. Don't invest your heart in that bitch; her heart can never belong to you because it belongs to another man."

"Nah, Ma, you're wrong. She's about to have my baby. That proves that she is over that nigga," I foolishly argued.

Tamika had me so gone I couldn't see past her wet pussy and sweet deception. The bitch was smooth with her shit, I give props on that. But what she hadn't realized while she was tryna recreate me into another CJ is that she had created a beast. Now I was gonna use everything that she taught me to bring down the nigga that she had truly loved.

I returned my attention to my peoples. I looked from one to the other as I spoke. "This is not the time to party yo. For every action there's a *reaction.* We gotta expect that CJ is gonna come back at us sooner than later. Right now we got him throwed off because he's probably still fucked up about his bitch. So let's hit the nigga again while he's tryna clear his head. Strap up and stay on point, its war around this bitch."

Later That Night

Man Dog was behind the wheel of the stolen van. I was riding shotgun up front. Big Nasty and Talib were in the back. The four of us were dressed similarly in black hoodies and jeans. We turned left onto the street and crept up the block.

"Dead the headlights," I whispered, fighting to control my anxiety.

Man Dog killed the lights.

It was a cold windy night due to the recent rain. Winter was still a month away but the temperature felt like it was already in the 60's. The street was dark and quiet on one end; on the other end where one of CJ's main trap houses sat it was business as usual.

Fiends stood in a long line that led up to the side door of the dilapidated house, and armed lookouts patrolled the area like hood militia. I counted two up the street and two in front of the house. All four held sub machine guns.

It was well known that CJ could operate his drug houses out in the open, with no worry about them boys, because he had Newark's crooked ass Police Department in his pocket. I didn't give a fuck who his protection was, I was on a mission to smash everything associated with him.

Man Dog brought the van to a stop at the curb in front of the house. "Turn your muhfuckin' headlights on and pull down the street some," barked a lookout. He was wearing a dark hoodie and a thick jacket. He pointed with the Uzi to where he wanted us to park.

Man Dog ignored his command.

I rolled the side window down and yelled, "Yo son, we're lookin' for some weight. How much y'all charge for a half block of glass?"

"Fuck is you? Nigga, y'all feds or something?" he spat, raising the Uzi to chest level and approaching the van warily.

"Nah fam. We're from Trenton. I'm Premo's people," I said, calling out a name he would recognize.

That relaxed him a little and he lowered the Uzi back down to his side as he came up to my side of the van and peered inside. Quickly, I stuck my fo-fifth out the window and shot him in the face twice.

Boc! Boc!

His body fell to the ground with his right leg twisted underneath his torso. The Uzi laid inches away from his hand but with half of his face blown off, he was in no shape to grab it.

I hopped out of the van and stood over him. His body involuntarily twitched as he began his journey to the afterlife. I looked down at him with no remorse. "In your next life don't work for a bitch ass nigga," I snorted, then I crushed him with no regard.

By now Big Nasty and Talib had jumped out of the side door of the van. Big Nasty's AK-47 was going the fuck off. He chopped down the second lookout that was in front of the house. The kid's body jerked as he stumbled back and fell on the ground crawling toward the house. I aimed my banger at him and rendered him motionless.

Talib ran up the driveway waving his tool back and forth. The fiends scattered like roaches. I shot through the front windows of the house as Talib blasted shots through the side door.

The other two lookouts that were posted down the street ran toward us, lettin' loose with their hammers. The sound of their sub-machine guns echoed in the night.

Behind them crept a second van. Inside of it was Zakee, Quent and Show.

The van sped up, jumped the curb, and ran over one of the shooters, crushing him under its tires. A thunderclap of gunshots erupted from inside the van, cutting down the remaining lookout.

"Tell CJ he can run but he can't muthafuckin' hide," I yelled out.

We drove the two vans over to Weequahic Park and doused them with gasoline. I stood back, lit a blunt with a cigarette lighter and took a pull. Then I slung the lit blunt between the vans and watched flames erupt toward a moonless sky.

NINE

CJ

I was lying across my bed with my hands behind my head, staring up at the chandelier that hung from the high ceiling of the master bedroom. Music played on the iPod on the dresser. Every song reminded me of Tamika, intensifying my regrets. Empty bottles of Grey Goose sat on the portable bar by the bed and dozens of half-smoked blunts filled the ashtrays on the nightstand nearby.

I had gone back to the cemetery to sit and talk to my girl the day after Nard and 'em tried to ambush me at her grave site. Tamika had been dead less than three weeks and already I was missing her like crazy.

I turned my head to the side and stared at my face in the mirror above the dresser. My eyes were bloodshot red, my forehead was creased, and the corners of my mouth were forever turned down. Without ma I would never find a reason to smile again. Nah mean?

So many times I had taken her for granted. I had thought that because I was *that* nigga, I could do whatever I pleased as long as I gave her the material shit. As the green laces in my safe increased, I gave her more gifts but a lot less of my time. I had fucked around on her again and again, just being the typical nigga.

My eyes caught a glimpse of a framed picture of us that sat on the nightstand by the bed. In the picture, I was sittin' on the hood of my Q-45 with both of my hands full of stacks. Tamika stood between my knees holding my 9mm, aiming it up the block like a ride or die. The Rock and Republic jeans she had on fit her ass like cellophane wrapped tightly around a beach ball.

I smiled at those memories from a several years back, when I still hugged the block and Tamika was my one and only. Then came the mula and the street fame.

Being a nigga that was born with nothin' but a hope and a prayer, I had always thought that cheddar would solve any problem. But the old street axiom, *more money more problems* proved to be true.

"I let that shit change me," I muttered.

"You let what change you, baby?" asked my company, draping her naked thigh across mine.

I cut my eyes at her with disgust. She had shown up at my door last night when I was alone and wallowing in grief. We had knocked back glass after glass of Goose and passed blunts back and forth while sharing our losses. I had known where it would lead when she said that she just wanted to talk to somebody who would understand.

I didn't respond to her question because now her voice irritated the fuck out of me. She ignored the meaning of my silence and ran her hand down my chest. It traveled down further until it encircled my wood.

"You wanna fuck? It would take your mind off of her," she whispered in my ear, running her tongue across the lobe.

I pulled back and looked at her. "You ain't shit, yo."

"But I can make you feel good," she cooed.

She slithered down my body and took me into her mouth. The feel of her lips and tongue working the head of my dick felt so good and so muhfuckin' bad at the same time. The good feeling could not be denied, the bitch was a bonified headhunter.

I gritted my teeth at my own weakness. This was one of the very things that had torn me and Tamika apart.

"Get the fuck off of my dick yo!" I spat, feeling foul as hell.

"Shhh! We both need this tonight. Ummm, CJ, this dick tastes so good. Push it to the back of my throat and make me gag." She took me deeper into her mouth, slurping, and bobbing her head up and down. Her eyes stared up into mine.

"Don't look at me, yo!" I growled. She lowered her eyes but didn't miss a beat.

This thirsty ass bitch ain't shit. I shook my head because I was no better.

"You like how I spit all over your dick and slurp it up?" she asked.

"Don't talk. Just suck!" I spat.

"Ummm. That shit right there turns a bitch on, daddy."

"Didn't I tell you not to talk, yo?" I grabbed the back of her head and made her gag. I tried to drive my dick out the back of her neck, but the bitch was a pro. She deep throated me with ease.

I closed my eyes and reluctantly surrendered to the feeling. When I opened them again she was straddling my waist, about to guide me inside of her. "Hold up!" I stopped her. Then I reached on the nightstand for a condom.

The picture of me and Tamika seemed to stare at me reproachfully. My hand froze, suspended in air.

"What's wrong?" she asked

I looked down at her to see if there was any guilt in her eyes. There wasn't a trace of remorse in her scandalous eyes. She leaned over and placed the picture of me and Tamika face down. Then she picked up the Magnum, tore it open with her teeth, and stuck her tongue out at me.

"I'm going to ride this dick, and I'm not going to feel bad about it. Life has to go on, CJ," she gabbled.

"But not like this. This some foul shit ma, and you know it."

"Is it, CJ?" she refuted. "Really, who are we hurting? We've always had a thing for each other, you can't deny that. And it's not like we haven't fucked before. Tell me you don't wanna point my toes toward that chandelier?" she pointed.

Everything that she said was true, but it still didn't make it right. There was nothin' weak about me so I couldn't place the blame on her. I was a dog-ass nigga and she was a grimy ho. Point blank period!

"A'ight, you want some more of this dick?" I said in spite of the guilt that tugged at my heart.

"Yes, daddy," she moaned, covering me with the condom then lifting up to guide me inside of her warm pussy.

"You foul, ma. Real foul!" I uttered through clenched teeth.

If she heard me, it didn't deter her from gettin' fucked. "I'ma ride this dick real good, daddy," she repeated.

I said nothin' at all. The whole time that she was grinding her pussy back and forth on my stiff pole, moaning and screaming out my name, I remained quiet. For all the response she got out of me, she might as well have fucked herself with a dildo.

I couldn't get my mind off of Tamika. Ma was dead because of my bullcrap, and I was still shittin' on her. It had to be the stress, the weed, and the liquor that was controlling my decisions.

I had to get my mind right! What I was doing was not boss shit. Ass was the average hustla's downfall, but I was not average yo.

Her arms were around my neck; her face was to the side of mine, and her lower body moved in a fast, circular motion. "Oooh baby, you got some good dick," she moaned. "I want to cum all over this muhfucka! Cum with me, daddy."

I fought hard to hold back the nut that was building up in my balls, but her sopping wet pussy had a slippery grip on my rock hard dick.

"Ooh, CJ, you're making my pussy feel so damn good," she cried as she bounced up and down on my dick almost as if she was tryna break it off inside her.

My hips involuntarily moved up to meet hers. I couldn't help but to fuck her back, so I tried to injure the bitch's spinal cord. That was a mistake though, 'cause the harder I pounded the more she loved it.

"Ooh, baby! Keep doing that shit. Oh, my god, I'm about to cum!" she screamed.

We bust at the same time then she slid down from on top of me with her arms around my neck and her head on my shoulder. Her hair was wet from sweat and she panted heavily from exhaustion. "Damn, nigga, your dick is the truth," she exclaimed. "I'm glad it can be all mine now."

I pushed her up off of me and onto the floor. "You not my bitch, so get that out of your head, ma." I made myself clear as I stood up over her. "Now get the fuck up and go get a washcloth so you can wash me up."

She climbed to her feet, keeping her head down. "Dang, why do you have to talk to me so rough?" she whined.

"I talk to you like the ratchet ho that you are. Now go get me a towel."

"Where is it at?" she asked.

"Put your nose to the floor and sniff it out, trifling dog ass bitch."

She looked up and rolled her eyes at me before going to the bathroom.

"While you're in there make sure you take a ho bath because that's what the fuck you are," I called out behind her.

"Fuck you, CJ," she yelled over her shoulder. "You like it."

I sat on the edge of the bed and sparked a blunt, blowing the smoke out slowly as the guilt over what I had just done quickly turned into anger. A Bruno Mars song played on the radio; its lyrics were exactly what I wanted to say to Tamika.

Same bed but it feels just a little bit bigger now
Our song on the radio but it don't sound the same
When our friends talk about you all it does is just tear me down
'Cause my heart breaks a little when I hear your name
Too young too dumb to realize that I should've bought you
flowers and held your hand

Ca$h

Should've gave you all my hours when I had the chance . . .
My eyes focused on a large portrait of Tamika that hung on the wall, and I felt the wetness on my face before I realized that I was crying.

My pride, my ego, my needs and my selfish ways
Caused a good strong woman like you to walk out my life
Now I'll never, never get to clean up the mess I made
And it hurts me every time I close my eyes . . .

Nee Nee came into the room with a soapy washcloth. As I sat there with a blunt in one hand, my strap in the other and tears streaming down, she stopped and her eyes followed mine.

She walked over and turned the station, then moved over to the portrait and ripped it off the wall. The sadness she had shown immediately after Tamika's death was gone. "She's dead, baby. You don't need pictures of her around. Let me be everything you need," she said.

I looked up at her and something in me just snapped!

TEN

RAHEEM

I was rolling with Lil' Eric when my cell phone rang with back to back calls from Premo and Flip, two of CJ's lieutenants. I decided to hit Flip up first since I had just missed his call.

"Sup, fam? How you?" I answered.

"Not good. You seen CJ?" he asked in a harried tone.

"Nah, I been trying to call him but he's not answering."

"Fuck yo!"

"What's up? Everything is a'ight, ain't it?" I questioned him as Eric looked over at me from behind the wheel of his Lexus LX 570.

"Hell no, everything ain't a'ight. Those niggaz hit three of our spots tonight. The one on 11th and Clinton Ave, the one in the *Spis*, and our main spot over by Branch Brook Park. We lost seven of our people."

He listed the dead boys' names, one by one. I recognized each one of them as I put faces with the names. Blood rushed to my brain and my face sagged.

"What about their side? Did they lose any?" I asked, trying to calculate the damage.

"Not that I know of," he reported grimly.

I let out a loud sigh and quickly whispered to Eric what I had just been told.

Flip said, "Fam, I don't know where CJ at and ain't nobody heard from him. I just hope he's not laying up with no pussy while those niggaz are killin' up our people."

Flip's statement rubbed me the wrong way because we both knew that he would never question CJ's actions to his face and live to tell the story.

"Who the fuck are you questioning, yo!" I snapped.

"I'm just saying, fam. It's gettin' ugly out here. Those niggaz not playing. Over in the Spis muhfuckaz were laid out on the pavement, domes splattered and their noodles leaking out on the ground. We gotta ride or niggaz are gonna start thinking that shit is sweet."

"Flip, do you think for one second CJ is gonna give the people who did that a pass? Are you slick trying to question his gangsta?" I calmly asked though inside I was seething.

"Fuck is that nigga saying?" asked Eric, getting riled up.

"Fuck is *he* saying?" Flip barked, overhearing Eric's comment.

The last thing they needed was beef with each other. I was concerned that something had happened to CJ, so fuck being humble I had to take control.

"Flip, I know how you're feeling right now but you're talking reckless and that's just gonna cause beef within the team," I warned.

"Nah, this shit just has me heated," he sighed.

"Yeah, well don't let it get your shit pushed back. It's all love my nigga, but don't get it confused 'cause if you doubting my man's gangsta we're about to have a problem that only a wake can fix." I made myself clear.

There was silence on the other end. Finally he replied, "I'm not questioning nothin', I just wanna lay somebody down."

"A'ight, call everyone up and tell them to go to the after-hours spot. This is mandatory yo. I don't give a fuck what they're in the middle of, tell them to dead that shit and get there. I'ma try to find CJ, y'all stay there until you hear from one of us."

When we got to CJ's house, he let us in. He had a bottle of Goose in one hand and his banger in the other. Blood was all over him and all he wore was a pair of boxers.

"Fam, you a'ight? What happened?" I asked, wondering if he had encountered Nard somehow.

"Yeah, I'm good but that punk bitch ain't," he said.

I looked at him curiously. I could tell that he was gone off the Goose.

He turned and headed up the spiral staircase. Me and Eric followed behind wondering what was going on. We both had our tools out as we followed him into the bedroom.

Lying in the center of the floor in a pool of blood was Nee Nee. "What happened?" I asked CJ.

He sat down on the edge of the bed and turned up the Goose, gulping it down like it was water. He brought the bottle down and pointed to a portrait of Tamika that was on the floor on the other side of the room.

"I told that stupid bitch not to fuck with it. It wasn't enough that we were shittin' on Tamika, the ratchet ass ho had to humiliate her memory. Well, that's what the fuck she gets."

He leaped up off of the bed and fired two more shots in Nee Nee's body.

Boc! Boc!

"Punk ass bitch!" he growled. "This what you thought you wanted, ain't it? Well, now you got it and everything that comes with it." He spat on her body and pumped another shot in her head. "Gutter rat!"

I walked over and took the gun from him. "Fam, this is bad, yo." I felt sorry for Nee Nee but there was nothing I could do for her now.

"She shouldn't have fucked with Tamika's picture," he mumbled, barely coherently.

"Bruh, we gotta get back on point. Shit is ugly in The Bricks. They hit some of your spots and murked seven of your mans," I said, taking a seat next to him and repeating what I had been told by Flip.

CJ listened without interruption. As I called off the names of those that got killed, CJ's head dropped into his hands. I had never seen him like this and I was glad that no one besides Eric and myself was witnessing it. Losing Tamika had him reeling already and now this.

I knew that he needed me now more than ever. In spite of my social consciousness and my disdain for the streets, I was my brother's keeper. I could not turn my back on CJ.

Immediately I took charge. "Eric, do something with Nee Nee's body," I ordered. "Take her and leave her somewhere she'll be found. And fam, handle her with care." That was the best I could do.

Nee Nee hadn't deserved what was done to her, but my concern for CJ trumped my regrets at having to discard her body somewhere like a pile of trash. From this point on it was G-mode.

An overwhelming feeling of trepidation bubbled up in my gut. Something told me that this was going to be a street war unlike any CJ had ever faced.

Disregarding a voice in my head and the tugging of my conscience that told me not to get involved, I made a vow to myself to hold my nigga down until we eliminated his foe or until we died side by side. At the end of the day, my loyalty to CJ outweighed everything else, even my strive not to mess with the streets.

***

I put on my seatbelt and prepared myself for my quick journey back to the *A*. I needed to put business in order with my nightclubs so that they would run smoothly while I was away. Once I handled that I was returning to The Bricks with two Dirty South thugs, DaQuan and Legend, that were trained to go.

When I first moved to the 'A' six or seven years ago to attend Morehouse, I was still dabbling in the streets. DaQuan had been one of my lieutenants, helping me get acquainted with the way brothers hustled in the South. Now he managed my nightclubs by night and flipped bricks in the daytime. He had proven that his G was official and his loyalty to me was bulletproof.

Legend was the Dee-jay at my nightclub, Sparkle's. He and I had met while I was serving that bid a few years ago. Neither he nor DaQuan would hesitate to ride when I told them about the trouble CJ was having back home.

CJ's team was official but I was coming back with the enforcements.

It took three days for me to set my business straight. Every night I called up top to check on my fam. CJ was on a warpath. They had murked a couple of Nard's people in broad daylight outside of IHOP on Bergen. Another night CJ slumped two of Nard's cousins but so far they hadn't caught up with Nard or any of his top goons. That was going to change as soon as I returned.

The day came for us to head up top and help CJ crush his enemies. Legend was all packed and ready when I went to swoop him up. At twenty-two years old, and childless, there was no one to stand in the way of his departure. His background was typical of many 90's babies who were born to crack head mothers and imprisoned fathers. The streets had raised him so anywhere he went was home.

DaQuan, on the other hand, had a queen and a seed at home. He and Tanisha had been together for five years. Their four-year-old daughter, Mayabi, was a little princess. I had second thoughts about asking him to leave his family because I didn't want to contribute to the possibility of another black child growing up without a father. That contradicted what I was returning to The Bricks to do but it was prevalent in my mind.

Inside I knew that no matter how I justified killing another black man or taking a life period, it was wrong but my allegiance demanded that I ride.

DaQuan's loyalty to me was just as intense as mine was to CJ. "Shawdy, I could just as easily get killed here in the 'A' as I can in

75

Newark. I'ma ride with you, bruh bruh. Tanisha is just gonna have to understand. You know how I rock, its ten toes down," he declared.

But Tanisha didn't understand at all. She let me and Legend in the house and eyed us with contempt as we helped DaQuan with his bags.

"DaQuan, I cannot believe this shit! You're just going to up and leave us?" she cried, hugging their daughter.

"Tanisha, stop being dramatic. I'll be back," he said.

Tanisha wasn't trying to hear that. "Mayabi, your daddy don't love us," she said in an attempt to make DaQuan reconsider.

"Don't tell her that!" he scolded.

I saw the hurt in his eyes when Mayabi began crying too. DaQuan was ruthless when he was in the streets, but like most head bangers that I knew he was a gentle thug when he was around his girl and his seed.

"Mayabi, come to daddy," he gently cooed.

He sat his garment bag down and held open his arms. Mayabi came to him and hugged his legs. He bent down and lifted her up into his arms. "Don't cry, baby." He tried to soothe his little angel, kissing away her tears.

"Daddy, you don't love me and mommy anymore?" she asked, sniffling hard.

"Of course daddy loves you, baby. And I love your mommy too. She's just a little upset right now," DaQuan replied tenderly.

I headed for the door to allow them some privacy. Legend did the same.

DaQuan caught up with us outside by the whip. "Let's roll," he said.

I leaned my forearms on the hood of the car and looked back up at the house. Tanisha was standing in the doorway glaring at us. "Black Man, stay here with your family. I can understand where Tanisha is coming from," I reconsidered.

DaQuan eyes followed mine. He disregarded what he had to be feeling. "Fam, I can't allow my girl's emotions to come in the way of business. Shawdy gon' be a'ight," he insisted.

"Nah, son, I was wrong to even ask you to go up top with me. Love is love, but your first priority is your Queen and that little princess," I argued.

"Hold up, Rah. I'll be right back. A man gotta do what a man gotta do."

"A man has to put his family first," I reminded him.

"Like I said, hold up," he repeated. Then he walked back up on the porch and he and Tanisha engaged in a heated conversation.

DaQuan stalked inside and came out carrying the bags that Legend and I had left at the door. Tanisha followed him, pulling Mayabi along by the arm.

"Go back in the house, shawdy. I'll call you when I get to Jersey." DaQuan's voice was full of irritation.

Tanisha's eyes were full of tears. "Mayabi, ask your father why he's leaving us if he loves us so much."

DaQuan scowled at her.

"Ask him Mayabi," repeated Tanisha.

DaQuan ran a hand down his face and let out a long sigh. "Mayabi, go inside so that daddy and mommy can talk."

Mayabi, who was well behaved, immediately did as her father instructed. Me and Legend got in the truck. From the inside of my 2012 Lexus RX Hybrid, I could clearly hear DaQuan and Tanisha shouting back and forth.

"Don't ever use my daughter to fight our battles, shawdy. That was some foul shit!" he streamed.

"It shouldn't be a battle! You don't choose your freaking friends over your woman and your child. How in the fuck am I supposed to feel about you going out of town for months? I heard you on the phone the other night. I know what you're going up to

New Jersey to do," ranted Tanisha. She pushed DaQuan in the chest. "Boy, you must be outta your goddamn mind."

"Calm down," he pleaded, reaching out to comfort her.

"Don't touch me! Don't you dare fuckin' touch me." She snatched away from him and threatened, "I swear, DaQuan, if you get in that car, it's over for us. You will never see Mayabi again."

"Shawdy, you don't mean that," he said. He knew that she loved him too much to walk away. And he loved her in return.

Tanisha was short and petite with the most alluring greenish eyes. In the 'A', where dudes preferred thick females, Tanisha wasn't considered a dime piece. But in DaQuan's eyes she was a dime plus some.

What I loved and respected about the young sistah was her perseverance. When Tanisha and DaQuan first met five years ago, she was in the Job Corps. She was a young wayward female with a whole lot of issues caused by growing up in a very dysfunctional environment in Gary, Indiana.

I had watched DaQuan's love for Tanisha fertilize her potential. Although DaQuan flipped bricks, Tanisha was not content with being the typical hustler's wife. She didn't sit in the house all day and wait for him to come home and toss the bands on the bed. Shorty held down a nine to five and she was getting a degree online.

I felt bad about asking her man to risk his family to go to The Bricks to fight a street war that didn't concern him. "Son, you don't have to do this," I said. "Go back in the house with those two precious queens."

DaQuan slid into the backseat. "Shawdy, you say anything?" he replied.

Tanisha ran up to the driver's door and glared at me. Her eyes were squinted in anger and her mouth was a tight line. "Raheem, for all of that shit you talk about elevating the black race, deep down you're nothing but a hypocrite. You're as fake as a three dollar bill," she hurled.

I had no comeback because her words mirrored what I felt inside. I turned and looked in the backseat at DaQuan. "Bruh, stay with your family," I tried again. But it's impossible to tell a man what to do when his mind is made up.

"Let's bounce, fam," he said.

I held his gaze and knew that he wasn't going to change his mind. I looked from him to his woman, feeling trapped in the middle of something that I should have never started.

"I apologize, Queen. But I promise—"

"Miss me wit' the speech!" She cut me off. "You ain't nothin' but a fake ass Muslim. I used to have respect for you but you ain't shit. You preach one thing and do another; it wouldn't surprise me if your ass eat chitlins when ain't nobody looking."

The insult hurt me. I put the car in reverse and slowly backed out of the driveway and drove off.

"Rah, you know shawdy got love for you. She's all in her feelings right now," said DaQuan apologetically.

As we hit the expressway headed up top, Tanisha's words rang in my ear. Was I really a hypocrite? Or was I just a loyal ass friend? I asked myself.

"Shawdy, don't let that shit bother you. We gotta focus because from what you've been telling me, The Bricks ain't no ho," said DaQuan correctly interpreting my silence.

He was dead ass—The Bricks wasn't no punk—but I couldn't get Tanisha's accusation out of my mind. I turned on the music and Nas and Lauryn Hill was spittin' powerful truth that spoke directly to my conscience.

If I ruled the world (Imagine that)
I'd free all my sons, I love 'em love 'em baby
Black diamonds and pearls (Could it be, if you could be mine,
we'd both shine)

Ca$h

If I ruled the world (Still living for today, in these last days and
times)

ELEVEN

RAHEEM

When we reached Newark, CJ already had an apartment set up for DaQuan and Legend at the Executive House on Prospect Street. He met us outside the security gate in his pine green 2012 Dodge Charger, one of many cars in his fleet. We followed him to the unit that he had leased.

Parked outside the building I got out of my truck and met my dawg at the front of his ride. Rick Ross's *Diced Pineapples* was hittin' hard from the sound system. "Sup family," I said, embracing CJ with a brotherly hug.

"I'm good. How you be?" he asked, holding the embrace longer than usual.

"I'm blessed, yo." I stepped back and took in his visage. His True Religion jeans were fresh and he wore a jacket over a black crew neck T-shirt. The thumbnail-sized diamonds in his ears sparkled as brightly as the sun against his dark skin.

When I looked closer I noticed that he was rocking a new platinum chain around his neck. A diamond-encrusted medallion the size of my fist hung down to his chest. I took a step closer and inspected it. It was a replica of Tamika's face. *RIP* was written in diamonds at the bottom.

My nigga remained a stunna in spite of all that he was going through, but stress lines creased his face like those of a man with the weight of the world on his shoulders. No amount of expensive jewelry or gear could cover that up.

I glanced over his shoulder and peered inside his ride. "Why you rolling dolo fam?" I asked. "Where is Eric, Snoop and 'em?"

"They're making moves. Niggaz still gotta eat, nah mean?" he explained.

81

"Nah, somebody should be with you at all times." I frowned. My head immediately went on a swivel, looking for any sign of the adversary. My strap was inside the truck but I would've taken five to the chest for my dude.

"I hear you, Rah, but those lames ain't gonna stop me from riding around this bitch doing what I do. This is my city, nah mean? I'll slay Nard's entire team." He lifted up the bottom of his shirt revealing two burners in his waistband.

Too many people on the outside, CJ came off as being cocky and arrogant, but I overstood. Where we came from modesty got the average brother stepped on. I was humble by nature while CJ's personality exuded a straight in your face confidence that offended those that didn't really know his heart. I wasn't worried about his attitude though, I was concerned for his life.

"Fam, I'm about to change things around. From now on somebody will be with you at all times. If you go take a piss one of our people better be posted outside the bathroom door or it's going to be a problem," I stated seriously.

CJ chuckled. "Yeah, nigga, that's why I need you here." The worry lines across his face seemed to fade away.

DaQuan and Legend got out of the truck and walked up to us. CJ gave DaQuan some dap and a chest bump. "Welcome to the Bricks. I hate that it had to be under these circumstances, but I know you're about this life. When this is all over I'ma fuck wit' you," The look in CJ's eyes conveyed his sincerity.

"It's all love, bruh bruh. Real niggaz do real shit," DaQuan affirmed. The sun reflected off his gold teeth.

I introduced CJ to Legend who was a real thin dude with a deep voice. His dark complexion was the same shade as CJ's and his murder game was second to none. He had four small teardrops tatted under each eye—one for every nigga he had put in the ground.

CJ gave him a half hug.

"Legend, huh?" he remarked. "You live up to that name, Slim?"

Before Legend could respond, a silver Honda Prelude crept up on us. The driver's window slowly eased down. Tension quickly invaded our space as Legend's Desert Eagle came out in a flash. Beside us DaQuan whipped out his fo-fo. I jumped in front of CJ, shielding him with my body.

The driver of the Prelude squealed at the sight of Legend and DaQuan's ratchets pointed at her.

"Chill, yo," CJ barked just in time to save ma from catching a face full of hollow points. "I know lil' mama, she good," he said, stepping around me and walking up to the sistah's car.

Legend and DaQuan relaxed a little and lowered their tools. A few other innocent people drove by as we stood at the curb waiting for CJ to finish talking to baby girl. They carried on their conversation for another ten minutes before she pulled off.

"Y'all scared the shit out of shorty. Her hands were trembling and shit," CJ laughed as he rejoined us.

"Ma looks familiar," I said.

"That was Eternity, she works at Diamond Doubies on Market Street. She used to do Tamika's hair," he said, walking toward the apartments with us following behind him.

The living room was furnished with black and gray butter leather sofa and chairs, and chrome and glass end tables. The walls were eggshell white and the thick carpet under our feet was a darker shade of gray than the pillows on the sofa. A modern chrome entertainment center took up one wall and a Plasma TV took up most of the other.

A large bowl of *sour* sat on the coffee table. CJ picked it up and passed it to DaQuan, who hesitated to accept it. "I'm good. I don't fuck wit' the loud if I'm putting in work," he explained.

"Nah, I want you and Legend to kick back and chill for a day or two before we strike. We just put some niggaz on their ass; the

83

bodies are still gettin' scraped off the pavement so it's hot on the block right now."

"Let's make that muhfucka hotter," said Legend.

CJ looked at me. "Slim trained to go, ain't he?" he replied approvingly.

"Yeah fam, he's sick with that gunplay," I said.

As they got high and talked murder, I calculated everything that I knew about Nard. The young boy was hard to predict because he was real brazen about the way he attacked. I decided that we couldn't take anything for granted.

I walked over to the window and parted the blinds, looking down into the lot. Everything was quiet except for a few cars passing by. CJ was telling DaQuan and Legend what was needed of them.

"Don't nobody in The Bricks know your faces so it's gonna be easy for y'all to get up on a nigga and spray his thoughts up in the air. I want y'all to lay low and don't socialize with anybody. This is more than a street beef, it's personal. The niggaz we're going after murked my girl and her people," he reemphasized.

"Let's get to it," said Legend, getting crunk. He pulled a machete out a tennis bag that he had brought along and caressed the blade.

"You're gonna have to watch and pay attention to everything," I cautioned. "The Bricks are different than The Dirty. New faces are gonna be met with suspicion and y'all will stick out like a sore thumb because Newark dudes have their own style. When niggaz see you, that should be the image they take to their graves."

I walked back amongst them and sat down at the end of the couch, allowing myself distance from the weed smoke that CJ was blowing out. DaQuan and Legend were in chairs a few feet away. The three of them were going to end up giving me a contact high.

"DaQuan, call Tanisha and let her know that you made it here safely," I reminded him.

"I'll hit her later," he said.

"Man, I'm not trying to tell you how to handle yours, but you know she's already worried sick about you. The least you can do is call her and let her know that everything is peace."

"I feel you." He pulled out his cell phone and walked out on the front balcony.

"He don't want us to see him cry," cracked Legend.

I laughed, but overstood that thugs love and cry too. My thoughts drifted to Sparkle. I hadn't really had time to mourn because of everything that was going on with CJ. I thought about all the families that would have to mourn before this was over. I stood up to leave and CJ asked where I was headed.

"I need to go see Big Ma and tell her what's going on. It's going to break her heart but I don't want her to hear it from someone else."

"You want me to go with you?" offered CJ as I headed for the door.

"Nah, fam, I gotta go alone," I replied.

The truth was going to break Big Ma's heart but I had been raised to be honest with her about everything. "It's better that I hear it from you instead of from someone else," she had always taught me.

This was about to seriously test that.

Ca$h

TWELVE

RAHEEM

"Raheem, I did not raise you to be a thug," cried Big Ma, looking up from her pillow into my face.

"I know you didn't and I'm not a thug, I'm just a loyal friend," I tried to explain.

She was in bed and not feeling too well. I felt bad burdening her at a time like this but I could not risk her safety. Once Nard realized that I had returned home to bust my gun side by side with CJ, my family's lives would be at risk.

Nard had not hesitated to murder Tamika's family, I could not take a chance that he would spare mine.

"Raheem, I've been trying to tell you for the longest to leave CJ alone. The streets are all he knows or cares about. I hope to God that I'm wrong but CJ is gonna die on these same streets that he loves so much. And before he does, he's gonna cause a lot of people to lose their lives. I don't want you to be one of them," Big Ma's voice choked with weariness and emotion.

I was sitting on the edge of her bed, holding her plump hand in mine, looking down into her tear-stained face. Her gray hair was tousled and she seemed to grow very old before my eyes. I reached down and stroked her hair.

"Big Ma, you know how I am. You know that I'll lay my life on the line for family. CJ is my brother. Maybe not in blood, but right here." I tapped my chest with a fist.

Big Ma turned her head away from me.

"I can't turn my back on him no more than I could turn my back on you or LaKeesha or my nieces and nephew. That's the man that I am Big Ma. I stand on loyalty and principle."

Continuing to look away from me she said, "You're not supposed to stand on the side of wrong Raheem," she corrected.

"Big Ma, I understand everything you're saying, and I won't argue with you—I have way too much love and respect for you to do that. I know that I don't always do the right thing at the right time, I just follow my heart. If I have not lived up to your expectations, I'm sorry. But you raised a man Big Ma. Not just a *man,* but a good one. Your job is done."

We both remained silent, almost overwhelmed with emotion. I could hear each tick of the old school wind up alarm clock on her nightstand. Big Ma slid out the other side of the bed, straightening her cotton gown as she stood up to her full 5'2" height. Today she looked every day of her seventy years of age. No doubt I was adding to her load.

She turned to look at me with eyes that brimmed with tears. "So I'm supposed to pack up and move out of my home at the snap of a finger? All because you want to involve yourself in CJ's bullcrap," she mumbled.

I respectfully kept quiet.

"His mother and sister got killed because of him, and I hear that he's the reason that Tamika was killed. Lord have mercy! Your sister already worries me bad enough running around here having babies by all these different no good men. Now this!" Big Ma rattled on, moving around the bedroom aimlessly.

"Big Ma, may I say something?" I asked.

"Might as well, you done already said a mouthful. Don't see what else you gonna say, though."

"The move will be real good for LaKeesha. At least it will get her away from Newark. In Atlanta she can make new friends and start a new life."

"Who can start a new life in Atlanta?"

The question came from the direction of the doorway. My head snapped toward the sound of my sister's voice. LaKeesha stood there with her arms folded, ready for a fight. She had dyed her hair red and the leggings and top that she wore fit her tighter than a scuba diver's suit. To have given birth to three kids at such a young age she had bounced back remarkably, but I wished that she would find a more subtle way to show it off. This was not the proper time to raise that issue again, though.

Let he who is without sin cast the first stone, I could hear Big Ma saying.

"Sup, La? Where the kids?" I asked, attempting to change the subject until I had things worked out with Big Ma, but LaKeesha wasn't going for it.

"Who's moving to Atlanta?" she demanded to know.

"We are. And don't raise your voice in this house," Big Ma intoned.

LaKeesha stormed into the room and planted herself in front of me. "Uh uh, Rah! I'm not moving to no country Georgia." Her hands shot to her hips.

"Yes, you are," Big Ma asserted.

LaKeesha rolled her eyes at me, then turned back to Big Ma. "Why do we have to move Mama?"

"Your brother will explain it to you. Now where are the kids?"

"They're over to Ant Man's mother's house. I have to go get some things to send him a package and I didn't feel like carrying the kids in and out of the mall with me."

"Chile, you would do better at finding a man if you chose the next one with your eyes closed," Big Ma said as she wobbled to the bathroom.

Her comment wasn't far from the truth, LaKeesha chose all the wrong dudes to fall in love with. Ant Man, her youngest child's father, was just the latest in a long line. He was on lock serving a double life joint for murder and home invasion.

Lakeesha plopped down on the bed beside me. She looked at me questioningly. "What's going on Rah?"

I put an arm around her and explained everything.

"But why would Nard come after me and Big Ma?" she asked.

"La, ain't you listening? Niggaz are grimy like that."

"I ain't letting him run me out of town, I'm not no scary bitch," she said, keeping her voice low out of respect for Big Ma.

"Sis, don't fight me on this. The move will be good for you, ain't nothing here in The Bricks."

"All my friends are here. I'm not going. I don't care what nobody says," she stubbornly maintained.

"You're moving to Atlanta if I gotta tie you up and drive you there," I stressed.

"That's the only way I'm going," she spat.

"That's how you'll go then because I refuse to lose somebody else that I love." I stood up and walked out into the living room as thoughts of Kayundra rushed to the forefront of my mind. I hadn't been able to protect her but I would not let anything harm Big Ma and LaKeesha.

I sat down on the sofa and tried to gather my thoughts. Before I realized it I was strolling through the pictures of Kayundra that I had stored in my phone. I wanted to dial her number and tell her how life was taking me down a different path; one that might not have a return.

I wanted to hear her laughter or simply tell her that I love her, and that I was ready to set my pride aside and open my arms to her again. I wanted to hold, touch, and feel her. Just one more time.

I looked up from my phone when I felt Big Ma sit down next to me. She put her loving arms around me and held me like she did when I was a little boy.

A week later, I watched Big Ma board a flight to Atlanta. LaKeesha was nowhere to be found, she had run off with the kids to keep from having to leave Newark. As the plane ascended into the sky, I felt an uneasiness in the pit of my stomach because my sister was not aboard it.

Now it became more imperative that I help CJ annihilate Nard. Or die trying.

Ca$h

THIRTEEN

CJ

The night was darker than my murderous intentions and as quiet as a bitch nigga with a banger to the back of his head. The clock in the dashboard read 3:13A.M. We crept pass the targeted house for the second time in the last five minutes. Everything seemed quiet and still inside. A lone light shined from a room upstairs.

A white Tahoe was parked in the driveway just as Flip informed us it would be. "This where the nigga lays his head." I pointed at a two story home as I drove by and parked a few houses down.

"How many people are inside?" asked Rah from the passenger seat.

"Three. All of them are in their twenties." I repeated what Flip had reported back to me.

Rah pulled on a pair of black leather gloves then tied a scarf over the lower half of his face. In the backseat, Legend and DaQuan strapped up too. We all had on bulletproof vests under all black gear. Tonight I was gonna find out if their murder games were vicious enough for The Bricks.

"The nigga we're after is short and stocky with a nappy fro. Word on the street is that he was with Nard when they killed my lil souljahs on Chadwick. Nigga been running his mouth to the wrong muhfuckaz," I said.

"No women and children, and no elderly people, right?" asked Rah.

"Not according to Flip. I asked him specifically and he knows you don't rock like that."

"A'ight. Before we move out overstand that there are three young brothaz up in there, and all of them are likely to be strapped.

We know at least one of them, Talib, will bust that toy. But we'll have the element of surprise on our side." Rah took charge.

"Smash anything that move yo," I added. "I wanna snatch Talib up without murking him right away, but if he bucks go ahead and flatten that ass. When we get inside I want Rah and DaQuan to take the upstairs, me and Legend will take the downstairs."

"What about a lookout outside?" DaQuan asked.

I pointed to a car parked a house down on the other side of the street.

"That's Flip. He'll get in position as soon as we make our move. Everybody strapped and ready?" I asked as I pulled on my own ski mask and gloves.

"Let's get to it," exhorted Legend.

"I'm ready," added DaQuan.

"Me too," joined Rah.

I gave them each a pound. "One love," I said in case one of us didn't make it out.

We got out of the whip and moved toward the back of the house like trained hit men. The ground beneath our boots was frozen with traces of an early winter snow that had fallen yesterday. I released the safety on my Nine as I climbed the four steps that led up to the back porch. My hit squad was right behind me, stepping lively.

I put a finger to my lips as I opened the screen door and stepped aside. DaQuan and Legend stepped in front.

"One—two—three," DaQuan canted, and then both of them kicked in the door. It slammed against something, making a loud noise. The four of us rushed in, weapons out, seeking to send a bitch to his grave.

Rah found the stairway and raced upstairs with DaQuan hot on his heels. Me and Legend ran through the downstairs until we located two niggaz in the living room. One was asleep on the couch. The other one scrambled out of a chair and reached under the seat cushion.

Boc! Boc! Boc! Boc! Boc! Nina in my hand screamed out five shots in quick succession, dropping him to his knees. Blood poured down his back. A sixth shot put something sizzling hot in his head.

Legend stood over the second boy with his fo-fifth pressed to his forehead. The boy was awake now with a petrified look on his face. "Don't kill me blood. I'm just visiting. I don't have shit to do with whatever is going on here," he pleaded.

"Well, now you do." Legend slapped him across the face with his tool.

I stepped closer and looked him over. He was not who I was looking for. "Where's Talib?" I questioned, turning on the lamp beside the couch.

He pointed upstairs. "Second room on the left."

"Snitchin' ass bitch," Legend said and shot him twice in the chest. Then he lowered the gun and blasted him once in the head. "Straight up," he rasped.

When we looked up, Rah and DaQuan were walking a young male and female toward us. They both looked to be in their early twenties. The dude was short and stocky, and he fit the description that I had been given of Talib.

He was butt ass naked with his hands covering his genitals like he was embarrassed of what he packed. Fear flashed in his eyes as they moved from one dead friend to the next.

The girl with Talib was a cutie even after being awakened out of her sleep by armed gunmen. She was pecan brown with a short bob hairstyle and big brown eyes that had teared up. A sheet was wrapped around her body covering her nakedness. She shook with fear and turned her head away from the sight of the bullet-ridden bodies.

I looked back at the dude.

"What's your name, B?" I asked.

"Talib," he admitted in a shaky voice.

"Do you know why I'm here?"

"No."

"You roll with Nard, don't you?" I removed my mask so that he could see that he had chosen the wrong side.

Recognition shined in his eyes but he held a poker face. "I don't know anybody by that name," he denied.

"A'ight. I see you wanna play games," I chuckled.

Boc!

I shot him in the foot. He squealed and hopped around on one foot. "I got all night, yo. And a clip full of bullets." I aimed my banger at his knee.

The chick began shivering, but I paid her no mind. "My nigga, don't insult my intelligence. You know who I am, and you know what this is about. I'm gonna ask you some questions, and every time you give me a wrong answer I'ma put some pain on your muhfuckin' ass."

"Man, my foot hurts," whined Talib, falling to the floor wincing.

I looked down at him in disgust. Is this what the fuck being gangsta had come to? When a muhfucka was on the other end of that tool he was all dick and balls, but when he found himself facing the barrel he turned pussy.

I shook my head. "Son, you not built for this shit. Tell me what I wanna know and we'll be out," I said.

"Okay. What do you wanna know?"

"That's better. Let's take this from the top. Do you know who I am?"

He nodded *yes*.

"Good. Now where is the money and the product?"

He gave up that info too. I sent DaQuan upstairs to check it out. He returned a few minutes later with a stuffed pillowcase. I inspected its contents then nodded my approval.

"Man, I'm going to bleed to death," cried Talib.

"No you're not," I promised, staring down at him with no compassion. "Where does Nard live?"

"I don't know."

"Wrong answer." I shot him in the knee. His bitch screamed. "Shut her up!" I barked.

Legend raised his gun to her head and was about to puff her shit out. "I got this," Rah intervened. He snatched ma by the arm and drug her out of the room.

Talib was rolling around on the floor howling in pain.

"It's only gonna get worse homie. You better tell the man what he wanna know," said Legend.

"I swear, I don't know where Nard lives, but I know where his brother Man Dog stays," cried Talib.

My eyes lit up. "Talk!"

Talib turned into a GPS.

As soon as he divulged the information, I nodded my head at Legend. He slid a hunter's knife out of a sheath strapped on his side and stepped behind Talib who was on his back, clutching his knee. Blood seeped through his fingers and ran down his arm in a river. He kept squeezing his eyes open and shut, tryna endure the hot pain of the gunshots.

I nodded again at Legend.

He bent down behind Talib and wrapped his arm around his neck, yanking his head back. I looked on unmercifully as Legend put the sharp edge of the knife against Talib's throat.

"Somebody should've warned you not to choose sides against me. See you in hell, nigga," I gritted.

In one swift motion, Legend slashed his throat. Talib gurgled blood and put his hands over the long deep slash in a futile effort to staunch the blood flow.

We stood there and watched Talib choke to death on his own blood. When his body stopped jerking I looked at Legend and

DaQuan; now was the time to demonstrate to them that I was a boss and a gangsta, unafraid to get blood on my own hands.

I looked down at Talib, whose head was almost severed from his body. I lowered my gun and blasted him in the chest six times. "You ain't gonna bleed to death now, you're already dead."

I stepped over the body and went in search of Rah and the girl.

We found them in the kitchen. The young chick was seated in a chair with her head between her knees, crying. Rah was leaned against the counter scowling. Our eyes met in the soft glow of the kitchen's light.

I walked over to my nigga and whispered in his ear. "Fam, she's seen my face. I'ma have to do what I gotta do."

Rah's eyes held mine for a long, silent moment, then without saying anything he left out the back door.

The girl looked up and started sobbing. "Please don't kill me. I just turned twenty-one last week. I don't want to die."

I steeled my eyes at her and gritted, "You should've been more selective about the niggaz you fucked with. If there's a next life and you come back, find yourself a church boy."

"Please!" she begged, but I had no mercy. The niggaz she laid with hadn't shown Tamika any.

I turned to Legend and said, "Handle your business, yo."

He raised the bloody knife and stepped toward lil' mama. I heard her scream then she was silent.

FOURTEEN

RAHEEM

I was silent, trying to stem the rage that was building up inside of me as we left the scene and rode out to East Orange where CJ owned a small warehouse.

As soon as we got there I hopped out the car and moved toward the door. Once we were all inside and had discarded our black gear, I exploded on Flip. "There was a young girl up in there. I think you knew that before we ran up in the house," I accused.

"Fuck off me, nigga!" He shoved me. "If a lil' bitch was up in there, I didn't know it."

"I think you did," I refuted, stepping back up in his grill.

"Fuck what you think. Who is you?" We were nose to nose. Our breath was hot on each other's faces. CJ, Legend and DaQuan silently looked on.

"I'ma show you who I am if that shit happens again, yo," I threatened.

"I hear you talking, son. But you ain't saying nothin'," Flip shot back. "Pull your thong out ya ass, this shit is war. We not sparing nobody. Man, woman or child, if they get in the way they can get it."

I raised my fist and punched him right in the face. Flip stumbled back and I caught him on the temple with a hard left hook that put him on his ass. "I told you *no women or children*!" I stood over him sneering down.

He pounced to his feet and charged at me, throwing hard haymakers that bounced off my head and forearms. My fight game was crazy nice so I easily slipped inside his wild punches and two-pieced him in the eye. He staggered back and reached for his waist but my draw was faster.

"Go ahead, make me put some hollow points in your life," I dared him.

Flip looked at me like he was considering testing my G, but the look in my eyes must have warned him not to do nothing stupid like that. With a grimace on his face he let his hand fall away from his waist.

"Ain't nothin' pussy over here, son. Test this shit and get ya face blown the fuck off," I clenched my jaw.

"Rah, chill," CJ bellowed, stepping up and pulling me back.

Flip wiped the blood that ran from his busted lip and glared at me. It felt like he was sending an unspoken warning my way.

"What's on your mind, son? You feeling some kind of way?" I challenged.

"You tryna punk me?" he shot back.

"Nah, but you can make me send some heat your way," I spat.

"Send that shit." He called my bluff.

He had just bought himself a one-way ticket to the pearly gates. I leveled my ratchet at his chest and was about to make it jump when DaQuan and Legend pulled me to the other side of the room.

"Nawl bruh bruh," said DaQuan, hopping in the way of my gun.

Flip reached for his shit again but CJ took it away from him and pushed him over in a corner. I could see them talking heatedly. Flip's arms were flying around and though he was talking to CJ he was staring at me.

"I know that's your man but I ain't no ho. I'll put six in that niggaz' dome," I heard him say.

"What'd you say?" I shouted across the warehouse, prepared to show him why Jesus wept.

"Be easy, dawg," whispered DaQuan. He held me in a bear hug, preventing me from stalking across the floor and showing Flip that a humble man is real dangerous when provoked.

Flip was talking mad noise. I knew he wasn't pussy but it didn't matter, I would not hesitate to serve him the same injustice he had served shorty.

CJ and 'em kept us separated until our tempers cooled down. Flanked by my mans, I strolled back across the warehouse to where CJ and Flip stood. The vein on the side of my head pulsated and my chest heaved in and out. Just that quick my anger returned. I stopped about twenty feet away from CJ and Flip to calm myself down again.

"Sup, Rah? How we gon' play this?" whispered Legend.

"I'm peace," I assured him as I restarted toward CJ and Flip.

We met up under a light hanging down from an overhead rafter. CJ looked us both in the eyes, trying to gauge our mindsets. "Y'all cool?" he asked.

"I'm good," grumbled Flip, never breaking eye contact with me.

"Me too," I said. "I been good."

CJ shot us both a warning stare. Stepping off, he said, "I'ma let men talk it out like men."

For a minute or so nothing was said; we stood there allowing our blood to cool off. Really, I was out of character because in this shit you let your gun talk for you. Otherwise silence ruled the hour. Cemeteries were full of people that said the wrong thing at the right time.

I knew with a street dude like Flip this was about to be a pissing contest if I came at him aggressively again. So I chose to speak humbly.

"My brotha, from the onset I explained to you how I rock. All I asked is that you respect that. To you that girl up in that house may have been just another body on your street resume. But to me she was a young sistah with her whole life in front of her. No different than my little sister. Nah mean?"

Flip didn't respond so I went on.

"Shorty wasn't about this life. What did she do to deserve to die? She laid up with a thug who had beef in the street? She probably didn't even know that yo," I vented.

Flip chuckled and waved off what I was spitting. He looked at me with his head cocked to the side and a crooked smile on his face. "Nigga, this is war," he said. "Don't nobody have time to figure out all of that shit. When you bomb on a muhfucka, civilians get caught up in the blast. If you can't accept that, you're not built for the game. This is The Bricks, ain't no love or mercy up in this bitch. Georgia has turned you soft."

I looked from him to Legend, then to DaQuan. I saw in their eyes that they felt lightweight disrespected. I shook my head, letting them know to let the insult pass. Obviously Flip was still a little hot. He knew that it didn't matter where you were from, it's what you're about.

I had to concede that Flip was right about one thing he had said. In war there is always innocent lives lost on both sides. I knew this as surely as I knew that the sun rises in the East.

I thought about the girl we had just murdered, Tamika and all the other young sistahs that had lost their lives over nothing more than loving a thug. The game spared no one.

"It's do or die out here in the streets," said Flip, correctly interpreting my anguish.

"I hear you," I concurred. But even amongst killers there had to be principles.

I told myself that that's what separated me from a heartless killa like Flip. But did it really? And while I was trying to show compassion Nard was somewhere out there plotting all of our demise.

FIFTEEN

NARD

I sat inside the Manalapan Diner with my hands folded on top of the table, ignoring the food in front of me. My concentration was on the man sitting on the other side of the table. He was well known throughout the state, but especially in Newark, which is why we were meeting in South Jersey right outside of Freehold. He had sent word through Jamaican Black that he wanted to make me an offer that would elevate my hustle and help me dethrone CJ.

No one knew that he was a drug supplier and for reasons obvious to me he wanted it to remain that way. In fact, he had asked me to come alone so that his identity remained a secret between us. I understood why he took such precautions, but with the beef going on between me and CJ, I wasn't rolling nowhere without my goons close by.

I looked up and saw Big Nasty seated at a table nearby. He was dressed in a business suit and tie with a folded newspaper in front of him on the table. I knew that inside that daily edition was something that would make the news real interesting if this was a setup.

At a table on the other side of the room was Man Dog and Lemora, pretending to be a happy couple sharing lunch. Both of them were strapped with automatic handguns that were locked and loaded, and easily accessible. Outside the restaurant was a car load of my most thorough men. They were under orders to drive straight through the front door and jump out blasting at the first sign of a flex move.

The man across from me had no idea that he was surrounded by my gunners, they had arrived at the restaurant an hour before our scheduled meeting.

I looked at the prospective connect and said, "I'm not the sociable type. You asked me to come here for a specific reason. Say what's on your mind and let's part ways."

He looked up from his platter and attempted to smile but it was more like a twitch. "I'm going to eat first. We can talk afterwards."

He was a man used to calling shots. I saw no need to challenge him, at least not until I had heard his proposal, so I just sat there studying him while he ate. He didn't seem fazed by the scrutiny at all nor did he speak again until he had pushed his plate away. When he spoke his voice commanded my attention, and when we were done talking I knew that soon the streets would be mine.

I remained seated until he left out the door. Big Nasty looked at me and I nodded my head, letting him know that everything was good. I looked over and nodded to Man Dog and Lemora too, I flashed them a quick smile and we all stood up to leave.

I zipped up my jacket and jogged over to where Big Nasty had parked. The wind was brutal today, it felt like the weather had dropped to forty degrees and it was only November. I told myself that I was gonna move to the South one day to escape these cold ass winters.

Big Nasty rushed ahead of me and held the door of his Durango open for me to get out of the cold. The heat inside the whip felt better than a nigga's first brick. I leaned forward and held my hands close to the vents, rubbing them together to warm them.

"It's cold as shit out there yo," I said as we drove off.

Big Nasty turned the heat up to full blast. "You good?" he asked when the hot air began blowing out.

"Yeah," I replied. I was a little distracted because my eyes were on the streets, watching every car in the vicinity.

I had been surprised when the man that I had just met with sent word through Jamaican Black that he wanted to meet. One minute the Dread was warning me not to test CJ's guns and the next he was playing intermediary for me and the connect.

"If this is a set-up Dread, I'ma kill you," I had warned him.

"No worry my youth. This is legit," he had vowed.

I relaxed when we jumped on the turnpike and headed back home with my people in cars behind me. I hit Quent up where he waited back in Newark and uttered a prearranged code. "I'm safe."

Now he wouldn't run up in Jamaican Black's barber shop and crush him.

My cell phone rung almost as soon as I hung up from Quent. I leaned over and turned the heat down, then I put the phone back to my ear. "Yeah bruh?"

"How did it go?" asked Man Dog.

"It went well. They can supply us with the *white girls* at fifteen apiece."

Man Dog let out a long whistle. "That's two bands less than we're paying. What about delivery?"

"It'll come through the Dread."

"It can't get no sweeter than that. Why is he tryna fuck with us yo?" asked Man Dog suspiciously.

"He says the nigga he's been dealing with is on some hot boy shit and he don't want their heat latching on to him," I explained as J. Cole played in the background.

"You trust him?"

"I trust *no* man. But I'ma fuck with him. The first delivery of twenty-five will be Saturday. Plus he has guns. AK's, AR 15s—a whole arsenal yo." I was excited.

"Bruh, that sounds too good to be true," cautioned Man Dog. "Don't it sound a little shaky that he would step to you right now with all the bloodshed going on? Shit, the nigga he's talking about can't be hotter than we are right now. Unless it's CJ."

I had already thought about that.

"Nah, it ain't him," I discounted. "You'll just have to trust my judgment on this one. This is the opportunity we needed to put the game in a chokehold. From here there's no looking back yo."

My other line rung with a call from Show. "Bruh, let me catch this call. We'll finish chopping it up at the crib." I hung up and clicked over to Show. "What's good, cuz?"

"They got him, yo," he blurted out in a voice full of anguish.

"They got who? Fuck you talking about?"

"They got Talib."

"Who got him? The rollers?" I asked.

"Nah dawg. Some niggaz ran up in the spot on that ski mask bullshit. They killed him. They killed everybody in the house and all the money and work is gone."

I banged my hand against the window. "Don't tell me that shit!" Talib was Lemora's first cousin, his death was going to have her fucked up.

"Yeah dawg, they killed my nigga." Show broke down. I understood his pain, him and Talib had done a bid together on the island in New York and they had ran hard together on the bricks.

I ran a hand down my face and let out a long sigh. I had just spoken to Talib yesterday. "Who else was killed?" I murmured.

"Two of his young boys and a shorty he just met the other day."

I dropped my head in my hands and tried to take in the reality that Talib was dead. One minute he was here, and the next minute he was gone. I lifted my head and sucked in my breath then let it out slowly. My heart ached but my mind was clear. "Okay, meet us at Man Dog's house," I said then hung up the phone and dropped it in my lap.

"You a'ight?" asked Big Nasty, keeping his eyes on the traffic in front of us.

"I don't even know. They got Talib," I replied, disheartened. It tugged at my heart that Talib had only been home from serving a bid two short years and now we were gonna have to bury him.

Big Nasty allowed me a few minutes of silence before grumbling, "Sometimes the enemy strikes back. To prevent that from happening again we have to eliminate CJ's whole team, sparing no one."

Big Nasty seldom spoke so I gave his words much weight. I nodded my head, letting him know that I felt him. Besides the money and the work we had lost a valued comrade. It was time to turn the fuck up.

"Blood, I'm gonna bring CJ to his knees," I promised.

SIXTEEN

CJ

The only thing niggaz in the streets understood was blood for blood. You had to show them that if they touched yours you would make the punishment fit the crime by murking twice as many of theirs. I was born and bred on that merciless mentality so it wasn't shit to me. Nah mean?

Now Nard knew what it felt like to have to look down in a casket and say goodbye to someone he loved. It was only the beginning, before it was over I was gonna show the young boy why muhfuckaz bowed to this boss shit.

In the meantime the streets was blazing. Hot Top, aka the punk ass police, was everywhere tryna get a handle on the sudden spree of murders. Nard was so preoccupied with burying Talib and 'em, and staying out of po po's dragnet, he had no choice but to sit his young ass down somewhere and let me live.

In spite of all the bullets flying around and bodies dropping, I remained a stunna. I wanted the streets to know that nothing had changed. I was still that muhfucka and my team still reigned supreme.

Me, Rah and Eric were rolling in my Maybach; that pretty bitch turned heads as we mobbed through the hoods. Behind us my peeps were in their whips, twelve cars deep. Snoop, Premo, Flip, and other members of the team were pushin' everything from BMWs and Benz's to Navigators, Infiniti's and Escalades. Everybody's whip was freshly washed and waxed, sitting on big boy chrome.

We pulled into the parking lot of the Top's Diner. It was a Saturday evening and the sun was just about to surrender to a premature nightfall. Earlier we had paraded all over The Bricks and Lil' City, letting muhfuckaz know that we were still on top.

As I parked and got out of my ride letting my boots touch the ground, I saw the flyest honey that I had seen in a long time. Ma was a model-type with a light brown skin complexion and long hair that fell pass her shoulders and blew in the wind. Her waist length jacket allowed me to peep that she had some sick curves to go with that beautiful face. As she turned and looked toward the restaurant I caught an eye full of all that ass in those jeans. *That right there don't make no sense*, I said to myself.

Baby Girl was jocking me just as hard as I was sweating her, maybe harder. I busted a little smile her way, flashing platinum. Her and a girlfriend had just gotten out of the passenger side of a dark colored Lexus RX that was parked right next to me.

Two niggaz got out the other side of the Lexus and walked around the whip to claim Shorty and her friend. The taller of the two dudes was saying something to baby girl, but ma wasn't really listening, her attention was all mines.

"You gon' stand there sweatin' another man or you coming inside with us," I heard son say.

Ma put one hand on her hip and stood back on her legs, cocking her head to the side. "What?" she asked with that hood girl 'tude that I recognized immediately.

I had to smile because that shit reminded me of Tamika.

"I'm saying. Don't be disrespecting me like that yo. Fuck I look like?" He stepped toward her aggressively.

Shorty turned to her girl and said, "Papaya, I'ma call a cab to take me back home. I'll catch up with you later gurl. I don't know who Weez thinks he's talking to but I'm not that bitch."

I watched with a smirk on my face as she went in her bag and whipped out her cell phone. By now Rah and Eric was out the car checking out the drama too. The rest of my team were parking and getting out of their whips.

The other dude with baby girl and 'em tried to diffuse the conflict. He said, "Just chill, Shy. My man is just asking you to show him a little respect."

"Yo, fuck that bitch," his mans hurled.

That set shorty off! She threw her hands on her hips and rolled her neck. "Boy, you's the bitch. Ol' broke ass nigga. You're thirty years old and still pitching stones and borrowing the next nigga's chain. Clown ass muhfucka," she blasted on him.

He took two steps toward her with his fist balled, about to knock some of that hot shit right back where it came from. But his boy quickly stepped in the way. "Dude, chill out! You know them boys don't play the radio out this way," he barked. He turned to baby girl and said, "Shy, you're dead ass wrong. Fa real ma."

"Fuck your bitch ass boy," she spat. She reached in her bag and threw a handful of change at the one she was clowning on. "Buy you some toothpaste nigga, 'cause yo breath is a beast!" she said.

Weez went ham. His boy could barely hold him back. I looked at Rah and said, "Yo son, let me borrow your cape."

Rah chuckled. "You got your own."

All my goons were out of their cars and standing by my side. "Ma, come here," I called out to Shy. I had already decided that she was gonna be mine.

She turned and looked at me for a minute like she was tryna feel me out. A few seconds passed then she came on over to where I stood. I put my arm around her waist as if I had known her for a lifetime. "Is that your man or your baby daddy?" I asked.

"Hell no." I could see her breathing heavily.

"A'ight," I stated. "Stay right here, you're with me now."

Flanked by Rah and my goon squad, I stepped over to Weez and his man. The closer I got to where he stood, the harder Weez stared me down.

I planted my feet right in front of him and met his gaze with a harder one. "You got a problem with your eyes?" I said, hand on my strap.

"Nah, cuz, he's cool." His man jumped in. "We're just tryna chill with our ladies, we're not lookin' for no trouble."

"Good. But I guess your man right here ain't as smart as you. He look like he wants trouble to find *him*," I replied, never taking my eyes off Weez.

I had noticed local tags on their car when I pulled up so I knew that they were from The Bricks or somewhere not far away. That meant they had to know who I was, but Weez was determined to act hard.

I pulled out my tool and stuck it dead in his face. "What's on your mind? You feeling some kind of way?" I challenged.

"Nah man, I'm good," he gnashed his teeth.

I slapped him across the face with the steel and gritted back, "Fix your tone when you talk to me yo. The name is CJ and I slump niggas like you and piss on their grave."

I saw his whole expression change when he heard my name. He was shaking so hard I started to offer the nigga a stage and a pole.

I reached in my pocket and pulled out some bands. I popped the rubber band and tossed a couple dead faces on the ground at his feet. "Find somewhere else to eat tonight," I advised.

The money blew all over the parking lot.

Weez and 'em wisely got back in their car and backed out of the parking space. My squad watched them closely in case they tried something stupid. The front passenger window came down slowly and Papaya yelled out, "Shy, you know you're real foul. This is some bullshit!"

"You don't need me to hold your legs up, do you? Push with them niggaz if you want to. I'm good."

"You sad." She shook her head at Shy as if her choice to stay behind was a downgrade.

Two of Shy's fingers shot up in the air. "Deuces. See you later bitch," she hollered.

"Whatever!" Papaya fitted back into her seat as they peeled off. Clearly choosing dick over her ace.

"I can't stand a hater. Ugh!" exclaimed Shy. "She my girl and all but I'd snatch that ho's weave out."

I shook my head and laughed. Shorty was going in.

"What?" she asked with her head tilted to the side, displaying a sexy little bad girl smile on her face. Yeah, she was just like Tamika, all sassy and shit.

"You wild, yo," I chuckled.

"No I'm not. But she knows I don't play with her ass." She poked her chest out.

"You too muhfuckin' pretty to be fighting. Come on, let's go eat," I said.

"You serious?" she asked.

"Twenty-four seven." I took her hand in mine and we walked toward the entrance.

I had reserved the right side of the restaurant for our dinner party. Five or six tables had been pushed together to form one long rectangular one. I took my rightful place at the head. To my right closest to me sat Rah. To my left sat Shy. The rest of my mans sat around the table talking raucously. I stood up and quieted everyone down once the platters of food and the drinks had been delivered.

I held my hands out at my sides and bounced from foot to foot animatedly. "Who put this shit together? Me, that's who!" I shouted, mimicking Tony Montana in Scarface.

My niggaz went ham laughing and cheering me on. A couple of waitresses that were nearby looked on humorously.

"Who do I trust? Me, that's who."

I pulled out two fists full of money and tossed it up in the air. "Cam'ron Jeffries and his Brick City gangstaz up in this muhfuckin' bee-otch!" I screamed, slapping one of the waitresses on the ass as she passed by.

She giggled and hurried to join the other two waitresses in scooping the money up off the floor.

I reached out and pulled Shy up to her feet, guiding her into my arms. "Y'all see this pretty muhfucka right here?" I said.

My men hooted and hollered, whistled and barked.

I palmed shorty's ass with both hands and kissed her neck. The smell of her oriental vanilla fragrance had my dick banging at my zipper. She smelled so good I wanted to bury my nose in the crook of her neck and never come up for air.

"Damn ma you smell like heaven," I remarked, kissing her neck.

"How would you know how heaven smells?" she giggled.

"Shut up, you messing up my mack."

I held her back at arm's length and looked into her pretty brown eyes. "The first time I laid eyes on you I knew I had to have you. I said to myself, that girl right there is a tiger. She's the one for me," I had the Scarface Cuban accent down pat.

Shy showed me those thirty-twos.

I was fuckin' up the lines but she was loving it. Ma was cheesing mad hard. I pulled her back to me and put my nose in her hair. Her arms went around my neck and my soldier saluted her. "You're mine now," I said. I needed someone to dull the pain I had been tryna suppress lately.

She looked in my eyes and saw that I was dead ass. My swag had her hypnotized. "If that's what you want," she replied.

I planted a kiss on her lips then guided her back to her seat. I looked around the table at my mans and exclaimed. "Now that's boss shit yo!"

"Real boss shit!" A couple of my people chimed.

114

I grabbed a bottle of champagne and popped the top. I held it up in the air above my head. "In salute of my team. We still run The Bricks. Let no other crew rise above us."

I poured them all some champagne then we brought our glasses together at the center of the table and clinked them. "Death to our enemies," I toasted.

"Death to the enemy." Everyone chorused except Rah, who just nodded his head in agreement.

I didn't give Rah's response a second thought because I knew that although he was reserved, he turnt up when it was called for. Out the corner of my eye I noticed Flip looking at Rah sideways.

I grabbed the champagne bottle by the neck and turned it up. I took a long swig then sat it down on the table. "Family over everything," I said.

Flip caught my slight warning. He raised his glass in the air again and repeated, "Family over everything."

I believed that he was sincere but only time could answer that. I looked at Rah and saw that same humble expression that he always wore. Whatever his thoughts were, I knew he would not be the first to violate that pact.

I shoved the issue aside and addressed my people. "Let's eat like we feast off the streets," I said, sitting back down and looking over at Shy.

Shorty smiled at me with awe in her eyes. The waitresses stepped up and began serving us from the heaping platters of Tilapia, Lobster, Crab Legs, Shrimp and Hot Wings.

"This is living," I proclaimed.

"It sure is, baby," Shy agreed.

I looked at Rah, his hands were folded under his chin, and his elbows were on the table. The look that he returned was not one of approval. I wasn't vexed, that was just his get-down. He had never sought the spotlight, but I was born to shine.

Shy whispered my name.

I turned my head in her direction and she motioned with her finger for me to come closer. I leaned over so that she could whisper in my ear. "Your swag has a bitch's panties soaking wet," she said seductively.

I knew right then that she was my type of bitch, bold and sexier than sin. All she had to do was play her position.

SEVENTEEN

SHY

"Baby, I have to go to the ladies room," I whispered to CJ.

"A'ight, ma," he said, and then told two of his mans to escort me there. "Make sure my girl makes it back safely," he added.

My nipples tingled inside my lace bra and my clit hardened as I stood up. The way he commanded other niggaz was such a turn on. I felt like a mob wife. I knew that he was looking at my ass as I walked with my "bodyguards," so I gave him a peep show.

The purple suede Prada pants that I had picked up from a boutique in New York last week hit my pockets for a rack. They hugged my hips and ass so snugly, it was as if Picasso had painted them on me. Now was the perfect time to make the $1,000 investment pay dividends.

I used my muscle control to make my cheeks bounce provocatively with each step I took in my authentic Red Bottom six inch stilettos. My 36D's stood perky and firm inside the purple satin V-cut shirt that fitted me tightly and swished as I sashayed toward the bathroom with the eyes of CJ's whole team on me. I enjoyed the attention but this pussy was reserved for the Boss.

A bitch was stuck from the moment he pulled up in the parking lot. There was only one paid ass nigga riding around Newark in a Mayback and every female in the city old enough to use a Tampon knew who he was. I didn't have to think twice about clowning broke ass Weez. I was only rolling with them because my girl Papaya was tryna get in his boy Akon's pockets. So when Mr. Cam'ron Jefferies showed me some interest Weez ass became *soooo* expendable.

"I'll only be a minute," I said to my escorts and sauntered into the restroom.

Ca$h

As soon as the door closed behind me and I saw that I was alone, I let out a little scream and started spinning around in circles, waving my hands above my head like I had found love at first sight.

I put my hand over my heart and looked at my reflection in the mirror over the sink. My face was flushed with excitement and a strand of hair from my $2,500.00 Brazilian weave covered one eye. I swept it out of my face and said to my reflection, "Bitch, you bad."

As I freshened up and re-applied a peachy flavored gloss to my lips I tried to decide whether or not I was going to fuck CJ tonight. Street niggaz was quick to classify a girl a ho if she was too easy; the longer you made them wait, the more they respected you.

First night pussy usually ended up being a booty call bitch, but that didn't apply to the wet pinkness between my thick thighs. Once CJ dipped into this hot, creamy treasure I was going to have him running around with my name tatted on his neck. The pussy was the trap, I would just have to make sure that he didn't find out about my past.

When I came back to the table I leaned down and planted a kiss on CJ's lips. "Was I gone too long?" I asked coyly.

"Nah, shorty, you good," he replied, receiving my kiss tenderly.

I sat back down and listened to CJ control the conversation amongst him and his men as we all ate our food. Like most dudes in that life, they talked arrogantly. He introduced each one of them to me, which made me feel good, like he planned on keeping me around. His boys seemed to embrace me in their company. CJ was the boss and if I passed his test, I passed theirs, I concluded.

There was nothing more attractive than a man that commands the respect of other thugged out niggaz. My kitty purred as my mind floated on every syllable that CJ uttered.

After the dinner we went to the strip club Jersey Girls in Elizabeth. CJ and 'em fell up in there and took over the VIP room. Everyone except CJ and Raheem were getting a private dance from the strippers. The whole team was poppin' bands and bottles, ballin' hard. Rah seemed to ignore all of the naked titties and big asses that jiggled and bounced around him.

I leaned over and whispered to CJ, "What's his problem? He don't like pussy?"

CJ's eyes turned cold and he grabbed me by the chin. "Watch your muhfuckin' mouth yo! That's my nigga. Don't you ever speak against him again. You understand me?" he snarled.

I nodded my head and looked down at the floor. "I'm sorry," I apologized.

CJ put a finger under my face and lifted my head. When I looked at him his face had softened. "Ain't nothin' homo about my peeps, he just don't trick off," he explained.

"Oh," I mumbled. And from that point on I knew that CJ's and Raheem's bond was not to be tested.

CJ leaned over and gave me a kiss. "You good ma," he said. The medallion that swung on the end of his chain thumped up against me. It was heavy with ice, and looked like it had cost a quarter of a million dollars, but I could not make out what the face of it was.

Pop That by French Montana featuring Rick Ross, Lil Wayne and Drake blared from the speakers as a thick, chocolate girl worked the pole on stage.

Drop that pussy bitch
I'm some young Papi, champagne
They know the face and the know the name
(Drop that pussy bitch)
What you twerkin with?
Throw it, buss it open
Show me what you twerkin' with

Ass so fat, need a lap dance
I'm in that white ghost chasin' Pac man

The stripper slid up and down with the pole between her bubble butt. Her oiled body glistened under the strobe lights as she squatted down and opened her legs, showing off her money spot.
I love my big booty bitches
My life a Godfather picture
Local club in my city
I fell in love with a stripper
Bitches know I'm that nigga
Talkin' four door Bugatti
I'm the life of the party
Let's get these hos on the Molly
You know I came to stunt
So drop that pussy bitch
I got what you want

A redbone with big titties, a small waist, and a bodacious ass walked by our booth in a blue G-string and clear stilettos. CJ reached out and stopped her. "Honey Bee, give my shorty a lap dance," he said, smiling at me.

Where these bitches get these names from? I thought, wondering if Honey Bee had a stinger.

She looked at me for the okay.

I nodded my head and she straddled my lap, pressing her titties against mine. I didn't do kitten but this was all in fun. On cue the DJ played *My Girl Got a Girlfriend* by Young Dro.

I locked eyes seductively with CJ as he watched Honey Bee wrap her arms around my neck and grind on my lap. She started off moving slow then picked up the pace. "You want some pussy baby?" she breathed huskily in my ear.

"Uh—no," I muttered.

She giggled. "It's okay. Pretend that you do, it will turn your man on and get you fucked real good when you get home."

I giggled back and took her advice.

I had a feeling that tonight was going to turn out to be the start of something much more than I'd ever had in all my twenty-four years of living. Men had pampered me with expensive gifts and they had taken me on vacations to remote islands, but only as a rendezvous. This felt like I had a chance to become wifey. The feeling almost astounded me.

I sat back and let Honey Bee put on the show that CJ wanted to see. If I was a two-way bitch she would've had me panting to let her taste my candy. But the way I saw it the only thing a bitch could do for me was give me a mani-pedi and keep it moving.

I looked over at CJ and saw him grinning so I pretended to be all into the lap dance. Beside us, CJ's workers were turned up, they had strippers all over them and the Patron was flowing non-stop. Newark was definitely in the spot.

An hour later CJ leaned over and whispered, "You ready to go?"

That smooth black muhfucka had a bitch wanting to scream, "Hell yeah." But I kept my game face on and replied demurely, "Are you ready to leave?"

"Yeah ma, let's bounce."

My usually calm nerves twerked with anticipation as we stood up to leave. The only thing that dampened the mood for me was Raheem's attitude. Before we left he pulled CJ aside. I strained my ears to overhear parts of their conversation over the music.

"Dawg, you don't know nothin' about this girl. You can't afford to start taking chances like this, there's too much at stake and the other side ain't playing," Rah cautioned.

CJ put his hand on his man's shoulder and replied, "Trust me fam. Shorty ain't rocking like that."

"A'ight, bruh, but take her to a hotel. Don't take her to where you rest your head."

"You worry too much. Shorty is what I need right now. You can call and check on me in the morning," said CJ.

They embraced then CJ went around the room saying good-night to his other mans. Rah slid up to me. He looked at me with an intensity that wasn't threatening or unfriendly, but it communicated to me that I had better take heed to what he was about to say.

"Shy, I don't know you. I don't know who your people are or where you came from. I'm not going to judge you on what I've seen tonight because if I did, it wouldn't be good. But I want you to know that if any type of tragedy should befall my man while he's with you—be it a car accident, natural death or a stray bullet. I'm going to hold you personally responsible," he intimated.

Then he turned his back to me and stood watching CJ with his arms folded across his chest. I wanted to ask him if he was always that serious but I had a feeling that he wouldn't catch the humor so I just kept my mouth closed and nodded my head up and down.

It turned out that CJ stayed out in New Haven, Connecticut in a house as big as a department store. I saw three or four expensive cars and trucks in the yard when we drove up.

"Uh, does your mother allow you to have company at this time of night?" I teased.

"You got me fucked up. This is all me," he clarified needlessly.

"I was just kidding," I sang. *Oh, I know you're the man.*

I imagined myself behind the wheel of either one of those whips with my Chloe glasses on, headed to the mall with our daughter strapped in her car seat in the back. If I could bag CJ I would be whistling Dixie, getting fed grapes as some Asian ladies messaged my feet.

The outside of the house was impressive, it looked like a mini castle. Inside, the downstairs rooms were expensively decorated with a masculinity that was so CJ. Following him up the winding staircase, I brushed his man's apprehension aside. If anything befell CJ in my company, it would be this kitty cat. He was my winning *Power Ball* ticket. I would slice off my left nipple before I'd let harm come to Mr. Jefferies.

A light was on in the bedroom as I followed CJ inside holding his hand. The drinks that I had consumed at the club had me as giddy as a schoolgirl. We had removed our jackets downstairs so when CJ stopped at the foot of the bed, turned around and smoothly pulled me into his arms, my nipples brushed up against his chest through the material of my top.

My arms went around his neck so naturally it was as if I had belonged to him forever. He looked deep into my eyes and whispered, "Damn, Shy you're soft. I can't wait to feel you underneath me."

"Who said I'm giving you some?"

"You can't turn me down, you belong to me," he stated confidently. And with that my panties came off. *Figuratively speaking.*

"Make me yours, daddy."

"I'ma fuck you so muhfuckin' good, shorty, you'll wake up in the morning and fix me breakfast."

"Quit talking shit and do it," I moaned as he pulled my body tightly up against his to let me feel that grown man in his pants come alive.

He covered my mouth with his and kissed me so tenderly, considering the hard thug that he was. Our breathing quickly became heavy as the urgency to unleash our carnal desires took control. Inside my suede pants my pussy was having a fit. CJ's tongue tasted like the Patron that he had been drinking all night. Mine tasted like the mints I had popped in my mouth throughout the evening. The mixture of our saliva heightened our lust and within seconds our clothes started coming off. CJ placed his gun and chain on the nightstand and stepped out of his black Polo boxers.

I snuck a peek past his waist and saw something long and fat, standing at attention. He took my hand and guided it down to that beautiful black pole. I encircled it gently, measuring its girth. *There is a God,* I said to myself because I didn't do Negroes with bite-size sausages—not for free anyway. I had to have some shit I could feel all up in my uterus.

CJ laid me down on the bed and pressed that hard body of his on top of me. I parted my thighs to accommodate him. The temperature in the room was comfortably warm; the heat between my thighs was threatening to inflame the bed sheets.

He pinned my arms over my head and sucked on my collarbone, sending a jolt of desire through my entire body. "Shorty, you're mine now. Are you ready for this shit?" he asked.

"Yes, I'm ready," I moaned while grinding my fatty up against him.

His mouth traveled down to my breasts. He sucked one then the other. Then he pushed them both together and pleasured them equally. His hand eased down my body and his long fingers traced my shaved lower lips. When he stroked the hood of my clit my pearl popped out, swollen with indescribable need.

"Oh, my God. CJ, you have me so fuckin' wet," I panted the moment I felt the tip of his finger slowly circling my clitoris.

His fingers slid inside and moved in and out as he kissed me deep. My juices coated his fingers and my hips begged for something fatter. I felt what I wanted and needed pressing against my thigh. "CJ, put that black ass dick in me and make me cum."

"Chill, ma, I got you." He removed his fingers from inside of me and brought them up to my mouth. Nothing drove me crazier than the taste of my own juices. I sucked his fingers greedily then grabbed the back of his head and pushed my tongue in his mouth.

He reached down and rubbed the head of his rock hardness up and down my moist slit. My legs opened wide on their own beckoning him to take me. I was so anxious and he was so poised. "Stop teasing me," I said almost pleadingly.

"Why?" He toyed with me.

"CJ, this girl is on fiyah." I breathed heavily.

He reached over on the nightstand by the bed and grabbed a condom. "Hurry," I said as he tore it open and covered up.

I felt him enter me gently. I sucked in my breath as he pushed all the way inside. My pussy contracted and gripped his dick tightly as our bodies automatically began to move in sync.

"Damn, your pussy feels so good," he whispered in my ear.

"It's *your* pussy now baby," I corrected as I put my feet on his shoulders, encouraging him to go deeper.

"Oh, you want me to beat it up."

"Yes, CJ. Do whatever you want to it, it's yours. You can get it any way you want it."

He lifted his body off of mine and pulled me down to the end of the bed. With my ass up in the air and his feet firm on the floor, he plowed deep.

"Yes, baby, fuck me," I cried.

"Like this?" He gave it to me harder, deeper, and stronger.

"Yes," I elongated my moan. "Hurt me."

"That's what you want?" His breathing became labored.

"Yes, baby, cripple me," I screamed.

CJ took my words literally. He held me by the ankles and dicked me down until I called him every different type of good dick, black muhfucka in the book. But I loved every stroke.

Just when I began to pop the pussy up at him he went so deep I sucked in all the oxygen in the room and started begging for mercy. "CJ, you're going to break something up in there," I cried, trying to run from the dick. It felt like it had engorged into a baseball bat.

CJ held me by the hips so that I couldn't get away. "This what you wanted, ain't it?" He pulled it out to the tip then went back inside with command.

I swear I saw little balloons floating in a circle over my head. CJ gripped me tighter and punished my pussy with thrust after mind-altering thrust. I felt my volcano about to erupt. "Ooh, CJ, here it comes. Here it comes! I'ma cum for you, baby."

My body was vibrating on a wave length I'd never felt before yet it felt like I had to pee at the same time. *What the hell? Oh my Gawd. Am I coming or going? Literally. Aah, I'm about to nut for real.*

"CJ, I'm 'bout to squirt for you, baby."

He plowed inside of me deeper and I screamed out his name. My juices skeeted all over that thick long black bitch pleaser.

"Spread your legs," CJ said. "Open my pussy up wide."

I was weaker than a wet noodle but I obeyed his command. "Make me nut," he growled.

I summoned up the little bitty strength left in my body and threw the pussy back at him with purpose. "Nut for me, nigga," I said with no shame. "Feed this pussy."

"Fuck yeah, shorty," CJ growled and bust a fat nut.

He collapsed on top of me and looked down at me in amazement. "Shorty, did you squirt for real?" he asked, gasping like he had just ran from the police.

"Yes. You made me do it. I squirted so hard for you."

His chest inflated. "You're bullshittin'."

"No, I'm not, baby, that's the truth. I can make your pussy do whatever you command it to do," I replied, gulping for additional air to take in.

"I told you I had you, ma." His arrogance emphasized the good hurt he had put on my pussy.

I looked up at him and asked, "So, is that my dick?"

"We'll talk about that," he said, just sucking the wind from under the little cloud I was floating on.

I didn't push though, because I knew that I had the type of sex he would want to cuff to keep another nigga from getting it.

"Mmm hmm, sir," I moaned facetiously.

He rolled off of me and I fell asleep in his arms wondering who the girl was in the picture on his nightstand.

Ca$h

EIGHTEEN

CJ

For the next two weeks me and Shy kicked it every day. The more time we spent together, the more she grew on a nigga. I knew that the reason she stood out over all the other fly hos that were on my dick was because she reminded me of Tamika. She had that same slick mouth and jealous streak, but underneath it all she really cared about a nigga.

Sometimes we would stay up all night talking, blowing weed and fuckin'. I had told her a little about Tamika, but not much. I kept those memories to myself and dulled the pain by running up in Shy.

Shorty never talked much about herself, at least not about her past, and I didn't press. If she was hiding something it would eventually come out.

I had practically moved Shy in with me. When I came out of the streets I had to have her there. Her body next to mine didn't stop me from thinking about Tamika but it helped me sleep.

My cell phone rung, bringing me out of my contemplation. I reached on the nightstand and grabbed it, half expecting to hear that another one of my young boys had been killed.

"Hey, CJ. Why haven't you called?"

I breathed a sigh of relief and looked down at the screen. That sweet voice belonged to Kenisha, a little cutie that I had met at Short Hills Mall the other day.

"I was gonna get at you, baby girl, I just been caught up in these streets. Nah mean? Maybe we can get together this weekend."

"I would really like that."

"Me too," I said.

"You wanna cook me dinner at your place?"

"You wouldn't want that," I chuckled. "But I'll take you out to dinner."

"I guess that will have to do," she giggled.

We talked another five minutes, setting a date for Friday, then I told her goodnight. When I rolled over Shy was livid.

"You disrespectful black muthafucka! That was so damn rude!"

I reached out and spooned her to me and rubbed my dick up against all that ass. "Don't let that shit bother you shorty."

"Get the fuck off of me, CJ." She climbed out of bed with a pillow in her arms.

"Where you going?" I asked with my dick on swole.

"Away from you," she said and stormed out of the room. A few seconds later, I heard the door to the guest room slam shut.

I bounced up, went down the hall, and banged on the door. "Shy quit trippin' and come back to bed yo," I demanded.

"Call that bitch and ask her to come and get in bed with you. Nigga, you got the game twisted," she shouted.

"It ain't even like that lil' mama. Bring your ass back in here and stop acting like Tamika." The comment rolled off my tongue before I thought about it.

Shy went postal. She snatched the door open and hopped up in my face. "Don't compare me to that bitch. I'm tired of hearing about your little Miss Tamika, if you miss her that much go sleep on her grave."

My hand was a blur. *Whap!* I backhanded her so hard she hit the floor on her ass. "What the fuck did you say to me?" I gritted.

Shy pounced up and clawed at my face.

"Nigga, you put your hands on me about the next bitch?! Get the fuck off me! I'm leaving!" She yanked away from me and flew back into the other bedroom.

I stood there with my chest heaving up and down. Had I slapped her for getting slick out the mouth or was it because of the way she straight disrespected Tamika's memory? I asked myself.

I knew the answer even if I didn't wanna admit it. I also knew that if the shoe was on the other foot I would have no understanding—zero. I had been burning Shy's ears up for two weeks with stories about Tamika. I guess she finally let come out what she had been holding in.

As I walked down the hall to the master bedroom, I heard her in there crying and breaking things. I opened the door and looked around at the damage. The lamp was shattered against the wall and the nightstand had been tipped over.

I stood silently as Shy snatched her clothes out of the closet and began throwing them in bags. When she had all her shit packed she turned around and looked at me with tears streaming down her face. She was looking at me like she expected me to beg her to stay. That wasn't happening.

I remained silent as I led her downstairs to the front door. Behind me she was crying and sniffling. If I had a heart I had buried it with Tamika. Nothing else could hurt me. Nothing! Shy's tears were just water to me.

I opened the door for her and silently stepped aside. Her teary eyes met my cold ones. I was looking at a heartbroken woman. She was staring at a heartless man.

Shy blinked and a fresh stream of tears poured from her eyes. My expression remained unchanged as I held the door open wider. Shy took a deep breath and tried to speak but what came out was a sob.

After a couple of starts and stops, interrupted by hard crying, she finally got her words out. "You're still in love with Tamika, CJ. I refuse to compete with her memory. You don't want to let go of what y'all had, and you won't let me love you because you're afraid that if you do that you'll forget about her." She paused to allow me a chance to deny it but I didn't have shit to say.

"Take care, CJ," she said through pursed lips. Then she was gone.

NINETEEN

SHY

By the time I reached the exit of CJ's subdivision, I was overcome with emotions that blurred my sight and it felt like I couldn't breathe. I pulled over to the curb and my head fell against the steering wheel as I tried to suck air in through my mouth. I couldn't believe that this shit was happening to me again.

I was tired of being the side bitch or the one that finished second. That shit had happened to me way too many times in the past. It was hard enough competing with a bunch of other thirsty bitches, but to have to contend with someone who was dead made no fucking sense. If CJ thought he was going fuck me, whisper sweet nothings in my ear, and then toss me to the side like a half smoked blunt, he was about to find out just how treacherous a bitch could be.

I grabbed my Juicy Couture bag off the passenger seat and felt inside of it until my hand came in contact with what I was searching for. I pulled out my .380 and checked it to make sure the clip was inside of it. *This nigga don't know who he's fuckin' with.*

I put the car in drive and made a U-turn, headed back to his house to show him that I was the wrong bitch to cross. He should've done his homework before sliding up in this prime red pussy and getting my feelings all involved.

As I neared his house, the thought occurred to me that I didn't have to mess up my manicure in order to get even with his black ass. I knew what was going on in the streets and I knew just who would pay a lot of money for the information I could provide.

No matter how boss a nigga is, they always let their guards down around a woman. Not only could I lead Nard to where CJ laid his head, I could tell him about the Executive House apartments where Raheem rested. I had been with CJ when he rode through there one day to holla at his man.

I hadn't just kept my legs open for CJ, I had kept my eyes and ears open too. I knew all too well not to count on nothing until a man put a ring on it. I had watched everything, storing it in memory in case he did me dirty. I wished like hell he had let me see where his safe was at, I would rob him blind. But since I couldn't take his money, I was going to help take his life. Then he could be with Tamika forever.

When I reached his house, I drove right on pass and headed out the neighborhood in the other direction. I thought about getting a room for a couple of days until I figured out exactly what my next move should be. I didn't really want to go to my own apartment that I shared with Papaya because she was still upset with me and I didn't want to have to snatch her weave out. But that was my bitch so we would be good. We had a pact that no man would ever come between our friendship. Besides, my name was on the lease of the apartment too. *That bitch better recognize.*

I put on Kelly Rowland's CD Talk *a Good Game* and set it on repeat as I made the long drive back to Newark. When the song Dirty Laundry came on it reminded me of the last time I had given my heart to an ungrateful nigga and let it come between me and my sister.

Let's do this dirty laundry, this dirty laundry
Let's do this dirty laundry, this dirty laundry
When you're soaked in tears for years, it never airs out
When you make pain look this good it never wears out
This dirty laundry, this dirty laundry
While my sister was on stage, killing it like a motherfucker
I was enraged, feeling it like a motherfucker
Bird in a cage, you would never know what I was dealing with
Went our separate ways, but I was happy she was killing it
Bittersweet, she was up, I was down

No lie, I feel good for her, but what do I do now?
As the lyrics played my emotions went back and forth between hurt and anger. I had promised myself that I would never love again. The only thing a man represented to me was a quick come up, but in the two weeks I'd spent with CJ he had really gotten in my heart and now I was all in my feelings, thinking homicidal and shit.

Hours later I let myself in the apartment and dropped my bags at the door. Papaya came out of her bedroom rubbing sleep from her eyes. "Bitch, what you doing here?" she asked in an unfriendly tone.

Then she looked at me and realized that tears were streaming down my face. "What did that muthafucka do?" she asked, instantly brushing our conflict aside.

I walked into her arms and cried my heart out. By the time my tears dried I had a clear game plan. With Papaya's help I was going to get even with Mr. Jefferies. His black ass was going to suffer for doing me dirty.

Ca$h

TWENTY

NARD

CJ was beginning to let his guards down, riding around flossing like this shit was a game or like he couldn't be touched. I knew it would be just a matter of time before his arrogance led me to him.

In the meantime my squad wanted to ride for Talib and 'em but I had to pull the reigns in for a minute because we had to get to this money. My new connect had just dropped more work in my lap than I had ever fucked with at one time before.

"Everybody move with caution because those niggaz are out there lurking. It's not just me, everybody is a target," I cautioned my people.

Just the other day some of CJ's killaz had tried to kick in Man Dog's door, but we had fought them off in a fierce gun battle that miraculously left no casualties. I warned my mans that there was to be no unnecessary hanging out.

As I looked around Big Nasty's basement I saw that I held everyone's attention but Zakee's. He was staring at his phone, texting. I walked over to him and slapped it out of his hand. "Pay attention. I don't wanna have to dress you in a suit," I said.

"My bad," he replied not taking offense. He knew that it was love. We were all on edge because there was no telling when bullets would come flying through the windows of some place we were chilling.

"I hear Raheem is back," I continued. "That's CJ's man who moved down South. If he's back in Newark it's to ride with his man. From what I know about him he's a thinker, not erratic and impulsive like CJ but just as deadly. Maybe more. His people live over there in Georgia King; he has a sister named LaKeesha, a little freak bitch. We can get to Raheem through her, and we can get to CJ through him."

"Let's try to flip one of CJ's people or a bitch that he fucks with," suggested Quent.

I thought about that for a minute. If Raheem was back and calling some shots, it probably caused somebody over there to feel slighted. "A'ight," I agreed. "Let's do that. Lemora, try to find out who CJ's fucking with now. Tamika always said he has to have a bitch up under him. Zakee, you get on Raheem's grandmother. Show, you get the sister. Don't touch them yet just collect info. Man Dog, I want you to step to Flip or Premo and find out if either one of them can be flipped. Every team has at least one member that ain't solid."

My own words made me pause and think.

I looked at each one of my people. Big Nasty was above reproach. Me and Man Dog came out the same wound so there was nothing CJ could offer my brother to cross me. Lemora was a down ass bitch and she despised CJ because he had slumped her cousin. Chinese torture couldn't get her to go against me for CJ. I trusted the others too but I let them know that if their loyalty ever came in question I would not hesitate to spin their tops.

Nobody said a word because the only muhfucka that could be offended was a muhfucka with treason in their heart. Nothing foul showed in anyone's eyes, further convincing me that my peeps were concrete all around.

Now that I had given them the game plan we weighed and bagged up work, counted money then took to the streets with a purpose to get money and eliminate CJ and his number one. By any means necessary.

RAHEEM

Finding Nard was turning out to be more difficult than any of us had anticipated. The young boy wasn't a slouch. Whoever had jeweled him on hustlin' and the art of war had taught him well. He didn't hit the clubs or leave himself open to being set up by a female. He wasn't being seen but he was being felt.

As the first days of winter took a stronghold on the city and snow covered the ground, bodies from both sides were being left frozen in vacant lots or inside abandoned cars. As the body count continued to rise I lost more and more of my soul each time I pulled the trigger and caused another black mother to grieve over her son. There was an internal conflict going on inside of me. I knew that justice was Allah's to serve, but I quieted my conscience by reminding myself that I was not the aggressor.

Each time the other side deaded one of ours, it made it easier for me to crush one of theirs. It was truly hard not to let vengeance become my sole mission when I was laughing and kicking it with a homie one day and the next day the other side filled his chest with holes.

Nard remained insulated by a growing crew of loyal soldiers who could not be flipped so in the meantime we targeted his killaz. I had a special interest in two in particular because I had been told that they had rode through the hood asking questions about Big Ma and LaKeesha.

Big Ma was down in Atlanta out of harm's way but LaKeesha's stupid butt was still in Newark somewhere. If they found her before I did I knew what would happen. So I looked for *them.*

Me and Eric had been tracking they're moves ever since I received that report. Today one of them was about to pay the ultimate price for posing a threat to my family.

"That's Show right there yo." Eric pointed to a short light skinned brother who was rocking stylish square frames. He slid out of a dark green Lexus where someone remained waiting behind the wheel.

I shook my head. The kid didn't look to be a day over seventeen years old. He had his whole life in front of him when he woke up this morning, now it was all behind him. In just a few minutes I was going to make sure that he didn't turn eighteen.

Parked across the street we watched him walk into Paul's Hotdogs, a deli that was famous for its Italian sausages. "Is that Zakee in the car?" I asked.

"Nah, Zakee is a fat ass nigga. I don't know who that is but he's getting it too."

There was nothing else to say. I got into beast mode by reminding myself that Show would probably murder LaKeesha if he found her. Best to get him before he got her. I pulled my skully down over my brow and tied a black scarf over the lower half of my face. Eric pulled on a ski mask and checked his banger. "Leave the car running," I instructed.

We slid down in our seats and waited patiently for Show to come out of the restaurant. As soon as he emerged from inside, I was out of the car with my strap gripped tightly in my hand. Eric quickly caught up to me and we trotted across the street with murder on our minds.

Show's arms were full of bags but his head moved from side to side as he scanned the block. He looked in our direction and saw us moving quickly toward him, and his street instincts kicked in. He dropped the bags and reached for his tool but mine was already out and spitting at his chest.

Three shots found their mark and slammed him into the side of the Lexus. A fourth shot hit him in the face and sent his glasses flying. His body slid down the side of the car and crumpled into the snow.

Eric raced around to the driver's side bursting off shot after shot as the driver threw the car into reverse and tried to pull off.

Boc! Boc! Boc! Boc! Boc!

Bullets pelted the side of the car as it skidded sideways and the tires tried to gain traction on the slippery pavement. "Bitch ass nigga!" shouted Eric when the driver finally zoomed off and left Show to die in a puddle of blood mixed snow.

I looked down at the body that laid at my feet and I was frozen in that spot. Was that how it was going to end for all of us? Could it end any other way? What plans had Show had for later that evening? Whose heart was going to be shattered by his death?

"Rah, let's go!" Eric's beckoning jarred me out of the trance.

As we moved swiftly back across the street, we passed in front of a Dodge Caravan. I let Eric continue on then I ran up to the passenger side of the van. The driver looked at me with fear in his eyes and tried to pull off but he was boxed in by a car in front of him and one behind him. I got right up on the window, raised my gun, and squeezed the trigger.

Glass flew inward and the bullet struck the man in the side of the face. I stuck my hand inside and pumped several shots in his head. Quickly, I snatched the door open and grabbed his cell phone.

I had the presence of mind to wipe down the door handle before dashing over to where Eric waited in the ride ready to peel out.

When I reached the car, Eric had removed his ski mask. I took off my hoodie and untied the scarf from over my face. "Why did you murk him?" asked Eric as we tore out of the lot with the sound of sirens nearing.

"Slow down and drive at a normal speed."

When we were safely out of the area Eric again asked why I had killed the man in the Dodge Caravan. I held up the dead man's cell phone and replied, "I had to kill him; he took our pictures."

Ca$h

142

TWENTY-ONE

NARD

Everyone was quiet as I walked down into Big Nasty's basement and posted up on a stool facing them. I looked in their faces and saw the pain that came behind the loss of another comrade.

Lemora's eyes were red from crying. Man Dog sat next to her on a couch with his arms around her shoulder. Quent sat on the far end of the same couch with one leg slung over the arm. He had his banger out caressing it, and the look on his face was one of barely controlled fury.

Zakee was pacing the floor with an AK-47 in his hands. From now on I would have his full attention because now he saw how one innocent trip to the store, one fuckin' slip up, could get a nigga fitted for a casket.

Big Nasty stood to my left with Lil' Nasty at his side, growling and baring his teeth. I looked down at Big Nasty's feet and saw someone on the floor with his feet bound together and his hands tied behind his back. His face was so swollen and covered with blood I could barely make out who it was.

"Elijah?" I looked up at Big Nasty confused but it was Zakee who answered.

"He was with Show when they got him and he drove off and left him." He stopped, drew his leg back, and kicked Elijah in the face.

The boy groaned through his bloody lips and tried to look up at me through his swollen eyes. "Nard," he moaned out my name.

Elijah wasn't part of my squad but he was Show's first cousin. I saw several bloody teeth lying on the floor beside him but I had no pity for a coward. "Why you leave him?" I snarled.

"I—wasn't—strapped," he grunted.

143

"You had the car. You should've ran one of those muhfuckaz over yo," I gritted. I knew that I would have fought a gun with my fist before I'd leave Man Dog or any one of my fam to fend for self.

"Them niggaz," he spat blood onto the floor, "was bussin' hard."

"Fuck that mean!" I snapped. "Show was your blood. Your mother and his mother are sisters. Y'all was raised in the same muhfuckin' building and whatever he had you had yo. You should have died by his muhfuckin' side 'cause you're about to die anyway."

Elijah started shivering. "Nard, I wasn't strapped," he cried.

"I heard you the first time, pussy ass nigga. Appeal denied!"

"Let me do his ass," spat Zakee.

"We're all gonna do his bitch ass, for Show," I said. I looked at Big Nasty. "Do what you do."

He smiled menacingly.

Lemora stood up and went upstairs, she was 'bout it but she could not stand to see what she knew was about to happen. When she was gone Big Nasty patted Lil' Nasty on the head and gave the command.

The pit went straight for Elijah's throat. Elijah let out a terrifying scream as Lil Nasty's teeth dug into the soft part of his throat and clamped down on his windpipe. The taste of fresh blood sent Lil' Nasty into a frenzy, his jaws locked and he thrashed his head from side to side so hard the violent movement flipped Elijah over on top of him.

Elijah's body shook but he couldn't scream or fight. I calmly looked at my watch and counted how long it took a bitch nigga to die. The killa pit bull held its lock until Elijah's body went still thirty seconds later.

144

Big Nasty gave the command and the dog released its death lock and went and sat down on its hunches at its master's feet. Blood coated Lil Nasty's mouth as he quietly panted.

Elijah's body laid in a twisted hump. I walked over to where it laid and whipped out my tool. "This is for Show. He would've never left you."

I aimed the gun at his head and squeezed the trigger.

Man Dog, Zakee and Quent lined up behind one another to bust a shot in Elijah's corpse. "For Show," they each chanted after they did so.

I called Lemora back in the basement and handed her my Glock .50. "Show was family to all of us," I said. Then I directed her on what she was to do.

Ma didn't tremble or hesitate. She stepped to her business like a real bitch.

"For Show," she repeated after me, and then she emptied the clip in Elijah's body.

I looked at her and smiled.

"That's what I'ma do to CJ," she vowed.

TWENTY-TWO

CJ

"The killings have to stop and this is the last time I'm going to fucking warn you." The Police Commissioner is seriously considering calling in the federal boys and that's not good for business. Do you understand what the fuck I'm telling you?" spewed Cujo. Nasty ass chewing tobacco flew out of his mouth as he spoke and his whole face was red with anger.

Beside him sat Michael Solaski, the federal drug enforcement agent that was really the one supplying all the drugs. He was watching me intensely but it was going to take much more than a hard stare to make me sweat.

I sat behind a desk in the office of my warehouse. My hands were folded on top of the desk and my voice was unusually calm when I replied. "Did you just say you're warning me?" I asked Cujo.

"Yes, that's what I said." He sat up in his chair. Solaski put a hand on his elbow and Cujo scooted back in the chair and let his shoulders relax a bit

I chuckled.

"You find this humorous?" asked the Fed boy.

"Yeah, I do. Y'all some comical muthafuckaz. What? Is this where I'm supposed to become frightened?" I met his stare with a colder one.

"Don't fuck with us CJ. We made you who you are and we can bring you back down just as fast," he threatened.

"Suck my black dick."

Cujo shot up out of his chair, placed his palms on my desk, and leaned down in my face. His neck was now just as red as his face. "Who in the fuck do you think you're talking to?" He challenged.

I grabbed ahold of his tie and tightened it around my fist. "Fuck up outta my face, yo."

Now Solaski was on his feet reaching inside his overcoat. The office door squeaked open and Rah stepped into the room with his tool already out. "Never mind me," he said real smoothly.

Solaski's hand slowly fell back down to his side. I let go of Cujo's tie and he straightened himself up. They both knew who Rah was because they had helped fix a case that him and DaQuan had caught in Georgia a few years ago. Cujo had always admired Rah's cool and calm demeanor and had often asked me to bring Rah into the folds so that we could expand the operation. I had always refused to step to my mans with that because he had been tryna live the legit life.

Cujo looked at the gun in Rah's hand and realized that a quiet storm was the deadliest. Rah looked at him like he already had Cujo's epitaph in mind.

"Have a seat gentlemen," Solaski broke in. "We're all men up in here and men can talk."

Later, I laughed about it with Rah. "Fam, did you see those crackers faces when you stepped up in that piece? They looked like they had just seen a muhfuckin' ghost, yo."

"Yeah, I think they were about to bang on you before I stepped through the door."

"Nah, they were flexin'. I'm their meal ticket and they're some greedy ass muthafuckaz. They would rather take some dick in their ass than murk me."

"I don't trust those devils, son. You know that what y'all doing can't last forever. Whenever it crumbles, they're going to sell their souls. You know that, right?"

I leaned back in my chair and propped my feet up on the desk, smiling like the cat that ate the rat. "Son, I don't trust them either.

That's why I told you to be here today. As soon as I don't need them no more I'm putting them on their ass. Believe that."

Rah nodded because we both knew that there was no other choice.

The conversation turned to Show.

"Nard is going to respond to that. I'm trying to anticipate where he'll strike," said Rah contemplatively.

"Let's hit his ass again. Fuck what Cujo and 'em talking about. This shit ain't gon' ever be over until one of us is in the dirt. Nah mean?"

"I feel you," he understood. "But don't stress over it. I got it. What you need to do is get away for a weekend and clear your head."

"In the middle of a war? Nah, I ain't going," I declined.

"The mind works better when it's rested CJ," countered Rah. "Why don't you go beg Shy to come back? Take her somewhere and blow a couple hundred bands on her." A sly smile crept onto his face.

"Oh, you Kevin Hart now?" I laughed.

"I'm just saying yo." He chuckled

"Nigga, you can't talk. Your cape is world famous," I cracked back. Then I recounted all the incidents where he had come to a woman's rescue.

By the time I was done, we were both laughing like we did when we were shorties and life wasn't so muhfuckin' serious all of the time. It was just me and my nigga, clowning on each other. Fuck the world.

Suddenly we both got quiet. Something was different and we both knew what it was. I could no longer crack basehead jokes about Kayundra, she was dead. And Tamika was no longer around to help me clown Rah, 'cause she was dead too.

The sadness in Rah's eyes matched what I felt inside but we were dealing with the deaths of our girls in totally different ways. I was tryna move on, looking for someone just like Tamika while Rah wasn't focusing on anything but the beef with Nard. I think that was his way of blocking out Kayundra's death.

"You know what fam? A short vacation might be just what I need," I said. "I'm gonna rent a cabin up in the Hamptons for the weekend and not even think about the streets. Just lay up in some pussy and smoke about a zip of sour."

Rah liked that. "That's a good look for you," he agreed. "You want me to call Flip or Premo and tell them to go find Shy?"

"You'sa funny ass nigga," I laughed. "Nah, I'm about to switch up styles on these hos. Fuck Shy and those types, I'm cuffing myself a plain Jane."

"Who? Kenisha?" he asked with a smile. Rah had met her a few weeks ago and had been impressed.

Kenisha was mad different from any female that I had ever kicked it with. She was only eighteen years old, green as lettuce, and she wasn't a trophy type. No one outside of Rah could see what had caught my attention. She only had a cup full of titties and a handful of ass. She was brown skinned and pretty, but in a toned down manner. She was not strikingly beautiful or sexy like Shy, or like Tamika had been, and her mouth damn sure wasn't slick.

Kenisha had an aunt named Jada who was about six years older than her. Jada was the classic dope boy's chick. She had the long weave with blond highlights, phat ass, designer nails, and the attitude that some baller was going to sponsor her.

Jada met Rah when the four of us went out to dinner one night. Afterwards she was on Rah's dick hard but my nigga ran from thirsty bitches like her.

In Kenisha though, I felt I had a lil' somethin' special.

"Take that beautiful, young sistah up to the Hamptons and spoil her," encouraged Rah.

I took my feet off the desk, sat up and grabbed my cell phone. "I think that's what I'ma do. We'll chill in front of the fireplace, ride a snowmobile, and act like white people for a week," I said, piping up to the idea of a little R&R.

The day came for me and Kenisha to leave for The Hamptons. All of a sudden I started stressing about going on a vacation while trouble still brewed.

"I'll handle everything my brotha, you don't have to sweat that," Rah assured me as we stood in the center of the warehouse.

One hundred and fifty bricks of that white girl and ten kilos of boy that I had just received from Cujo was stacked against the wall in boxes.

"I don't know Rah," I wavered.

"What you saying Cam'ron?" he asked, using my government to express his displeasure with me doubting his ability to hold things down.

I shoved my hands down in my coat pockets and stared at all the work lined against the wall. "I don't want to leave all of this on you," I explained.

Rah placed a reassuring hand on my shoulder and his eyes lifted up to mine. "Dawg, this is me—the one person in this world who will never let you down. If I tell you I can handle it, I can. I'll distribute the yack exactly how you told me to do it. Eric, Premo, Snoop, and Flip will redistribute it to our people around the city. Legend and DaQuan will watch my back like they always do—its business as usual, fam. This shit ain't difficult B. If Nard surfaces I'll do him ten times worse than anything you can imagine. Go enjoy yourself with that lovely young Queen. Shorty is the one dawg," he said.

"I feel you but she's not really cut out for the game. Lil' mama don't even know my get-down. Nah mean?"

"Fam, you're just looking for a reason not to go," he read me correctly. "It can't be because you don't trust me to hold things down while you're gone, so it has to be that you got Shy on your mind."

I laughed quietly. He was just tryna ease my mind off of the business.

"This ain't about Shy, but she does reminds me of Tamika," I confessed.

"I already peeped that yo. But you can't recapture that love. That was once in a lifetime."

"You're right. Anyway, Shy's not going anywhere. I just talked to her yesterday. She's playing hard but she's ready to come back to a nigga. I'm not really trippin' that. I'm really worried about Nard tryna strike while I'm away."

"Let him come with it. This shit right here ain't what he want."

"It really isn't. But just to be on the safe side give that bitch nigga a funeral to attend. That will keep him occupied until I return."

"No doubt," he replied.

I saw in his eyes that something was worrying him. Before I could ask what it was, Rah added, "Take Legend with you. I don't want you traveling without someone to watch your back."

"Nard's a peon. His arms aren't that long. He can't touch me way up in The Hamptons, fam. He's a local joker, nothin' more. Don't worry I'ma be good, and I'ma have my baby wit' me." I slid my Nine from under my Goose Down coat.

"Just comfort me fam. Take Legend along," he impressed upon me until I relented.

"A'ight." I tucked my strap back in my waist and we locked fists. "I love you, man. No homo."

"I love you, too, son. Be safe," implored Rah.

"You too."

As we parted ways I had a feeling in my stomach that something bad was going to happen while I was gone. I just didn't know what.

TWENTY-THREE

KENISHA

I was nervous as heck from the moment CJ picked me up from my aunt Jada's house. First of all, I had told my mom that I was going to visit a classmate in Boston. Lying was foreign to me and I was not good at it. Jada would cover for me but I still felt that my mother had looked at me suspiciously when I left last night.

Legally I was an adult. But I still lived at home with my mom and she would not have approved of me going to spend a week in The Hampton's with a man. In fact, Momma wouldn't have approved of CJ at all.

He's too old for you He looks like a thug. He smells like a marijuana factory.

I could picture her saying all of the above whenever I built up the courage to introduce him to her.

Daddy was going to be a different matter altogether. He would also look at CJ and conclude that he was a gangster, but Daddy wouldn't be able to put CJ down because he had been a hustler himself back in the day when he first met my mother.

He had gone to prison when I was still in diapers and he hadn't come home until I was sixteen. By then him and my mother were no longer together. Momma had embraced the Baptist church and Daddy had joined The Nation of Islam while doing his bid up at Rahway. Now that he was home he was Minister David X, a well-respected figure in the NOI and a rabid adversary of crime and drugs in the black community.

My mother and father did not see eye to eye on religion, but they were both in harmony when it came to what was best for me. Cam'ron Jeffries definitely would not make the cut in their eyes.

Honestly, I never envisioned myself with someone like CJ. And I didn't think a man like him would be interested in me. When

CJ had first approached me and Jada at the mall, I thought that he was coming to spit game at my aunt. That's how it had always been when I was with Jada; nobody gave me a second look. Jada was all eye candy and designer labels. I was a ponytail and jeans girl in Air Max's. My only indulgence was designer bags.

Jada and I were standing at the check-out counter in Nordstroms when CJ approached. We had seen him get out of a Maybach in the parking lot and he seemed to follow us from that point on. Not like a stalker though. His swag emanated confidence and purpose.

As he approached, I took in his dark skin tone and the diamonds in his ears. Usually that was a turn off but he rocked the earrings with a masculinity that was unmistakable. And he had the prettiest smile.

I elbowed Jada and whispered, "Here comes your future baby's daddy."

"Maybe so." She smiled and poked out her booty.

"Girl, you're a hot mess," I laughed.

CJ walked right up to us. "Excuse me. How y'all doing?" he asked with his deep baritone voice.

"Fine," we both replied at the same time. Jada was grinning so hard it looked like her eyebrows were on the side of her head.

"I saw you in the parking lot and I just had to come and ask you your name." He reached out and gently grabbed my arm, bringing me in close to him.

His cologne smelled so good my head started spinning. My heart skipped a beat and a surprised smile appeared on my face. He returned the smile and looked into my eyes before he pushed his fingers through my hair. His touch made my knees so weak I thought my legs would fall right out from under me.

I took in a quick breath of air and watched his lips as they began to move. "What's your name, Miss?" he wanted to know.

I must've told him because he said, "Kenisha. That's a beautiful name and it fits you."

I didn't know how to respond so I just nodded and said, "Thank you."

"Kenisha, my name is Cam'ron but you can call me CJ. Do you mind if I pay for that for you?" he asked, taking the Tory Burch bag out of my hand and sitting it on the counter.

It felt like I had a lump in my throat and was at risk of choking. I gulped my saliva down but the anxiety made it hard to swallow. Now Jada was elbowing me. I opened my mouth but nothing came out.

CJ chuckled. "Don't be so shy. It's all good, I don't bite."

Before I could protest, he pulled out a roll of hundred dollar bills thicker than both of my fists put together. Beside me, Jada's eyes were bulging out of her head. The money hadn't impressed me, it was CJ's style that had me walking on air.

"Thank you, but you didn't have to do that," I said once I found my voice.

"What's wrong with me making you smile?" he asked, flashing those pearly whites that complimented his sultry eyes and chiseled cheekbones perfectly.

I was stuck.

"Nothing, I guess," I mumbled.

CJ's cell phone rang. "I'm sorry beautiful, but I have to take this call," he politely said. "Here, pay for that. And go pick you out something else."

He placed the large roll of money in my hand.

"No, CJ, I—"

"Shhhh," he hushed me with a finger to his beautifully thick lips. "I gotta step off and take this call. I'll be right back."

When he stepped off Jada's mouth ran a thousand words per minute. She was trying to coach me on how to play CJ. "You gotta get on your grown woman shit real fast. That muhfucka is a boss, you can't let him slip away," she said.

"I don't care about all of that. I'm just going to be myself. If he likes it, fine. If not, oh well."

When CJ returned, he told me that an emergency had come up and he had to go. "Call me later," he said.

"Okay, what's your number?" I asked, taking my cell phone out of my pocket and handing it to him. He programmed his number in the phone and handed it back.

"Hit me up yo," he said.

"Hold up. You're forgetting something." I reached my hand out to give him back his money.

"Nah ma, that's you right there," he said. Then he was out.

I moved to catch up to him but Jada had a grip on my arm like the Jaws of Life.

"Let go of me, I'm not keeping this," I declared vehemently.

"Oh yes you are," she insisted.

We stood there wrestling until I finally snatched free. But now CJ was nowhere to be found. "Ugghhhh!" I stomped my feet in frustration.

Beside me Jada was all teeth and gums.

"You can wipe that smile off your face because I'm not spending any of it. I'm going to call him and give it all back."

"Whatever," she replied flippantly.

As we headed over to the food court Jada was shaking her head and wearing a screw face. "Damn, no offense, but I don't get it," she blurted out.

"Get what?" I asked.

"What he sees in you."

I hunched my shoulders and giggled. I didn't have the answer to that question either. Jada was on some hater type shit but I took her statement as a compliment because he saw something in me other than my appearance. I had to be mighty special for him to even give me the time of day.

Since then CJ and I had gone out three times. I had returned his money on the first date.

"Shorty, you could have kept it. I told you that was you," he said. But I could tell from the look in his eyes that it had made a good impression on him.

I had met his little brother, Eric and his boys. Rah was the coolest of them all. It was super cool that Sparkle had been his fiancé. When he talked about her I could hear both the love and the pain in his voice. He didn't try to act all hard, he admitted that he wasn't over losing her yet. I liked that about him.

When Jada met Rah she practically acted like a groupie. It tickled me because usually she was in diva mode and men fell at her feet. Not Raheem. He was polite but it was obvious that Jada wasn't his cup of tea.

"Rah, why don't you like my aunt?" I'd asked him one day.

"You want the truth or the politically correct answer?" he asked.

"The truth." I giggled, punching him in the shoulder.

He seemed to contemplate before responding, and then he replied, "Let's just say that I have too much going on right now to even entertain the idea of getting involved with a woman intimately," he expressed.

I smiled and responded. "Sounds like you opted for the politically correct answer anyway," I kidded.

Rah laughed. "I don't care to cast stones," he said.

On the subject of Tamika, whom I was curious as heck about, Rah said little. "I believe those are questions you should ask CJ," he told me.

"But he won't talk about her much." I sighed with frustration.

"Give him time, he's still dealing with her death," Rah explained.

I could deal with that because honestly I was still confused as to what he saw in plain old me. I was so afraid that once he really got to know me I wasn't going to be what he wanted. That was the cause of my anxiety about spending a week on vacation with CJ. But I put on my game face and hoped for the best.

TWENTY-FOUR

CJ

"I'm lovin' this, yo!" I exclaimed as I sped down a snow-covered hill.

"Go faster!" cried Kenisha. She was on the back of the snowmobile, hugging me securely, and squealing with youthful excitement.

"You ain't said nothin' slick to a can of oil," I said. "Hold on tight shorty I'm about to make it do what it do." I floored the gas and we hydroplaned over a ramp of snow.

We landed smoothly and I let up off the gas.

"Yessss! That was awesome," she screamed.

I chuckled. "You sound like a pink toe."

"What's that?"

"A crack."

"Huh?"

"A white girl, shorty." I laughed.

It was so cold our words seemed to freeze in the air, but we were dressed like Eskimos down to the boots. The wind whipped around our heads and snow blew in our faces as I raced off again.

Behind us Legend tried to keep up.

Kenisha was prodding me to go faster and faster but I had to slow down again as we came to a steep decline.

We reached ground level and ventured off into the woods. Squirrels and rabbits darted out of our path as I steered around the trees. This was a fun escape from the city where fun and laughter was hard to come by these days. I had been going in hard for so long I had forgotten that there were other things to life than money and mayhem.

We stayed out on the snowmobile until black clouds rolled in and choked off the daylight. Back at the bungalow, we heated up one of the pre-cooked meals that I had brought along. Kenisha set up the table and served us roasted breast of duck, cream and chive potatoes and sweet peas.

Later, Legend went to his room with an ounce of Kush and his X Box to keep him company while shorty and I sat on a bear skin rug in front of the fireplace roasting marshmallows and listening to the Miguel CD that Kenisha brought along.

"I'm gettin' soft," I said with a smirk. *If my niggaz could see me now.*

"Why you gotta be so hard anyway?" asked Kenisha innocently.

"Because that's the life I live, ma."

"What life are you talkin' CJ?"

"I plead The Fifth."

She sat the fire poker down and turned and looked in my eyes. "CJ, I'm not as naive as you may think. I see how you rock the best labels and keep a fat grip in your pockets. And you've never mentioned going to nobody's job. So I know what you do." She read me.

"Maybe you do, maybe you don't."

"Oh, I know," she repeated with certainty and with a look on her face like she felt some kind of way about how I got mines.

I squinted my eyes at her and straight up asked, "You judging me yo?"

"No." Her voice pitched and her eyes bucked with incorruptibility. "I'm sorry," she leaned in with an apologetic kiss that turned into something very tender.

Her tongue tasted like marshmallows as I wrapped her in my arms and kissed her deeply. My hands eased up her sweater and I unsnapped her bra. I gently guided her down on the furry rug and pulled her sweater over her head.

"Ummm," she moaned when my mouth covered her small breast.

I traced her chocolate nipple with the tip of my tongue and her back arched up off the floor. "Please excuse my hands," I whispered in her ear as they slid inside her sweats.

I could feel the throbbing of her pussy against the palm of my hand. A nigga boned up instantly.

In the background with the fire licking at the logs Miguel crooned.

These lips can't wait to taste your skin, baby, no, no
And these eyes, yeah, can't wait to see your grin, ooh ooh baby
Just let my love
Just let my love adorn you
Please baby, yeah

You gotta know
You gotta know
You know that I adore you
Yeah baby

Baby these fists will always protect ya, lady
And this mind, oh, will never neglect you, yeah, baby, oh, baby
And if they try to break us down don't let that affect us, no,
baby

You just gotta let my love
Let my love
Let my love adorn you
Ah, le-le-le-let it dress you down

I took her hand and guided it down to that Plymouth Rock so she could feel how much her innocence turned a thug nigga on. She held her hand closed, acting like she was scared of all this meat.

"I thought I told you I don't bite. And neither does he," I said in a gruff tone full of desire.

I nibbled on her neck and shoulders as I removed her clothes piece by piece. When she was down to her panties, shorty held on to them with both hands as I tried to ease them off. I figured that she wasn't comfortable out in the open where Legend might walk out and see us.

I lifted her up and carried her into the bedroom so that she would feel more at ease. I laid her down on top of the comforter and began to step out of my clothes. I got butt ass naked and climbed on top of her, kissing her and running my hands all over that still maturing body. She had curves that would blossom in five years or so. Or after she had a baby.

I took her hand and guided it down to that powerful muscle between my legs. "Stroke it for me ma," I coaxed.

"No, CJ." She panted hard, fighting the desire that had begun to mount between her thighs.

"C'mon, shorty, don't deny us this moment," I whispered in her ear as I continued encouraging her to pleasure me.

Her hand went stiffer than my dick.

Sighing, I used a knee to gently try to part her legs. Shorty became as rigid as a corpse. "No CJ, I'm not ready." Kenisha clamped her thighs shut like the door to a bank vault and the sexual energy in the room instantly evaporated.

I rolled off of her onto my back and stared up at the ceiling, saying nothing. Kenisha sat up and covered herself with both arms. "See, this is why I didn't want to come," she said.

"Why? What's wrong? You're not on your cycle. So what's the problem? You not feeling a nigga like that?" I asked with an undertone of anger resonating from my voice.

Kenisha didn't respond for a minute and when she did she shocked the fuck outta me. With her eyes averted away from me and her voice real low, she disclosed, "I've never had sex before CJ. I'm a virgin."

I damn near fell out of the bed.

"Say what? Nah ma you bullshittin', right?" She had to be. No girl her age was still untouched.

I looked at her and saw in her face that she was serious. I pulled her down on top of me, adjusting her right on my wood. "It's all good ma. Let me be your first, your last, your everything."

"I'm not ready, CJ," she resisted.

I wasn't about to press her like I was some bum ass nigga. Fuck she think? She should have felt privileged to give her virginity to me. I slid her off of me, sat up, and grabbed my boxers off the floor and stepped into them. "This is what the fuck I get for fuckin' wit' a little ass girl," I gritted

"Wow! Is that how you really feel?" Her eyes watered.

"That's exactly how I feel. You trippin', ma. All I'm tryna do is make you a woman."

"God already did that," she shot back. She got up, wrapped the comforter around herself, and began gathering her things.

"Fuck you doing?" I questioned her.

"I'm ready to go home. I should have never come," she said on the verge of tears.

Crying was the wrong thing for her to do because I was a nigga with no compassion. I looked her in the eyes and retorted, "You're right about that. And I should have never brought your young ass up here with me. You not ready for no grown ass man, you need a little boy; somebody who has time to play bump and grind games with you. I'm not that nigga. I fuck with grown muhfuckin' women not little ass girls that are scared of dick."

Now the tears fell from her eyes. "You think that I have to fuck in order to be a woman?"

"Pretty much," I replied, breezy as fuck.

"Really?" She asked, sounding offended but I didn't care.

Kenisha stormed out of the room and came back with her clothes in hand. I went into the other room and came back with Legend. "Fam, take this little ass girl home and bring Shy back with you."

I looked from Legend to Kenisha as I grabbed my cell phone off of the nightstand and dialed Shy's number. "I keep pussy on deck shorty," I hurled at Kenisha.

Fuck her. I'm a muhfuckin' boss. I don't sweat pussy, bitches line up like they're at the Welfare office for a chance to spread their legs for me.

Shy answered her phone on the third ring. "Hello."

"What's up ma? Pack some clothes I'm sending somebody to get you. This little ass girl I got up here with me ain't what's happening."

I cut my eyes at Kenisha and saw that she was crying harder.

"Legend, get her the fuck out my face," I ordered.

TWENTY-FIVE

SHY

"Trick, you're stupid as hell if you go running back to that nigga. Then," she rolled her neck and eyes, "he has the nerve to send one of his boys to pick you up. Who in the fuck does he think he is?" ranted Papaya.

I had just got off of the phone with CJ and he wanted me to come up to The Hamptons where he was lamping. Normally it would have taken flowers and furs for a nigga to get me back after being so rude to me but I was missing CJ like crazy. Besides, I didn't want the next bitch to slide in my place.

Papaya had been getting on my last good nerve anyway so getting away from her sounded good to me. She was my girl and all but the bitch was so damn thirsty it was driving me up a wall. Ever since I had come back home she had been constantly trying to get me to tell her where CJ lived so we could have some niggaz rob him. That had been my same thought when I was upset but the more I thought about it the more afraid I had become that if something went wrong CJ was going to know that it was me who had put them on him.

Papaya and I had discussed going to Nard and selling what I knew to him but I didn't know him like that and I was afraid that we would end up like Tamika once I disclosed the information.

As I began packing for my rendezvous with CJ I tried to recall what all I had told Papaya's grimy ass about CJ's business. I had no doubt in my mind that she would try to squeeze a band or two out of it.

I quickly grabbed a half dozen outfits, under clothes, toiletries, and a few other things. After everything was packed I went into the bathroom and fixed my hair in the mirror. Papaya was standing in the doorway with her arms folded across her chest, steady running her mouth.

"Bitch, find you some business and leave mine alone," I checked her. Sometimes she could be a true hater.

"I'm just trying to look out for your ungrateful ass. When he put you out whose shoulder did you cry on?" she reminded me.

"Thank you." I spoke facetiously. "But it's not like you've never cried on mine so don't throw it back in my face," I said, becoming more aggravated with her by the minute.

"As long as you jump up and run back to him as soon as he calls, he's gonna continue to treat you like sideline pussy. Damn, I thought your game was way better than that. That nigga say jump and your head hits the ceiling." She struck below the belt.

"I don't need you to tell me how to handle mines," I enlightened her as I applied eyeliner around my pretty browns.

"Well, you know the rent is due," she said, trying to find something else to pick a fight about since I wouldn't let her influence me about CJ.

Did this jealous ho think that I wouldn't have my share?

"That's not a problem." I sat the eyeliner pencil down and went in my Gucci bag and gave her my half of the rent.

Papaya counted behind me as if we weren't best friends and she thought that I might short change her. The money was all there but her mouth was still twisted up. I looked at her and rolled my eyes. "Um, do I detect an attitude, boo boo?" I confronted the situation head on.

Papaya didn't respond.

"Because really, it's not like we're bumping pussies bitch. I don't try to tell you how to manage your men and I don't need you to tell me how to deal with mines," I continued.

"That's your problem, you only care about yourself."

"Hold up!" My hand shot up in the air. "Please explain to me what this has to do with selfishness—I'm confused."

166

My hands were now on my hips.

Papaya said, "Ever since you clowned Weez at the restaurant that day Akon has been feeding me with a long handle spoon."

I cocked my head to the side and looked at the bitch like she had two dicks in her mouth. "Pap', do you hear what you're saying? You sound stupid. If Akon cut you off because I didn't want his broke ass boy, you must not have been sucking his dick right. 'Cause I can guarantee you that if I'm sucking and fucking a nigga, there's nothing the next bitch can do to make him give up this pussy between my legs. You need to step your game up, boo." I dipped my head to look down my nose at her. "Start with Kegel exercises. Maybe you need a tighter grip."

"Ho. I don't know what you're tryna infer but my shit is not loose. You're the trick who's been flying coast to coast selling pussy on the internet. Ratchet ass bitch."

I started to reach for the canister of Mace that I kept inside my purse but I kept my cool. "That sounds like something you've been wanting to say for a long time. You must be jealous?" I laughed.

"Jealous of what? Bitch, don't get brand new over here. Don't forget I know you."

"And?"

"And I know you done had so many different niggaz running in and out of your bedroom it looked like the Million Man March," she spat.

"Are you mad? Check your bank account, boo. It's funny how Akon doesn't have time for you but he's steady blowing up my phone with texts."

"Ha! Bitch you're lying. That's all you do is lie, suck dick, and lay on your muhfuckin' back," shouted Papaya, turning red in the face.

"No, sweetie, you have it all wrong. I don't lie on my back; I like to ride, so niggaz don't forget who's in control. And when I suck dick, best believe it's with a purpose— that's why I do it well. And as far as lying about Akon blowing me up..." I paused and grabbed my cell phone off the sink counter. I strolled down to Akon's latest text. It read: *I'm not feeling ya girl, I'm tryna fuck wit' you. What's it gonna cost a nigga?*

I tossed my cell phone to Papaya and said, "I don't have to lie about no man. See for yourself."

The expression on her face changed from a smirk to a frown as she saw the proof. But, of course, she turned her anger on me. "You backstabbing, ratchet ass ho!" Her eyes were on fire.

She flew at me swinging wildly. She got a couple of licks in before I grabbed the front of her shirt and slung her against the wall. Her titties popped out and my fist popped her in the mouth. She reached out and tried to grab my hair but I had anticipated that.

"Un-uh bitch," I said, leaning back. I spun around and grabbed my bag.

Papaya jumped on my back screaming, "I'm gonna fuck you up."

We tussled around, bumping into the sink and falling over the toilet. She ended up on top of me but my bag was on the floor not far from my reach.

I managed to flip Papaya off of me, and then I grabbed the bag strap. She clasped my wrist knowing that I was reaching for my .380 or the mace. We rolled around on the bathroom floor until I was able to snatch my arm free and dig the mace out.

Papaya tried to turn her head and slither away but I was so not having it. "Nah bitch, don't run now," I sneered and aimed it at her.

I pressed down on the lever and squirted her dead in the eyes. "Ahhh! I can't see! Bitch, I'ma kill you!" she screamed.

"You don't need to see ho. Now you know how to stay in your lane." I climbed to my feet and kicked her in the side several times trying to break a few of her ribs.

She was writhing on the floor, choking and gagging. Her eyes became watery and her nose was running.

I looked down at her and spat, "And just so you know, I didn't take Akon up on his offer; I wouldn't do you like that. The only reason I hadn't told you about it until now is because I know how you are. You need dick in your life. Therefore, you'll believe anything a nigga tells you. Now let this ass whooping stay on your mind so you'll know I'm not that bitch."

I went back into my bedroom and finished getting myself together, and then I sat down on the bed and called CJ to see how long it would be before his boy arrived.

Ca$h

TWENTY-SIX

RAHEEM

"So what did wifey say? Is she and Mayabi hanging in there okay?" I asked DaQuan as soon as he got off the phone.

"Yeah, bruh bruh, they're gucci. Tanisha just got a new job at Grady's Hospital working in Records. I'm real proud of shawdy she's come a long way."

"She definitely has. I'm proud of her, too. And Mayabi is her spitting image. You have a beautiful family yo. I know they miss you. Why don't you fly home to visit them for a couple of days?"

"Yeah I'ma do that but I'ma wait until CJ and Legend get back."

"You don't have to wait bruh. Everything is good up here. The streets are quiet and if somebody wanna make some noise I got Eric and 'em to watch my back," I tried to reassure him. "See if you can book a flight for in the morning and go spend some time with your Queen and your little princess."

DaQuan nodded his head but otherwise didn't respond to my suggestion. He was unusually quiet which led me to think that he had something altogether different on his mind. "I think Tanisha is pregnant. She keeps talking about this big surprise that she has for me, but she won't say what it is," he finally said.

"Word? You think you made a son this time?" I kidded, glancing over at him in the passenger seat. We had just left from scouting out this barbershop on Central Ave. owned by an old school G named Jamaican Black. Word was that Nard fell through there frequently. We had watched the barbershop for the past three days with no luck.

Now we were headed over to Hawthorne because I had been told that LaKeesha had been staying with a friend over that way.

I glanced over at DaQuan again; he was staring down at the picture of Tanisha and Mayabi that he had as the screensaver on his phone.

"Fam, when we get back to the spot I'm calling and booking you a flight ASAP," I persisted.

"Like I said, I'll go when Legend and CJ get back, I don't wanna leave you up here butt naked," he resisted, staring at the screen still.

"I'll be a'ight, son. I got Eric and 'em here to watch my back," I repeated.

DaQuan shook his head dismissively. "Eric is gucci, Snoop and Premo seem to be official but I don't trust that nigga Flip at all. Nawl shawdy you need a Dirty South nigga watching your back at all times. Some of these fools up here seem shady."

"I hear you fam, but I'm not listening. You know I never really felt right about asking you to come up here anyway," I admitted as we pulled up to the spot where LaKeesha was supposed to be.

"Rah save all that talk for somebody that wanna hear it," said DaQuan. But I wasn't giving up. The suddenness of Kayundra's death had reminded me that you should never take life for granted and put off going to see the ones you loved.

We got out of the car and went inside the building but LaKeesha had just left I was told by the girl she was apparently staying with. I slid the girl a grip and told her not to tell my sister that I had been by because I didn't want LaKeesha to get in the wind.

Back in the car I continued to try to get DaQuan to go back to the A and see his peoples. As we drove across town my persistence finally began to wear him down. He agreed to make arrangements to go back home for a few days at least.

A call from CJ came through on my phone interrupting my conversation with DaQuan just as we were pulling into the apartments where we were staying.

"Sup?"

"What's good?" he asked

"Everything is lovely bruh. Ain't no drama or none of that. Are you and Kenisha enjoying yourselves?"

"Nah, I had to send her back. Legend didn't tell you? Man shorty was on some Sister Theresa shit. I got Shy up here with me now so you know it's going down."

"Fuck outta here yo," I laughed.

When CJ told me how that had happened I just shook my head and changed the subject to Nard and Jamaican Black.

CJ said, "The Dread got that ganja. That could be the reason Nard goes to see him. I think he would know better than to form an ally with Nard against me. He knows that I'm the main reason coroner's are overworked."

"You probably right but either way I'm on it. Enjoy your vacation. I'm handling things here."

"A'ight. One."

"One."

I hung up from CJ and parked right in front of our building. Me and DaQuan got out and I started telling him about CJ and Kenisha. He was laughing and texting on his phone. As we proceeded up the walkway two masked gunmen stepped out of the darkness.

"Fam, watch out!" I screamed to DaQuan. My hand shot inside my coat and I dashed to the side.

It was hard for me to get to the Glock on my waist with the heavy coat I was wearing. Bullets whizzed past my head from no more than ten feet away as I half-slid, half zig zagged in the snow, darting behind a parked car. I looked back and saw that DaQuan had slipped and fell down. He was rolling on the ground desperately reaching for his banger.

One of the gunmen ran up and stood over my nigga. He aimed his gun down and shot DaQuan twice.

Boc! Boc!

His partna was beside him now. He pumped three shots into DaQuan.

Now my Glock was out and coughing at both of those muhfuckaz.

Boc! Boc! Boc! Boc! Boc! Boc!

I let loose. "This what the fuck y'all want? C'mon, let's do this shit!" I cried, rising up from behind the car going all out.

Boc! Boc! Boc!

They fired back and then took off running around the building. I chased behind them emptying my clip, but in my fury my aim was faulty. A car was waiting for them with its passenger doors open. They dived inside and the car zoomed off.

I was out of bullets and breath, but adrenaline pumped my legs. I skidded around the front of the building as I went back to check on DaQuan. I knew it would be bad even before I made it back to where he lied sprawled out in the snow. His blood had turned the snow around him crimson red.

I slung my banger up on the roof of the building because I knew that soon 5-0 would arrive. I fell to my knees by DaQuan's side and lifted his head onto my lap. His eyes were glazed over and his body was slack. Blood trickled from the side of his mouth and in the cold smoke rose from his chest.

"Bruh, stay with me. You a souljah fight that shit," I cried. Tears dripped from my eyes and splattered down on his face.

A crowd formed around us.

"I called 911 they're on the way," someone said.

I hugged my nigga with my forehead against his. "Fight that shit, fam," I tearfully implored.

I felt his hand grip mines as his eyes closed then fluttered back open.

"Tell Tanisha," he gasped, "and Mayabi I love 'em. Tell wifey to keep striving and don't ever look back," he groaned. Every word was a struggle as his eyes began to close again and his mouth hung open.

I shook my head in denial. "Nah, bruh, you're gonna get to tell them that yourself."

I kissed his forehead. No homo. All love.

"You my nigga, Rah. Legend too." His voice was fading.

"Fight dawg. Fight," I cried. I shook him a little thinking that would keep him alert.

"If Tanisha is pregnant—and she—has a boy—name him—Raheem."

"You not leaving us. You're going to be here to name him after you."

"Name—him—Raheem," he coughed out.

Those were the last words before his head fell slack.

"Nooooo!" I cried out to Allah, the most merciful and magnificent. Tears poured down my face.

Through my blurred vision I spotted DaQuan's cell phone on the ground next to him. The screen was lit up allowing me to catch a glimpse of his two angels. How was I going to be able to tell them that he was dead?

TWENTY-SEVEIN

CJ

Shy was on the bed on all fours with her head down and her phat red ass up. I took her by the hips and pulled her to the edge of the bed. "Yes daddy, give it to me," she moaned. Then she made her ass cheeks clap.

With both feet firmly planted on the floor I drove inside of her, eight inches deep. We we're on a sex marathon that was going into the second hour and her shit was still wet. I leaned back and let a stream of spit drip from my mouth down between her ass cheeks, and then I used my thumb to rub it around her hole.

"Ummm. Do that nasty shit daddy. Make a bitch pull her goddamn hair out," she begged.

I eased my thumb inside of her tightest hole and long stroked my dick in and out of her pussy real slow. Her walls gripped my black steel and caressed it with her wetness.

"Fuck me harder, CJ. This your pussy, claim that shit. Oh my god! This dick is so muthafuckin' good. I swear baby I'll do anything you say," she cried.

"You gonna act like you got some sense from now on? Huh? Answer me!" I went in deeper and harder.

"Yes, daddy. And if I don't, make me act right. You own me, CJ. I'm all yours. Tell me what to do. Show me. Make me. I don't care just keep fucking me, nigga." Shy was going in. This dick had her losing her mind.

I grabbed her hair and pulled her head back. "That's right. This my pussy. I own this right here," I grunted as I felt her muscles contact around my pipe.

"Oooh, daddy, I'm about to cum."

"I'ma cum with you. Throw that shit back at me," I groaned as I felt myself building up to a big nut.

I stood still and let Shy grind that catty back on this wooden beam. She worked this muhfucka so good she had me planning her a trip to Tiffany's in my head. But I was too smooth to moan like a bitch so I roared like a beast and we came at the same time.

Exhausted, we collapsed down on the bed and feel asleep in a knot of arms and legs.

Later, Shy woke me up with a cloud of weed smoke in my face. "That's what the fuck I'm talking about." I rolled over and took the blunt from her hand.

She looked at me with a smirk on her face. "'Sup, my dude?" I asked, like she was one of the homies.

"This pussy knocked your ass out. That's what's up son," she mimicked my flow.

"You think you did something, don't you?" I chuckled as I got my lungs right.

"Boy, don't play. You know I handled mines. I heard you moaning like a little bitch," she giggled.

"Nah, you heard me growling like a *beast*," I set her straight. "I bet that pussy sore," I boasted.

"I'm not gon' lie, it is. You did that."

I was about to say some more fly shit but my cell phone rung and cut off my reply. Shy picked it up from off of the nightstand and handed it to me. The caller ID told me that it was Rah.

"What's up my dude?" I answered.

As soon as the first word came out of his mouth I knew something was wrong. He sounded almost like he did the day Kayundra died.

I listened as he told me the sad news. The pain in his voice touched my heart. What hurt him hurt me.

"Bruh, I'm on my way back," I said in a solemn tone.

"A'ight. Let me speak to Legend." Rah's voice was calm but deeper than usual.

I got up out of bed and pulled on my silk boxers.

178

"Where you sneaking off to?" she mouthed.

"There's trouble back home. We gotta leave."

I walked into the other room where Legend was laid across the bed smoking a blunt.

"What's hood?" he asked, sitting up tryna read the expression on my face.

I handed him my cell phone. "It's Rah," I said.

He put the phone to his ear. "Sup, shawdy?"

I watched him as he listened quietly. His expression melted into one of grief. A second later his head dropped to his chest. When he lifted it back up, he exhaled slowly. Tears welled up in his eyes but he fought them back. He lifted the phone back to his ear and said to Rah, "They're gonna pay for this. Every. Single. One. Of. Them. That's on everything that I love, homie."

He listened to Rah's response then hung up the phone.

I put a hand on his shoulder. "I'm sorry about your man," I said.

His jaw twitched and he wrung his hands, and then he exhaled again. He was fighting hard to keep from breaking down in front of me but I understood his pain. It was like one minute his man and him was blowing weed smoke in the sky, cracking jokes on each other and reminiscing about shit that they had done in the streets, then, in the blink of an eye his man was laying on a cold steel table with a tag on his toe. I knew his pain because my own was still as raw as an open gunshot wound.

Sometimes the memories of Tamika were so vivid I would look up and see her walking through the house in her panties and bra. Or she would be preening in the mirror, combing her hair with her fingers. Or I would hear her voice in my sleep saying, "CJ, I love you so much." Then it would fade away.

Dead at 26 years old! Life was too short and the fucked up part was nobody knew when they would take their last breath. The game is a cold-hearted bitch. A lowdown heartless ho, I thought.

And even though I was starting to feel Shy, she could not replace my boo.

I looked at Legend, wanting to say something but knowing that there were no words that could take the hurt away. I tried to imagine how I would've felt if it had been Rah instead of DaQuan. I couldn't even take thinking about that.

I took in a deep breath. Damn, it was hard to breathe.

"What's the matter, baby?" asked Shy when I walked back into the room.

I gave her the short version.

She wrapped her arms around my neck and said, "I'm by your side through whatever CJ. Just tell me what you need me to do. How do you need me to be to make things easier for you?"

"We'll talk about that. Now is not the time."

I removed her arms from around my neck and began packing up. It was going to be a long quiet ride back home.

Legend appeared in the doorway. I looked at him and realized that tragedy could make a man age right before your very eyes.

TWENTY-EIGHT

CJ

Back in Newark, I dropped Shy off at her apartment with instructions to pack all of her things.

"Don't leave nothin' because you're not coming back," I told her as she got out of the truck.

"Okay," she replied, wanting to smile but containing it out of respect for my mood.

"What about my furniture, baby?" she asked, leaning back in the window.

Behind the wheel Legend looked straight ahead and ignored the bitter cold wind that crept through the window. He was seething, anxious to kill in revenge of DaQuan.

Shy stood in the cold waiting for my response.

"Forget about your furniture, Shy. Let your girl have it. You're not gonna need it anyway, I'm moving you in with me. Just bring your clothes," I decided.

I took the door key off the ring and passed it to her through the window.

"After you get all of your clothes, go to the house and wait for me. I'll be home later," I said.

"Okay, baby." She leaned in the window and planted a kiss on my lips, and then she straightened back up and turned to go.

I reached out and grabbed her arm. When she turned around my eyes bore into hers. "Don't make me regret it," I warned.

"I won't," she promised.

As we drove off, I watched Shy walk toward her building. She had that same confident strut that Tamika had displayed. Like, I'm a bad bitch and I know it.

A text come through on my cell phone as we headed to my spot on Avon Ave. where everyone was to meet.

I miss you. Please give me a chance to make it up to you. I'm ready.

The message was from Kenisha.

I texted her back. *U good. A lot going on. TTYL.*

I liked baby girl and her purity was a turn on, but I had to have a street bitch on my team.

***

Rah pulled up at the spot at the same time as we did. We got out of our whips and embraced. When he embraced Legend they held it for a long time. The bond they had forged with DaQuan in The Dirty was now missing a link. That had to hurt both of them.

I looked up and down the block. Familiar rides lined the street. All of my top lieutenants stood outside in the driveway. Their heads were ducked, and their collars were turned up against the cold.

Rah tightened the fur hood of his Goose Down coat around his face and the wind whistled around us as we stepped in a natural cadence, heading inside. Someone opened the door as we climbed the five steps onto the porch. Nightfall surrounded the faces of Malice and Young Stunna, two mid-level workers that stood on the porch. They were passing a blunt back and forth between them.

Snoop, Eric, and Premo entered the house ahead of me, Rah and Legend. Rah stopped at the threshold and told Flip, "Get some more of our people over here. Make sure that they come strapped with those choppas. Until they arrive I want you to stay out here with these two lil' knuckleheads. Fuck they going to protect us with a stick of loud in their mouths?"

Flip looked at me as if he expected me to intervene but I refused to undermine the authority that I had given Rah.

When we went inside Flip was right with us.

"You hard of hearing, yo?" Rah confronted him just inside the door.

"I heard you, but you not saying shit. Fuck I look like? Nigga I earned my stripes. You stand out there in the cold," Flip challenged.

Rah's banger was out in a fraction of a second. He stepped up in Flip's face and shoved the gun up under his chin. I stood there and let the scene play out, knowing that this was the moment of truth.

"You saying anything, yo?" Rah said in a gravelly, calm tone that typified his get-down.

Flip didn't fold though; there was no bitch in him. He scowled at Rah and stated, "My heart don't pump water, Blood."

Boc! Boc!

Two shots rang out and the inside of Flip's head flew out the top and splattered all over us. His body dropped at Rah's feet and twitched several times. My mouth was wide open!

Rah bent over, placed the tip of the gun against Flip's body, and shot him straight through the left side of his chest. "Now your heart don't pump at all," he said through gritted teeth.

Premo and Snoop looked at me. I knew what they were thinking. Flip had put in work for the team and they felt some kind of way about Rah killing him. I didn't know how I should feel. I knew that there was no one or nothin' that could make me side against my nigga but I had to say something or risk a flat out mutiny.

I stepped in the center of the circle that my mans had formed around Flip's body. Commanding their attention with the pitch of my voice, I said, "This is the type of shit that happens when insubordination invades the ranks. It has to be all love and everybody has to play their positions. A real souljah follows commands. No questions asked. Now were gonna give our brother a proper burial, then we're gonna come together closer than ever before. Is that understood?"

Each man nodded in agreement.

Rah added, "The other side isn't playing. From now on it's do or die. I don't have a problem with nobody in here. I'm here to annihilate the enemy whether that's Nard or one that's hidden in our own camp. That's how I rock and I'm immovable on that."

I threw an arm around Rah's shoulder and led him to the back of the house where we could talk in private. He was tensed up and ready to strike again. The murder of DaQuan had unleashed the fury inside of him.

We stepped into a spare bedroom and I closed the door. I expected to see his chest heaving up and down but he was as easy a Sunday morning. "You a'ight?" I asked in case he was holding it in.

"I'm peace," he replied. Then he looked me in the eye and said, "I tried to contain the beast but muhfuckaz wouldn't let me. Now they're about to find out why it's best to let a lion lay still. I'm flying DaQuan's body back to the 'A', and then I'm coming back to turn The Bricks into little tiny pebbles. "Write that shit in blood my nigga."

And from that point on Rah was a different man.

TWENTY-NINE

RAHEEM

"I hate you, Raheem! I hate you!" cried Tanisha, pummeling me with both fists.

I didn't even try to block her blows I just let her wear herself out until her arms fell down at her sides. Blood trickled from my nose but I didn't wipe at it.

"You got him killed. Oh, my God!" Tanisha sobbed.

I was standing just inside her door. Facing her was the hardest thing I had ever done. It would have been easier facing a firing squad. Behind her Mayabi hugged her leg. She too was crying. I felt like I had pulled the trigger and fired the fatal bullets that killed DaQuan. If I had never asked him to go up top with me, Tanisha would not be mourning her man and Mayabi would not have to grow up without a dad.

Over Tanisha's shoulder I could see friends and family members sitting in the living room. They all seemed to be staring at me with contempt. I had seen this reaction from Kayundra's people when she died, but this time I truly deserved the scorn.

"I'm sorry Tanisha." I tried to reach out and hug her; to let her feel that my heart was aching too.

She stepped back, shaking her head. "No—No—No!"

I looked down and saw that her belly was poking out a little. She noticed me staring and said, "I was going to surprise him when he came home." Then she broke down sobbing.

I pinched my eyes and inhaled deeply then I let it out very slowly. "He knew," I tried to assure her.

If it's a boy tell her I said to name him Raheem. I could not bring myself to tell her that. Instead, I tried to explain what happened. "Tanisha I know you hate me right now and you have every reason to feel that way. But you know I had real love for

185

DaQuan and I did everything I could to protect him. I tried to shoot…"

"I don't wanna hear it!" she screamed, clamping her hands over her ears. "Y'all got him killed. You and Legend! I hate both of y'all!"

The relatives watched and listened to our exchange without moving out of their seats. I was glad that Legend had elected to remain up in Newark until the day before the funeral because he would have taken Tanisha's blame very hard.

"I'm sorry," I tried once more.

"You're sorry?" she replied bitterly. Her red eyes were like flames. "Tell Mayabi that you're sorry. Explain to her where her daddy is. Tell these two little boys growing inside of me why they will never know their father, Raheem."

Two? Twins?

That made me feel so much worse.

I didn't know how to quiet the storm but I was not going to run away from it. I bent down and looked into Mayabi's watery eyes. Tears as big as rain drops ran down her precious little face. I reached out for her and she hugged my neck tightly, sniffling in my ear.

She didn't know the meaning of everything that was being said; she didn't understand that she would still have a daddy had I not asked him to go up to The Bricks to help fight a war that was not his to fight; a battle that had decimated their lives now. All that cute, doe eyed, dimpled cheeked Mayabi knew was that I had always been kind to her. Her innocence spared me the anger that I deserved coming from her.

"Rah Rah," she said.

"Yes honey?" My voice cracked.

"Did you kill my daddy?"

I didn't know how to answer her. Had I killed DaQuan? In a way I had.

Tanisha surprised me when she knelt down next to us, took Mayabi in her arms and said, "No, he didn't kill your daddy, baby. Raheem was your daddy's best friend. Hug his neck and give him a kiss on the cheek."

Tanisha's words and her sudden change of attitude touched me. It lessened my burden of guilt to hear her say that to her daughter. She did not hate me, because she had to know that I had mad love for DaQuan and that I had done everything in my power to come to his aid that night. She was much too real to let Mayabi grow up blaming me for her father's death.

"Thank you," I mouthed.

We stood up and embraced, and I let her cry against my chest. "I'll be here for you, Mayabi, and the twins when they're born. Here, take this. Put it away somewhere safe."

I handed her a book bag that I had brought with me. It contained $50,000 from CJ, $10,000 from Legend and $100,000 from myself.

"Thank you," she said softly.

I felt a little better but as I looked down at her belly one last time before leaving I thought, *No amount of money can bring their daddy back.*

Big Ma's wide smile lifted my spirits a little as soon as I walked in the door. "My baby!" she cried, hugging me tightly against her.

"Hey precious woman," I replied affectionately and kissed her on the top of the head.

"Oh no! Give me some real sugah," she said.

I bent down and planted one on her lips. "The sweetest thing I've ever tasted," I remarked.

"My baby," she repeated. "Tell Mama what's wrong. And don't you dare try to deny it because I know better. I can see it in your eyes."

"I'm okay, Big Ma," I maintained. "How are you getting along?"

That sat her off to complaining about all of her aches and pains. I listened patiently and offered to rub her swollen feet. She couldn't resist that, and I really enjoyed doing it. That was such a small thing to do for all that she had done for me.

Big Ma said that she didn't miss Newark at all, and she thanked me for hiring a lady to come over and help her every day and to drive her around.

"She's a sweet girl, she just talks a little too much. She can really clean up but I don't allow her in my kitchen. Nope, that child can't boil water," she said, laughing at her own joke.

We sat and talked about LaKeesha and I promised Big Ma that I would have her in Atlanta real soon. "You make sure you do that," she emphasized. "Now I'm about to fix you a good home cooked dinner. You look like you're about to disappear."

I couldn't say no to that.

Big Ma did her thing in the kitchen. Baked chicken, macaroni and cheese, candied yams, greens, cornbread, peach cobbler, and sweet tea.

After we got our grub on we sat at the dining room table talking. I didn't mention my reason for being back in the 'A'. When it started getting late I cleared the table and washed the dishes while Big Ma retired to her room. Her waddle-walk seemed a bit slower these days.

With an indescribable sadness I realized that she was getting old.

I dried the dishes then went and sat in the den. Framed pictures of Kayundra still adorned the walls. *I stumbled on this photo-*

graph... it kinda made me laugh... it took me way back... back down memory lane.

I felt a sharp pain in my heart as my eyes moved from one framed memory to the next. Now I was face to face with the ache that I had blocked out.

I could have saved her.

I put on a DVD of her music videos. As she moved gracefully across the screen, singing soulfully, the void in my heart widened like the distance between paradise and the projects. I longed to hold her in my arms, to turn back the hands of time to when she was so excited about winning at The Apollo. Or further back to when neither of us had anything but each other and our dreams.

Tears wet my face as I watched one video after another. My tears dried quickly and anger replaced sadness when the video she did with Scare Me came on. Why in the fuck did she betray me for that clown ass nigga? I had given her my love and devotion. She had cheated and aborted my seed. After everything that we had gone through why couldn't she have been stronger than the pressures that lurked in the industry? Was her love for me that fickle?

For the first time since she had taken her own life, I realized that I was mad as hell at her for destroying what we had. We were supposed to have grown old together.

To lessen the agony, I moved it from my heart to my mind where I could handle it better. My mental accepted that anger was just one of the stages of grief, not unlike what I had witnessed from Tanisha earlier. I fast-forwarded the DVD to Sparkle's video for her song *A Long Way Home*, the last video that she had made before her death.

I could see the hurt in her eyes even as she smiled and danced. And when she sung about a love that she hoped to earn back, I absolutely knew that those lyrics were written for me. I closed my eyes and thought about the good memories because there had been many.

I opened my eyes when I felt a familiar hand on my shoulder. "God will send you someone who will make you smile again," Big Ma prophesied.

I covered her hand with mine and wondered if her vision would ever come true. Sparkle was gone. With her went my joy.

Too many deaths and so many killings on my part had stolen my smile forever.

And I still had to lay DaQuan to rest.

THIRTY

RAHEEM

Legend and CJ came down for DaQuan's funeral. After it was over they immediately went back up top and started putting niggaz on their asses. I had remained in the *A* another three days checking on my nightclubs and plotting something that was long overdue.

When it was time for me to leave I said goodbye to Big Ma with a heavy heart and promised her that I would find LaKeesha and bring her and the kids to Atlanta soon.

I hugged her tightly and told her that I loved her.

"I love you too, baby," she replied on the verge of tears.

When I tried to let go of her she pulled me back in and held me tighter. "Raheem," she said, "I don't know what all you've done but whatever it is, it is changing you. I can see it in your eyes. It's like you're fighting against what you know is the right thing to do. Now I know you love CJ but don't sacrifice who you are to honor that friendship. God comes before all things. Go to the mosque, baby, and seek peace in the Word. Do that for me."

I looked down at her and saw a tear running down her face. That caused tears to pour down in my heart. I could remember when I was in college and making her proud. Now all I seemed to do is make her cry.

"Go to the mosque," she implored. Although Big Ma was a Christian she respected Islam because she had seen its positive effects on so many brothers.

"Okay. I'll go as soon as I get back. I promise."

She reached in her bosom and pulled out a small lacquered card and handed it to me. I kissed her goodbye then went outside where a cab awaited to drive me to the airport.

As we hit I-285 I opened my hand and looked at the card that Big Ma had given me.

English Translation of the Holy Quran by Maulana Muhammad Ali.

16:33 Await they aught but that the angels should come to them or that thy Lord's command should come to pass. Thus did those before them. And Allah wronged them not, but they wronged themselves.

16:34 So the evil of what they did afflicted them, and that which they mocked encompassed them.

Al-Baqarah — The Cow:

2:20 The lightning almost takes away their sight. Whenever it shines on them they walk in it, and when it becomes dark to them they stand still. And if Allah had pleased, He would have taken away their hearing and their sight.

"Surely Allah is Possessor of power over all things." I read the last sentence of the Surah out loud.

I put the card inside my coat pocket and drifted deep inside my own thoughts.

I took off my coat and neatly placed it in the overhead compartment, and then slid into my window seat in First Class. I buckled in and took a magazine from the pouch on the back of the seat in front of me and began reading an article about President Barack and Michelle Obama.

"Excuse me." A soft voice demanded my attention.

I looked up into the face of a beautiful ebony skinned sistah who appeared to be in her late twenties or early thirties. I realized that I had seen her earlier as we waited to board. She had been wearing a long wool coat and matching hat so I hadn't seen much of her besides her pretty smile and dark brown eyes.

Now that the coat was draped over her arm I saw that she had a nice figure to compliment her smile. I guessed that she was probably a size ten or twelve and she wore it nicely.

I stood up and helped her put away her carry-on luggage and her briefcase.

Standing so close to her I could smell the soft fragrance of her perfume. I didn't know the name of it but 'sensuous' would have been perfect. "Please don't be offended sistah, but you smell lovely," I politely complimented her.

"Thank you." She smiled beautifully.

"You're welcome," I replied, allowing my eyes to take in her beauty as we both settled into our seats. Her locs hung down her back in a ponytail. Her skin tone was the color of dark maple syrup. Her brown eyes looked friendly but smart, as if she could read you upon first glance. Her mouth was as sensual as the smell of her perfume and her lips made me want to lean over and kiss them.

"Excuse me for staring," I said. "You're a very beautiful sistah."

"Thank you. You're very easy on the eyes yourself," she replied.

I smiled. "Hi, my name is Raheem."

"My name is Malika. Pleased to meet you." She extended her hand.

I shook it and said, "That means Queen, doesn't it?"

"It does. I'm impressed," she replied.

We smiled at each other and I returned my attention to the magazine article because I didn't want to invade her space.

Once we were in the sky, a flight attendant served us dinner. I had a New York steak and baked potato. Malika had baked zucchini and a salad.

"It was decent as far as airline meals go," she said after our trays were taken away.

I liked that she looked at me when she spoke, that showed confidence and high self-esteem.

"So, Raheem, are you from Newark or Atlanta? Or neither?" she asked.

"I'm from Newark but Atlanta is home for me now. What about yourself?"

"I'm from Atlanta—well, actually the East Point area is where I grew up."

"I'm familiar with East Point," I said unable not to stare. "Uh, I hope I'm not making you uncomfortable."

"What do you mean?"

"My staring. Honestly, you're the first woman to have this effect on me."

"That's quite flattering," she said, flashing a smile that welcomed more conversation.

"So what's up in Newark?" I asked.

"A new job in system analysis with an upstart research company. I've only been there for a month. How long will you be in Newark?" I was surprised that she pronounced "Newark" like a true Jersey girl would instead of like it was two words like most out-of-towners pronounced it.

"I'll be there indefinitely. Maybe we can go out to eat or I can show you around." I glanced at her hand to see if she was married or engaged.

Malika smiled then lifted her left hand and held it close to my face. "Nope. Not married," she said and we shared a laugh.

Now she was the one doing the staring. She said that I looked very familiar. I told her about my nightclubs in Atlanta. "Maybe you've seen me there."

."I haven't gone out to a nightclub since my wild and crazy college days," she said.

"How wild and crazy?" I joked.

"None of your business." She laughed.

I liked the way her eyes brightened with her laughter. She looked down at the article that I had been reading and said, "Michelle is awesome. Don't you think so?"

"I do," I answered honestly.

That began a conversation that started with politics and moved to social issues in the black community. When Malika spoke on the drug epidemic in the hood I listened but offered little in response. The conflict inside of me heightened with each well founded statement that she made.

"Why are you so quiet?" she asked.

"I'm just enjoying listening to your views on the issue. I'll share mine one day if we decide to stay in touch with each other," I supplemented the truth.

She must have sensed that I was holding back because she changed the subject to one that was much lighter. Music.

She liked a little bit of rap and R&B, and a whole lot of neo-soul. I was diverse in my musical taste so I was familiar with all of her favorite artists.

She looked at me a little harder, and then said. "You know what? You kind of resemble Mystikal. I bet you've been told that before."

"He wish," I quipped.

Malika threw her head back and laughed. "I know—right?"

Before we knew it the pilot was announcing landing. We debarked together, then exchanged numbers before departing. As I watched Malika walk away I promised myself that if we ever went out I would keep her far away from that part of my life that could easily cost her *hers*.

Ca$h

THIRTY-ONE

RAHEEM

Legend and Eric was waiting for me at the arrival gate. I greeted them with a G-hug then we drove out to a new spot that Legend was resting at. CJ was up in New Haven. He called while we were in route to the new apartment. We talked for a minute then agreed to get together later tomorrow. I was tired and just wanted to take a shower and close my eyes.

The next morning was Sunday. I had given Big Ma my word so I had to honor my promise. I got dressed to go to the Temple in Harlem where Kenisha told me her father David X was over the service. With so much beef in the air Eric and Legend refused to let me ride alone. They rode shotgun and would wait for me outside in the car.

When we pulled in front of the Temple my heart was weighted with emotion. The anguish of the many losses I had sustained had begun to take a toll on my spirit. *Back to your roots* I repeated in my head as I stepped out of the car heading inside.

When I walked into the lobby an instant calm came over my mind. The sight of the brothers' welcoming faces reassured me that my decision to attend service today was the right one.

"As-Salaam-Alaikum, my brother." A tall brown skin brother walked over and extended the greeting.

"Wa-Alaikum-Salaam," I returned the salutation as we touched shoulders from right to left.

"Welcome home. Is this your first time to the Temple?"

"No, sir. But I have strayed," I said, feeling a slight bit of shame.

"Allah is most merciful my brother." He gave me a sincere eye. "Please come be seated service will begin in a minute."

"Thank you." I walked inside.

Ca$h

The sisters were seated on one side and the brothers on the other. My chest filled with emotion when my eyes settled on the children lined across the back row. My mind reflected back to me and my moms hurrying to Jumar prayer on Friday's and me struggling to be still during prayer service.

I walked down the aisle to the front row where guest where seated. A brother came to the rostrum and asked the believers to stand for the opening prayer. I stood and extended my palms upward, closed my eyes and listened to the words that flowed from the brother's mouth.

"In the Name of Allah, the Beneficent, the Most Merciful. All praises due to Allah the Lord of all the world, the Beneficent, the Most Merciful, and Master of this day of requital. Thee do we serve and thee do we beseech for help, guide us on the right path, the path upon those whom you have bestowed thy favors and not the path upon those whom thy wrath is brought down nor those who go astray,"

Go astray rang in my mind loud and clear as I lowered my hands and took a seat.

When the minister came to the rostrum and began his class I sat up straight and rested my palms on my thighs as I was taught. Each word from his lips seemed like it was being spoken directly to me. The minister spoke about the prodigal son who had asked for his wealth early from his father and took it and went into the world and wasted it on partying, drugs and women.

"That son was a disappointment to his father and his family, and then was struck with poverty. But after being brought low he came home to his father's house seeking only a job. Just let him be close to the house, he humbly asked.

The father was overwhelmed with love and respect for his son and welcomed him back with opened arms and placed him at the head of his kingdom for his son had knowledge of both worlds, the good and the evil and he could now help his father do his work."

I sat listening to how Allah was forgiving and that everything in history is already written as the Holy Quran says, "Not one grain of sand turns over in its resting place unless it is written in a book."

I felt relieved for some of my evil deeds but remained conflicted because I knew that I still had murder in my sights.

After service I walked outside and climbed in the backseat. I quietly stared out the window as Eric pulled off without him or Legend saying a word. When we arrived back in The Bricks a false sense of calm seemed to have settled over the city. Minister David X's words remained with me but so did visions of DaQuan dying in my arms. I closed my eyes and asked Allah to protect the innocent from the death toll that I was about to cause.

Ca$h

THIRTY-TWO

NARD

Raheem must've had an angel on his shoulder. I swear me and Man Dog had him right where we wanted him that night and he still managed to get away untouched.

Man Dog was furious but I had chalked it up to it just hadn't been Raheem's time to go. At least we took one of them down. Any day that we could make them bury one of theirs was a good day.

The next night they gunned down three of my boys in the parking lot of the Key Club, a spot on Park Place. Bodies on both sides were falling like raindrops. To put an end to so many dying over the beef between me and CJ, I sent word to him that we could settle the beef straight G-style.

"Tell that bitch ass nigga that we can meet in the middle of Sussex Ave, just me and him, guns blazing. If he can find his nuts I'll be there on any day and at any time he wanna do it," I told Jamaican Black when he had suggested that I turn down a little bit.

CJ responded like the coward I felt he was underneath all that street persona. He didn't meet me in the middle of the hood, instead they killed another one of my boys that same day.

I retaliated swift and mercilessly. We ran up in a spot of his and put four niggaz on their backs. Two days after that we rode through The Bricks seven whips deep, mocking CJ in the same manner they had shined on us after killing Talib. My message was clear: *An eye for an eye.*

There, in broad daylight, we hopped out of our whips and stood shoulder to shoulder with our choppas and AR 15's in our grips. I scanned the block; a handful of people trudged through the foot of snow that covered the ground but none of CJ's people were in sight. Regardless, I knew they were somewhere up in those buildings watching.

Speaking through a bullhorn I shouted, "Tell CJ that this murder shit ain't gonna stop until all you bitch muhfuckaz die! Anybody that fucks with him is my sworn enemy!"

My voice boomed up and down the block. I looked up in the windows of the apartments hoping to see an unfriendly face. I was gonna send a little semi-automatic heat their way, but no one appeared. I pointed my choppa toward the sky and made it go the fuck off. Beside me, Man Dog, Big Nasty, Quent, and Zakee did the same. It sounded like roaring thunder. I was just letting the hood know that I did not bow down to their king. Fuck Cam'ron Jeffries!

We hopped back in our whips and mashed out before them boys showed up.

"My youth, you a hot boy. I tell you walk easy," said Jamaican Black a few days after the episode.

I would've ignored his advice but business necessitated that we let our guns cool for a minute. My connect was about to hit me with fifty bricks, the largest drop he had made to me yet.

"You can't let anything go wrong," stressed my supplier when I talked to him on the phone at Jamaican Black's barber shop.

I assured him that I would not betray his faith in me.

While I waited for my connect to deliver the work I sat back and plotted. Getting to CJ was going to be easier with the help of lil' mama who had come to me with the information that Raheem and 'em had a spot in the Executive House apartments and had promised to find out where CJ rested at. But the more I thought about it the harder I worked to come up with a plan to get at CJ in a way that niggaz would remember forever. I no longer wanted to jump out and wet him up in the middle of the street. Nah, this had to be vicious!

I smiled as a wicked plan suddenly came to mind.

"Why are you smiling? Does it feel good?" asked Papaya. She was on her knees breaking me off."

"Yeah ma keep doing you." I grabbed the back of her head and closed one eye.

Never two because after Tamika it was *Trust No Bitch.* I let Papaya suck my dick and dream about being on my team because she had been useful. But I wasn't ever gonna fuck the grimy ho.

"After I nutted in her mouth and she swallowed, I gave her a mission and sent her on her way.

"I'll gladly do that," she agreed. "I owe that bitch anyway."

Since CJ didn't wanna come outside and play with guns, I was going to systematically eliminate everyone close to him.

Ca$h

THIRTY-THREE

SHY

I was sitting on the bed painting my toenails and watching *Catfish*, the reality show about people falling in love with someone that they met on the internet and that person turning out not to be who they claimed they were. I shook my head at how gullible some people could be. I mean, I had met clients on the internet back when I was in a certain line of work but I damn sure wouldn't look for love on no freaking social site. Ugh!

A bitch had to be bored out of her wits to watch that shit. I was way up in Bumblefuck, Connecticut where I didn't know anyone and the distance to the closest neighbor's house might as well have been a whole 'nother area code away because I seldom saw any of them. Like me, I guess they sat inside their big fancy homes all day staring at the television, surfing the internet, or getting all dressed up with no damn where to go.

I was surrounded by all of the splendor that I had ever dreamed of; I had a boss nigga that spoiled me with designer labels and fucked me so good I almost lost my sight every time he made me come. He had just copped me a brand new Mercedes Benz C-Class earlier today. I would have been jumping up and down with excitement except for the fact that I couldn't ride around making the bitches that knew me jealous, particularly Papaya's hating ass.

"Don't go to Newark," CJ had just ordered me. "Matter of fact, stay out of Jersey period."

I looked at his sneaky ass with my mouth twisted and one eye closed. "Why can't I go to Jersey? You must don't want me to run in to none of your hos," I accused.

"Just do what I said," he replied roughly, without even looking up at me as he continued getting dressed to leave.

"Do you talk to that little young girl Kenisha like that? Or is her supposedly virgin ears too tender for that," I asked sarcastically.

That got his attention because we had ran into Kenisha and her aunt Jada at Short Hills Mall a couple of weeks ago and Jada had put CJ on blast. I wasn't mad because CJ had already told me about Kenisha when we were up in the Hamptons but I didn't believe that he no longer talked to her.

CJ stepped out of the closet and put two guns on his waist. He looked up and said, "I don't have no hos, so don't hit me with that bullshit every time I walk out the door. For real shorty."

I could see the signs of stress on his face, underneath his eyes had gotten darker and the natural scowl that he always wore had become more prominent.

"I'm bored to death up here with no friends and nothing to do all day. I don't see why you even bought me a new car if you won't let me go anywhere," I pouted.

"Tamika used to complain about the same thing," he chuckled. But I didn't see a damn thing funny!

My head shot up and I breathed flames. "That was so rude! Please don't compare me to her again," I bristled. It was bad enough that he still had her pictures all over the bedroom and he still rocked a chain with her face engraved on the medallion in diamonds!

"My bad, ma," he quickly apologized and took a seat on the bed next to me.

He put his arms around me and kissed away my anger. Pulling back he asked, "You forgive me?"

I sat the polish on the nightstand by the bed and looked at him with sad eyes for full effect. "CJ, I'm bored," I whined.

He looked at me with a straight face and asked, "Do you want me to buy you a poodle or something?"

I looked at him reproachfully. "Sometimes you can be a real ass hole," I griped. I laid down on my stomach and covered my head with a pillow. A moment later I felt CJ's hand on my shoulder. "I don't want to talk. Go on in the streets I'll just sit at home and wait on you to bring me back a damn dog," I grumbled.

"Sit up shorty," he said in a serious tone that let me know that now was not the time for theatrics. I uncovered my head and sat up.

Staring deep into my eyes he asked, "Are you really ready for this life, yo?"

"Yes, baby, I am," I said confidently. I knew that I could be *that* bitch that he needed.

"Good, because I'm gonna need you to be a souljah. Nah mean?"

I nodded *yes*.

CJ took a deep breath and let it out slowly, and then said, "This is my get-down, Shy. When I walk out the door and step into the streets I step into a whole different world. Especially now because there's a war going on in The Bricks and this young nigga that I'm beefing with is going all out to take my life. You understand me?"

"Yes baby." My heart pounded with fear for him but I told myself that there was no way Nard could defeat CJ.

"When I'm away from home, I gotta be on point because one slip and my dick is in the dirt," he stated what I feared most. Then he continued. "I don't have time to worry about where you're at or who you might be creeping with behind my back. If you're disloyal or full of drama, you're gonna be a detriment to me. You may not love everything about me but don't try to change me. I'm not the kind of nigga you can mold. Just play your position and things will be a'ight. Nah mean?"

"Yes. And I apologize for acting so needy," I said.

"You good ma." He leaned in, kissed my lips and stood up.

"CJ can I ask one thing of you?" I dared.

"What's up?"

"Will you please take Tamika's pictures down? Please?"

He stood there looking like he was thinking real hard about my request. Then without saying anything he walked over and took the large picture of her off the wall and the smaller one off the nightstand. I saw sadness envelope his face as he carried them out of the room.

I smiled inwardly. Now I knew I was his bitch. I had endured the insult of another woman's picture hanging in our bedroom, but it hadn't been in vain.

THIRTY-FOUR

CJ

Packing Tamika's pictures away felt like I was burying a part of my soul, but it was something I had to do in order to move on. Shy hadn't said anything about the chain but I removed it from around my neck and put it inside a hidden wall safe in one of the guest rooms.

I stood there for a minute as memories tugged at a nigga'z heart. I picked the chain up and kissed the medallion. "I'll never forget you Mika," I said.

I put the chain back in the safe and locked it. But that chapter of my life wouldn't be completely closed until Nard laid dead at my feet.

I walked back in the bedroom where Shy was at and a smile came across her face when she noticed that I wasn't rocking the chain anymore. "Thank you," she said softly before standing and wrapping her arms around my neck.

"You good now?" I asked, palming her ass.

"Yes, I am" She smiled brighter. "And you don't even have to get me a poodle."

I let out a little laugh at that.

"I tell you what ma, I'ma do something nice for you. Your birthday is coming up ain't it?" I recalled her mentioning it a few days ago.

"Yep, in two weeks," she confirmed.

"I got you. You can throw a birthday party. We'll do it at Club 466 in West Orange, that's a nice spot. Fuck the beef in the street, I'm not letting no young boy stop me from celebrating my girl's born day."

Shy squealed with excitement. "Thank you baby," she beamed. "I'm going to start arranging it tomorrow. You can be so sweet when you want to." She hopped back up and hugged me.

"Let me bounce. I need to go to Newark and check on my squad. Don't wait up for me I'm gonna stay down there tonight," I told her.

"Okay," she accepted without complaint.

As I walked down the stairs and went and got in my whip, my phone lit up with an incoming call. Pulling out of my driveway I answered it. "What's up lil' mama?"

"Uh—I'm just calling to see what you're doing."

"I'm on my way to pick you up unless you've changed your mind?"

"No I haven't," replied Kenisha.

"A'ight, I'll hit you up when I get to Newark."

Anticipation soared through my body and caused my foot to get heavy on the gas pedal. A line from Wale's song *Bad* came to mind.

Is it bad that I never made love, no I never did it.
But I sure know how to fuck.

THIRTY-FIVE

KENISHA

When CJ picked me up I was so full of nerves it felt like my heart was going to jump out of my throat. I tried to do everything Jada had coached me to do in order to be ready, but I could not pull it together. As he drove toward Newark Liberty International airport my eyes roamed up his leg to his waist. I could see his dick print and it looked enormous. The thought of all of that going inside of me caused the very heat to drain from my body. I felt a panic attack coming on.

I quickly put my shaking hand on the door handle and lowered the window.

"You a'ight ma," CJ asked, looking over at me.

I wanted to answer but my lips wouldn't part. I forced a small smile and nodded my head.

"If you scared, I can take you back home, it's all good," he offered.

No. That reminded me of the disaster in the Hamptons. I had almost ran him away and later when I saw him at *our* mall with Shy I knew that I had to be more like her in order to win his interest back. I had blown his phone up and eventually his anger subsided and he agreed to give me another chance. I was determined not to blow it by chickening out. *Good girls are no fun.*

"I'm fine," I said taking a deep breath.

CJ gave me a little smile that only confirmed my fear, he was going to get to do something to me tonight that would make me more than a woman.

I clutched my purse and took a few deep breaths then instantly a slight calmness came over me. But when I saw the airport hotel signs my cool went right out into the night's air.

211

Ca$h

We pulled in front of the Marriot, parked the car, and then headed inside. At the elevator he reached down and took my hand causing me to jump.

"Relax, lil' mama, I got you," he said as we entered.

When the door closed, he pulled me in his arms and nestled his nose in my neck and inhaled. His heat settled against my skin sending chills up my spin.

"Don't be scared. I'ma make your pretty little kitty purr real good," he said while planting soft kisses on my neck.

His hand settled at the small of my back pulling me closer and for the first time I felt a gush between my legs. I closed my eyes and breathed in. All type of thoughts ran through my mind. What if I couldn't please him? Was he going to expect oral sex? Was he going to take my innocence then toss me to the curb?

The doors opened and he released me from his grip. Walking down the hall each step felt like my last. I began to say a little prayer because I knew that once I walked through that door I would never be the same.

CJ

When I stuck the plastic card in the door, my mind raced with flashes of how many positions I wanted to put shorty in. She was slim built and probably flexible as hell. I tried to anticipate how good she was going to feel. I don't give a fuck how much of a G a nigga claimed to be, excitement always took over a man's gangsta when he was this close to new, tight, virgin pussy.

I hit the lights and watched her little heart shaped booty bounce as she walked to a chair by the window and took a seat. I could tell that she was nervous. I needed to help her relax a little or it was going to be a struggle getting those tight walls to receive me.

I knew I was here for one purpose only and that was to be the first to conquer. I looked at the two queen sized beds and picked the first one I was going to damage. I walked over to it and pulled the sheets back.

"C'mere, ma," I called out to her and she slowly moved to where I stood. "You missed me didn't you?" I asked.

"Um hmm," she shyly replied.

"Well, show me how much." I pulled her into my arms and stuck my tongue deep into her mouth, taking her breath.

When I allowed her to come up for air, she was panting and blinking her pretty eyes. She was trying hard to maintain her composure and go with the flow. But everything I did damn near gave her a heart attack. I helped her take off her coat, then I took off mine and placed it on a hanger on the coat rack next to Kenisha's.

The room was nice and warm already, but I was about to make it hot. I pulled her back in my arms and softly kissed her neck. Little moans escaped from her mouth and she hugged me tighter while I rubbed her ass.

"Come in the bathroom with me so I can get you wet," I said, looking down into her eyes.

Kenisha swallowed hard as she tried to form a sentence. "Okay," she said a little over a whisper.

I took her hand and led her to her first level of pleasure. I stripped down while she looked on. When I rocked up and took my dick in my hand, she dropped her head and covered her face with her hands.

"We way past being shy, ma." I walked over to her and slid my hands up her shirt, pulling it over her head.

She jumped with my every touch, I allowed my hands to roam over her soft breast, and the light moans that pushed past her lips had a nigga ready to put in some work. But I knew I had to walk light or her scary ass was going to snatch away my key to heaven.

I moved my hands slowly to the top of her jeans and opened them wide. She closed her eyes tight as my hands roamed freely.

213

"CJ," she moaned when my fingers began to cause a flood between her thighs.

"Let this shit happen," I said sliding her jeans down until they hit her ankles. When she stepped out of them it was on. I turned on the shower and pulled her up in there with me. Her little nipples stiffened and my dick got harder. I released them from her bra and covered them with my mouth.

"Oh, my God," she whispered as my hands and mouth took over her thoughts.

I popped the side of her panties and let them hit the shower floor. When she gasped for air I stuck my tongue to the back of her throat. Soaking wet and squeezing me tight she began submitting to my every command.

KENISHA

I knew I was standing but my body felt like it was floating on a cloud. It was like his hands could read my mind. I turned my head to the side and saw my reflection staring back at me in the mirror and disbelief set in. The image of me standing in a man's arms totally naked caused my body to shiver.

"Sit right here," ordered CJ, lifting me onto the bathroom counter.

Opening my legs, he stepped between them with intentions that were clear. Fear took over. "CJ wait." I put my hand on his chest.

"Relax, let me make you cum," he said as he lowered his face to my waist.

My eyes grew when his tongue made its first contact with my body. He gripped me tightly and seemed to savor every lick. I tensed up at first and then it began to feel good. I grabbed the back of his head and threw mine back. The more he sucked the louder I got. Jada had tried to tell me how good oral sex felt but never in my wildest dreams could I imagine it would feel this good.

214

"I can feel it," I muttered as my legs began to twitch.

He sucked harder and harder trying to make me erupt.

"Wait, CJ I need to pee," I said pushing at his head.

"That ain't pee, ma, let that shit happen," he mumbled then went back to work.

Tears formed in my eyes as I experienced what words couldn't describe. My thighs shook and my waists made movements I never felt before.

Unable to catch my breath I looked down at CJ as he rubbed his lips in my wetness and placed gentle kisses up and down my inner thigh.

When he stood up I wrapped my arms around his neck and my legs around his back. "That felt good," I murmured.

"I can make you feel even better," he said, lifting me in the air and carrying me to the bed. When my hot body touched cools sheets I let out a soft whine.

CJ's muscular hard body was all over me. I could feel the tip of his manhood ready to drill. I knew there was no turning back. "CJ I'm scared, be gentle."

"Relax, shorty."

Just as the words left his lips I could feel him entering me. I squeezed my thighs to his waist as sharp pain accompanied his penetration. "CJ!" I called out, squeezing him tighter.

"Just relax," he repeated as a hiss left his lips.

When he was half way inside of me, his strokse quickened and my moans filled the room. Grunting, pumping and sweating he began breaking through the last of my innocence. I closed my eyes tightly and held on to him for dear life.

"How it feel, Kenisha?"

I moaned out something unintelligible and bit down on my bottom lip to help endure the pain and pleasure. It hurt so bad yet felt so good. I wrapped my legs around his waist and moved my hips like I had practiced at home with a pillow in preparation of tonight.

"Yeah, ma, give it up. Get your grown woman on. Gimme what's mines. Make me give you my seeds."

The things he was saying made me hotter. I wanted to say something back but the words wouldn't come out. Not verbally, so I spoke them with the sway of my hips.

"Aww shit, lil' mama," he groaned loudly and sped up his pace. Then I felt him come inside of me.

I laid there thinking did this make me a woman? Would CJ be a different man once he got up? The answers were probably no but either way, the reality that tonight I was *his* took away some of my pain.

An hour later, we made love again. He laid me on my stomach and entered me from the back. I was sore but I wanted to give it to him like a grown woman. *Good girls are no fun.*

With every stroke, I lost a valuable piece of myself, but in all honesty there was no one else I would have wanted to give it to.

THIRTY-SIX

RAHEEM

I had been back from DaQuan's funeral three weeks now. While CJ and them concentrated on moving the work that had recently dropped, I had taken full control over finding Nard and making sure that no one else in the crew died from his gun while we searched for him.

Me and Legend occasionally rode by Jamaican Black's barbershop in hopes of lucking up on Nard but so far we had come up empty.

"Let's run up in there and make that spaghetti head tell us where he's at," suggested Legend who was just as anxious as I was to avenge DaQuan.

"Let's chill, JB isn't the enemy," I cautioned.

Besides being strapped with a banger, Legend rode around with a big ass machete inside a tennis bag, hungry to spill some blood.

I convinced him to have patience, we would catch our prey eventually. In the meantime, we drove back over to where LaKeesha was supposed to be staying but again she wasn't there. Dejected but not defeated we went back to the new apartment.

I sat my strap and my gangsta on the shelf and got my mind off of murder and put it on my long planned date with Malika tonight. Due to her busy work schedule and the demands of my vengeance, we hadn't been able to hook up yet. We had remained in touch through text messages and nightly conversations on the phone but we both were dying to see each other again.

It was refreshing having someone to talk to on my level. Her intelligence and brutal honestly turned me on every time she parted her lips. The sistah was different from any woman I had ever dated and I was looking forward to seeing her like a kid anticipates the morning of Christmas day.

Legend was slick skilled as a barber so I asked him to give me fresh cut. I sat in the kitchen waiting while he went in his bedroom to get his clippers. He returned with his kit in one hand and the other hand behind his back.

I braced myself for some crazy shit.

"You ready?" he asked, wearing a smirk. Slowly his hand came from behind his back and he was holding that goddamn machete. I almost fell out the chair laughing.

"Son, you throwed," I said, shaking my head. Legend sat the blade on the counter and went to work on my head with the clippers. He was clowning around cracking jokes the entire time. "You're playing but you better not mess my shit up," I chuckled.

"Chill, nigga, I got this."

"I'm saying, yo." I frowned.

"You saying what? Don't you know not to talk shit to the barber while sitting in his chair? Fuck around and I'll have your hairline so far back it'll look like it's on somebody else's head."

I cracked up. It was the first time we had shared a laugh since the homie, DaQuan, got killed.

Once my cut was right, I took a shower, lotioned my body, and began to get dressed. I chose a Versace 'fit that I had picked up from Newport Mall the other day: black pants and turtleneck sweater, black Versace tie-ups. I splashed on some *Armani Sport*, slid into a grey leather Versace jacket and put on my black and grey leather hat. I was ready to go chill with the Queen.

Legend didn't wanna let me roll alone but I demanded that he fall back. He conceded but with reluctance.

"Why you mugging?" I asked as I grabbed my tool off of the shelf and reached for the door knob.

"I'm good" he mumbled.

"Son, I'ma be, a'ight," I assured him.

"That's what's up. Anyway, you the one mugging. How you gon' frown with that leather jacket on? Nigga, you look like a vicious ass wallet," he shot.

I was still laughing as I pulled out of the complex watching to make sure I wasn't being followed. Once I was certain that the enemy wasn't behind me I turned on some music and let Marvin Gaye keep me company during my drive.

When I arrived at Malika's house, out in Montclair, my body filled up with nervous energy. There was something about her that made every experience with her seem like my first. I pulled out my phone and called her.

"Hello," she answered full of excitement which slightly eased my nerves.

"Hey, beautiful," I replied as a smile came across my face. "I'm outside. You ready?"

"Almost. Can you come in for a minute?"

As the words left her mouth, I had a moment of paralyzing silence as I processed her request. "Yeah, I can do that."

"Why you paused?" she giggled.

"Nah, I just thought you were coming out, but here I come."

"Well, come on," she giggled again, making me feel like a teenage boy who was just told *hurry up, my parents aren't home*. I hung up, turned off the engine, pulled my hat down over my ears and stepped out of the car.

I hesitated again before I moved on instinct. I took the Glock off my waist and slid it under the front seat.

I stepped on the porch and rang the bell and waited for her to answer. Within seconds I was treated to her sweet smile and sexy body. She opened the door wearing a pair of dark green high waist pants that hugged her sexy full figure body just right and a black fitted long sleeve blouse that rested at the top of her pants. Her feet were bare, very well-manicured and suckable.

"Come in," she invited.

I looked at her polished hardwood floor and didn't want to move. In the corner was a shoe rack so I assumed she didn't allow visitors to keep theirs on inside her house.

"It's all good, you can keep them on," she read my mind.

"You sure?"

"Get in here," she said, pulling me in the door and closing it behind me. "Come into my office." She took my hand and guided me down the hallway, apologizing. "I'm sorry I'm a little late, I was waiting on a fax from a client who is very anal about his account so I wanted to make sure I had it before I left."

"No problem," I said as my eyes took in the decor. There were pieces of black art and cultural artifacts on the walls and on little stands in the hallway that she led me down, but the art of Malika's full figure was the best art in the room.

When we entered her office, I fell in love immediately. She had built in wall to ceiling book cases all around the room.

"May I?" I asked as I walked over to a shelf with a binder I was very familiar with.

"Please make yourself at home," she said as she walked over to her printer and grabbed some papers and began to look them over.

While she placed a confirmation call to her client I pulled the book from its place. *Beckonings* by Gwendolyn Brooks. I had been looking for it for a long time.

"That is one of my favorites," Malika said as she came to my side.

"Yes, mine too. I haven't read this since I was in high school. Mrs. Brooks is why I fell in love with poetry."

"Don't play with me, Raheem." She sounded genuinely surprised by my claim.

220

"No really." I tried to convince her but she was giving me the side eye. I reached back into my memory and pulled out a Mrs. Brooks gem.

I've stayed in the front yard all my life.
I want a peek at the back
Where it's rough and untended and hungry weed grows.
A girl gets sick of a rose.

Her eyes grew big and a huge smile formed on her pretty face. "Awww."

"Yeah you was sleeping on a brotha," I kidded then I put the book back in its place.

"I have never met anyone like you."

"And you never will," I joked.

"Come on before your head is unable to fit through the door," she teased back.

We smiled at each other and she again took my hand. This time she led me to the front door.

I watched as she slipped into her nylon ankle socks and black high heel boots. As she reached for her short wool jacket from the coat rack I took it from her hands and assisted her with it.

"You are such a gentleman." She complimented as she tightened the belt.

"I'm sure you're deserving of it," I said as we locked eyes.

Again we shared an uneasy moment of silence. "I need to get my keys," Malika said a little over a whisper and pointed at a small table behind me.

I turned and grabbed her keys from a dark red ceramic bowl then turned back to hand them to her. When I was fully facing her she grabbed me by the back of the neck and pulled my lips to hers. Closing my eyes, I welcomed her tongue in my mouth. She tasted as sweet as she smelled. I inhaled the China musk that saturated her locs. Before I could get my hands to her waist, she pulled back looking me in the eyes.

"What was that for?" I asked, licking my lips savoring the trace of flavored lip gloss she left behind.

"Just getting it out of the way so later when you drop me off you won't be so uncomfortable," she smiled and turned to the door.

I had to respect her forwardness it was sexy and classy at the same time.

We hopped in my ride and headed to Kyo Ya, a Japanese restaurant in East Village. We drove and talked listening to a new CD by Jaheim. When we arrived I got out, opened her door, and escorted her inside. I wasn't big on Sushi but Malika had expressed an appreciation for it so I was accommodating her.

"Please come this way," a small Asian woman said as she led us to our table.

I looked over the menu but it was all foreign to me. When I looked up Malika was smiling at me. "I have no idea what any of this is. I can make out the fish but that's about it," I admitted.

"Don't worry I will order for you," she eased my worries.

"As long as it ain't pork I'm good."

"I don't eat meat so you know I got you."

The waitress came back to the table and Malika ordered Sweet Potato Tempura for an appetizer, Smoke Salmon Sushi, Black Cod with Miso and some Spring Rolls as the entree.

"What you drink?" asked the meek waitress.

Malika ordered a small bottle of Sake. I, a glass of water.

Conversation was light until it drifted to the subject of our past relationships. Malika told a story about a relationship that had left her self-conscious about her weight and doubting her worth.

"Black is beautiful in so many sizes, shapes and shades. And love sees imperfections as uniqueness," I commented sincerely.

"Oh wow." She was awed but I was only spitting the truth. Too many beautiful sistahs allowed men to make them feel bad because they didn't fit into a size 8 or smaller. Confidence in your own skin was sexy as hell to me and I was glad that Malika had persevered over her insecurity.

"Enough about my disaster. Tell me about your past relationships. I know it's going to be profound because you're a deep brother. I love your intelligence but I see a glint of bad boy in you. So sir, whose heart have you broken?" She delved.

By the time I finished talking she was wiping tears from her eyes. I hadn't intended on divulging so much but it had been on my heart for months and getting it off felt cathartic.

"That's very sad. Her voice was beautiful and her death was tragic. So many people were rooting for her," she said.

We talked awhile longer then I paid the bill and we drove to Nuyorican Poets Cafe in Greenwich Village.

Once inside we took a seat at a front table in the dim lounge as a poet walked on the platform and spit her piece. The waitress walked over, "Can I get you two anything to drink?"

"Lemon water for me," Malika readjusted the position of her chair.

"Make that two," I confirmed as the lady retreated to another part of the room. I refocused my attention on Malika.

She saw me staring and placed her hand in mine.

We soaked up the energies in the building listening to one person's plight to another person love stream in the harmonies of rhymes.

The DJ announced a brief intermission. I excused myself and went to the restroom. When I returned to my seat the emcee was saying, "Let's welcome a crowd favorite to the stage. Flame! Flame!" He pumped up the audience.

A sistah took the stage and walked confidently to the mic. Her short locs accentuated the earth tone colors of her ankle length dress and the wooden bangles around her wrists. She looked radiant in a wise manner, as if she had been through a lot and had overcome it. She greeted the crowd before delivering a serious piece.

Nigga!
You think you can reinvent the meaning in that name?
Take the negative connotations off and somehow erase the shame?
You are what you respond to.
And a nigga ain't much to amount to.
Follow this.
Putting a dress on a boy won't change his gender.
Just like putting an (A) on nigger won't make that shit tender.
Ask yourself, are you working our oppressor's agenda?
Still with me?
No real man will allow you to call him a bitch.
No hood dude will condone you labeling him a snitch.
So why do you, the black gods of this realm, continue to denounce your throne?
Digesting their weak label of who you're not and calling it your own.
When I trace my ancestral tree.
Beyond slavery.
To ancient Egyptology.
There were no niggaz building pyramids, only recorded scientists and deities.
Dig this and let me make this plain.
There is much to the meaning of a name.
Remove the slave vernacular and those mental chains.
And never call a black man a nigga a-gain.
He's a god!

She threw her fist in the air, "I am Flame, watch me burn!" She announced as she exited. The crowd cheered, bobbing their heads with their fists held high to pay homage to her piece.

As I watched her walk off stage, I had the brightest smile on my face. I couldn't believe what my eyes had just seen. Flame was *Porcelin*, the girl that had been in drug rehab with Sparkle.

I leaned over and whispered to Malika.

"How ironic is that?" she remarked.

I had included Porcelin in the story I told her at the restaurant. "I'm going over and speak to her. Do you mind?"

"Not at all."

I went over to tell Porcelin how proud I was of her. She was happy to see me. We hugged and she introduced me to her husband who was a psychologist.

While I sat with them and talked the emcee announced that it was open Mic time. Several poets came up and shared their rhythmic energy. A young brother took the stage and rhymed poignantly about poison in the black community. His verses placed me in a melancholy mood as I thought about my own contribution to the atrocity that he spat about.

I was staring off into my conscience and battling with my justifications.

"Introduce yourself sis," I vaguely heard.

"Good evening, black people. My name is Malika and I will randomly speak from the heart."

My eyes shot up.

The crowd chorused different welcomes to her before silence befell the room. Malika closed her eyes as if to draw direction from deep down in her soul and then her passion flowed.

Wounded.
Hey world, I wear a mask.
Lashes on my back, torn spirit, broken soul.

I've been walking in a world that does not see me, struggling in darkness, calling for light.
Oh Lord!
Help me understand, why am I in a land that is strange to me?
I've been loved by men that did not see me.
Or feel me.
Or love me.
I'm wounded.
Sometimes all a woman has is what is in her chest.
That feeling that lies between her breasts.
And sometimes she'll let him put his face there,
  but then she fears that he will never hear the heart that beats there.
Hello?
Are you there?
Do you hear me? And Oh baby when I touch you do you feel me?
He wants to be there but he lets his fear tear him away from me,
  and then there's that lonely view,
  from empty places, looking in empty faces,
  and all along instead of feeling the very heart of me,
  he feels inside, then he's out of me,
Do you see my face?
I ask the question but the silence in your stare answers for you.
Because you're wounded.
It's been cold there in your shadow. Each breath I take releases a piece of you.
I feel for you but I can't reach you.
I'd heal for you but life won't allow me to be a resting post for you.
  You know, sometimes all a women has is her best,
  that which lies between her breast

beyond her chest it's the soul of you,
I feel for you but I can't reach you.
I'd take your heart in mine, but I'm wounded.
I'd kiss your mouth with mine, but I'm wounded.
Does the whispers from your lips, make my mind sane?
Or does it force me to refrain
from your love because I'm wounded.
And all the while, while wanting to take your hand and help
you stand,
I can't
Because the only soul I have left is wounded.

The crowd saluted. I stood up and met her back at our table. She radiated as she left a piece of her soul behind her. She looked at me bashfully as I studied her.

"Why are you staring?" she asked.

"You make me stare, Queen," I said proudly. I pulled her in my arms and held her.

When we broke our embrace, I took her over and introduced her to Porcelin and her husband. On the way back to our table I said, "I'm going up."

"Do it." She encouraged me with a kiss.

I stood on stage with the mic in my hand. I didn't know what I would spit because so many different emotions battled to be heard. I looked out into the room and saw a kaleidoscope of faces. Black, brown, and white. Hood, 'burbs, corporate, hustlaz.

Then I saw one. I wanted to tell her that I wasn't who she thought I was. I was educated and I was a conscious brother but I was living savage. I killed.

It was okay for her to look at me from afar but if she got too close the blood might stain her as it dripped from my hands. Or maybe it would be both of our blood as it dripped from the hands of my enemies. I couldn't let that happen.

You might think you know me but you don't
And really you don't want to
I'm a complex man that knows how to love but I wont
Although I really want to
But see, I'm wrapped in internal misery
Battling not to concede to fatal epiphanies
I don't ask for your tears or sympathy
I shed tears for those that die at my hands in infamy
I pray that the Most High is forgiving of me
I know right from wrong but my loyalty is my worst enemy
To stop me now it's going to take ten of me
I'm telling you now you don't want to be in my vicinity
Pay close attention to the signs that God gives to thee
I'm not on my Deen
There is more unseen than what is seen
I might greet you in peace
But I haven't learned to walk how I speak
I'm telling you, I'm still a slave to these streets

When I got back to the table Malika was silent. Porcelin rushed over with tears running down her face. She hugged me and said, "I know that's not you Raheem."

I didn't respond.

She looked at Malika and repeated with emphasis, "That is *not* him."

"Yes it is," I said as I held Malika's coat out for her to slip on.

THIRTY-SEVEN

KENISHA

He hadn't called or texted one time since I gave him my innocence. I was just another notch on his belt, a conquest. Some days I hated him, other times I stared at my phone trying to will him to call me. But his cold-hearted indifference was stronger than every single prayer I prayed.

My eyes were swollen from crying day after day and my heart felt like he had snatched it right out of my chest and stomped on it continually. How could he do this to me?

I tried to convince myself that he was just busy in the streets and would come through any day now and apologize for making me worry myself sick. I was an emotional mess. I hadn't been eating much of anything; I hadn't slept straight through at night in more than a week. This dilemma had made me withdrawn from friends, even affected my attendance with school.

Had I really been that awful in bed? I revisited that night to recall the look of what appeared to be satisfaction.

Why had I let Jada talk me into doing it in the first place? Why had I wanted him so bad? I had been perfectly happy with my own little insignificant life before he came along and casted a spell on me with his smooth talk and thuggish exterior.

"Let me make you a woman." he said.

And like a fool I had allowed him to do it! If I knew that this ill feeling came with it, I would have remained a *girl* forever.

I could still feel his persuasive hands cupping my breasts. His warm tongue flicking across my nipples while he moved in and out of me. He had been tender yet demanding, like he knew exactly what would make me yearn for him after he stole both my treasure and my heart.

I felt like ending my life. All four of my mother's prescriptions stared back at me, begging me to swallow them until I entered an eternal sleep.

And when he'd hear about my death he would feel what I've been feeling. The guilt would eat at his uncaring heart and he would suffer for having drove me to do it.

That'll show him!

I reached over and grabbed the first bottle off of the dresser and studied the label. *Will I attempt to save myself once I begin or will I be too lethargic and just succumb to the will of death? What will Mommy do when she comes home from work and finds me? What about Daddy, how will he react? Will he blame Mom?*

I didn't want that to happen because there was only one person that was responsible for this. I had already written and rewritten a letter explaining why I couldn't go on. But would CJ ever see the letter? Would that fucker even care?

Tears burned my eyes and cascaded down in streams. I was tired of balling and he wasn't going to call if I cried until my eyeballs fell out. He didn't care.

But maybe he did? I second guessed.

I sat the pills down and picked up my phone instead to try to reach him one last time before I'd go to the point of no return.

I took a deep breath and dialed his number. As the phone rang I imagined the conversation we would have.

"What up, shorty?"

"What do you mean 'what's up', CJ? Why haven't I heard from you? I've been calling and calling, going crazy over here."

"My bad lil' mama, I was locked up. Did you miss a nigga or what?"

"I don't know. I'm mad at you. You could've found a way to let me know. I thought you had played me."

"Nah never that. I love you baby girl. I just didn't wanna involve you in my troubles but er'thing good now. I miss the fuck

out of you Kenisha. I'm on my way to get you. Pack all your shit, you ain't never going back."

I was grinning from ear to ear until I realized that I had been sent to voicemail yet again. That accounted to 532 unanswered calls in the past four weeks, two days, nine hours and thirteen minutes.

He was never going to answer.

I slung my phone against the wall as a loud sob roared outwardly from within. I was done with him, with life. I threw five tablets in my hand to gulp down in a hurry. *I can do this!* I coached.

I ignored my sobbing, took a deep breath, and summoned up the courage to do it from deep within my gut. As I sucked in the air, I thought about the life growing inside of me that depended on me to breathe.

I put my hand on my belly although I could not feel anything. But the doctor had confirmed it just yesterday. I could take my own life but could I do that to our baby? I asked myself as more tears fell. Then the pills obeyed gravity and fell atop my bed right before I did.

Ca$h

THIRTY-EIGHT

CJ

Shorty was blowing me the fuck up. I should have never ran up in her because deep down I knew I didn't want her. She didn't have enough street smarts to be on my team nor enough ass or titties to warrant a second time around. I didn't have time to teach her how to fuck, suck and duck or the patience to wait on her ass to sprout out.

With Shy none of that was an issue, she came in the door with plenty to get the job done. The only reason I had to look at her sideways was because Rah had raised a good question the other day.

We were sitting around tryna figure out how Nard and 'em found out about them staying at the Executive House. I recalled Eternity, Tamika's hair stylist, riding up on us over there when DaQuan and Legend first came up top with Rah. "That bitch probably ran and told that," I had been quick to convict.

Legend jumped up with his machete in hand, ready to go serve her justice. But Rah deaded that. "We're not killing the girl on a whim," he rejected.

Of course I could've gave the order anyway or went and crushed her myself but we never went against each other. Besides, Rah's next statement made me consider some shit that I didn't like thinking about.

"Shy knew we rested there. She was in the car with you a couple of times you came through," he helped me recall.

My face twisted up immediately.

"Think about it, fam. I don't know whether she would cross like that; I mean, I don't see what she would gain but y'all was going through some things back then. Shy is an emotional female and on impulse she might do anything."

"Shorty wouldn't violate like that," I defended her.

Rah must've felt that he had offended me because he softened his response. "Maybe not," he allowed, "but we don't know for sure. I'm not questioning your judgment fam, but from the beginning you moved way too fast with her. I know why and I overstand. But DaQuan lost his life behind somebody's treachery, you don't want to be sleeping with the enemy."

As hot as I was over what he was saying, I had to admit that he was spitting real shit. I knew without a doubt that Rah was only trying to watch my back.

"I'ma get some answers, you can bet that," I assured him.

When I walked in the door that night Shy wasn't home. I hit her on her cell phone. "Fuck you at?" I asked as soon as she answered.

"Nowhere, baby. I'm just up the street at the drug store."

"Get here. Now!"

"Okay. Damn. Why do you have an attitude?" she asked with an attitude to match mine.

"Shorty, don't ask me shit just get your ass home," I ordered, tossing my phone on the couch and taking a seat.

As soon as she came through the door I grabbed her by the throat and pushed her up against the wall. "Who did you run your mouth to?"

"Get off of me, CJ," she gagged as her bag and keys hit the floor.

"Bitch, you better start talking." I held her firm, causing her to rise up on her tippy toes.

She snatched away from me screaming. "What are you talking about?" Her eyes were watery with confusion.

When I told her, she went off. "Do you really think I would do some grimy shit like that? Is that what you think of me?" She moved up in my face.

"Would you?" I asked tryna ignore the flood of hot tears that poured from her eyes.

"If you have to ask that, maybe I shouldn't be here?" She turned and stalked upstairs and began packing her things hastily. "I don't need this shit. You're not gonna be putting your hands on me. Fuck all this shit," she ranted as she grabbed and tossed things from one side of the closet to the other.

I walked up from behind and wrapped my arms around her. Something in me needed to believe that she wouldn't betray me. Shy jumped like she thought I was about to stick a knife in her back. "No, stop." She tried to wiggle away from me.

"Come here, shorty," I soothed. "The streets got me not knowing who to trust," I said.

"CJ, I would never do anything against you," she tearfully vowed. "Nothing."

I turned her around to face me and looked deep in her eyes. If she was lying she was the best that ever did it. "The only thing that is unforgivable is betrayal," I made clear.

"I love you. I would never betray you," she said a little over a whisper.

I held her tighter then led her to bed and stroked away her pain.

Ca$h

THIRTY-NINE

CJ

TWO weeks after I had confronted Shy with that crazy suspicion, I was laying back on the bed smoking that loud and watching her move around the room smiling and getting dressed. She had just sucked my dick for the third time tryna show appreciation for all the gifts I had been showering her with over the last forty-eight hours. The icing on the cake was going to be tonight's party at the 466 Club.

I knew that I would be taking a huge risk but fuck it, I wasn't letting that nigga force me into a hole. If I was gonna die it was going to be on my terms, doing all the shit I loved and was hood famous for. Fuck Nard he could suck my dick too.

"You gonna wear all that ice ma? You gonna walk up in there looking like that nigga on that movie *I'm Gonna Get You Sucka*," I joked.

"Don't tease me, baby," she cooed. "I love all of it," she said coming over to the bed and kissing my lips.

"It's all good, I want you to enjoy your evening."

"I will. Thank you so much," she said with a hungry eye and straddled my lap. Her pussy was so wet from excitement I could feel it through the silk of her thong. I rocked up in anticipation of how good she was getting ready to handle her business.

"You keep climbing up on this dick, you gonna fuck around and miss ya party."

"Let me make you come one more time before we leave," she whined, pulling her thong to the side and sliding down on my stiffness. I put my hands behind my head like the king that I am and let Shy thank me again.

SHY

I was beyond excited. I rode in CJ's Maybach damn near wiggling out my seat. When we pulled up to the club he had it set up like the academy awards. There was a back drop with my name written all over it, red carpet and a camera crew flicking pictures. CJ had his security team on point when we pulled up they moved to the car shielding us as we moved to the velvet ropes. I was able to stop and pose for a few pictures before we were whisked inside like celebrities.

When we got inside, the music went down and a spotlight put us on full display as all eyes moved to where we stood. I was in a fire red cat suit with a low back and a pair of red thigh high Louis Vuitton stiletto boots to match. I had on platinum and diamond everything: necklace, earrings bracelets, rings. A bitch was hot and cold at the same time with all my ice on display.

"Alright, everybody, y'all know whose night it is, let's make some noise for the King and Queen of the hour." The room erupted in cheers, whistling and clapping. "Now tell the Queen of the city happy birthday Stevie Wonder style." The beat came on and the crowd sung in unison. I was beyond gassed up.

CJ took me in his arms, hugged me tightly, and kissed me deeply. The room was on blast, the bottles started popping and the music went on high volume.

My bitch bad looking like a bag of money
That bitch bad looking like a bag of money
I go and get it and I let her count it for me
I fuck her good and she always ride it for me

We were escorted to our VIP section. CJ's mans were already there with their girls. Eric's young butt was with a grown ass woman and she was all over him. Premo and Snoop had dimes on their arms, and Legend had a line of thirsty bitches trying to push their titties in his face. Rah's anti-social ass was dolo.

238

I sat and drank, danced and laughed with the other girlfriends of the crew while our men talked shit and puffed that sour. Every hour of the night CJ had a different gift brought to our section. I had expensive purses, shoes, outfits, money and more ice. You couldn't tell me shit.

A bitch was living.

RAHEEM

I stood by watching Shy enjoy what she didn't deserve. We were at war and the other side was not playing. I didn't give a fuck how much my nigga was feeling her I just didn't trust that female. One slip-up would put the whole team in grave danger.

I had the team on high alert. Other souljahs moved around the room incognito and the souljahs outside rotated shifts so everyone remained alert.

My eyes scanned the room for the faces of any enemy that may have escaped detection. I made myself the last line of defense while CJ and 'em balled. With all the murders and hustling that had consumed us over the past six months it was good to see the family getting a chance to enjoy themselves.

Watching them with their girls made me think of Malika, and it further confirmed to me that I had made the right decision to let that sistah go on with her life before she got caught up in mine. I couldn't envision bringing her to something like this.

CJ came over to me talking loud on slurred words. "You ain't gonna have no fun nigga?"

"You have fun for me," I responded with a half-smile. I didn't want to make him too uncomfortable with my disappointment because win, lose or draw he was my man.

"You gotta live a little Rah you gonna fuck around and be an old man before your time," he said, taking a bottle by the neck and turning it up.

Before I could answer he turned back to where Shy was and pulled her to him and poured Champagne into her mouth. She opened wide and guzzled as he continued to pour. The liquid ran out the side of her mouth, down her neck and chest. CJ ran his tongue over her breast and the team cheered and laughed. *She's exactly what my dude loves but not what he needs.*

I had to quickly block that thought from my mind because only God can judge. My mind briefly went back to Malika, she was a quiet to my storm. I wanted to see her so bad but with all the death that was surrounding me I could not risk sucking her into the hell that was awaiting my soul. It had been hard ignoring her calls but I needed to put as much distance between her and me in order to keep her away from Nard's radar; that young boy had proven he would stop at nothing to reach out and kill what we loved and I was not going to lose another woman to the game.

I was getting ready to rotate the outside crew when I looked up and saw Kenisha and Jada coming in the front door. "What the fuck," I said as I looked at them scanning the crowd.

Kenisha was dressed in skin tight jeans that were caressing her frame much tighter than the clothes she usually wore. She had on a see through top which showed her red lace bra and perky breast. She looked like a rare diamond dressed in hood rat clothing. Niggaz took notice as she strutted to the bar in a pair of high heel shoes causing her ass to rock with every step.

I quickly moved to where Jada and Kenisha stood. When I got up closer it appeared that lil' mama had already had a drink or two. I knew what was going on between her and CJ, and I didn't want her to confront him tonight and play herself.

I spoke and gave them both a hug.

"Hey, Rah, where is your boy and his bitch?" asked Kenisha, sounding like she had switched tongues with Shy.

I looked at Jada and gritted, "Why did you bring her here?"

240

"We're trying to get our party on," she tsked, taking a glass to her mouth.

"You know what the fuck I mean."

Jada looked at me with her head cocked to the side and mouthed off, "If you want to talk to me like that, you're going to have to claim me as your woman otherwise you can miss me with that shit."

I fought back the urge to choke her. Turning to Kenisha I said gently, "You shouldn't be here, this ain't your crowd."

"I'm grown and I want to have a good time," she said, tossing the drink back then blinking hard as the hot liquor went down her throat.

"Where's ya boy? I got some shit I need to say to him," she said with a glare of anger in her eyes.

"Why don't you let Jada take you home? You don't need to talk to him while you're like this."

"Like what? I'm good," she said, looking past me to the VIP section. "I just want to holla at his heartless ass real quick,"

I looked around the room trying to keep a cautious eye while at the same time convince lil' mama she needed to leave. Before I could catch her she had wormed from in front of me and moved to VIP at high speed.

SHY

I looked up from my drink and saw CJ's little so-called virgin coming our way looking like she had recently gotten ahold of some dick. She was walking with a purpose and Raheem was trying to catch up with her. I tensed up immediately. I threw my hands on my hips and got ready to cuss this bitch out if she was coming to confront my man.

She walked right over to the ropes and began talking to security. When he denied her access she got loud and rowdy. CJ looked past me and then moved me off of his lap. "Watch out for a minute," he said.

"No, let me handle that bitch." I stood ready to go ham.

"Chill the fuck out, I got it."

"Yeah, you better have it." I looked at him with fire in my eyes.

He looked down at me with heat coming up off of his frame. "Don't get fucked up on your birthday. Act like you're number one, don't let some random pussy fuck up your position."

I threw my hands on my hips then turned my back and picked up a drink. *I thought you said she was a virgin.*

I stood sipping as he walked to where she was in an attempt to calm the situation down. Raheem walked up behind her and was trying to do the same. Somebody had better talk to the little girl or I was going to put a grown woman beating on that ass.

CJ

"Why the fuck you here?" I asked with venom dripping from my vocals.

"Why you not answering my calls?" Kenisha countered with water beginning to form in her eyes.

"Look, you know what it is."

"No I don't, why don't you tell me?"

"I'm chilling with my girl and my fam, I'll call you when I have time. Now take your ass home."

"You are a ruthless muthafucka." She tossed her drink in my face.

I reached back to slap fire out of her face. Rah put a hand on my arm and leaned in close to me. "Nah fam, don't do that shit. You know she's in her feelings, give shorty a pass," he shielded.

One of my souljahs rushed over with some napkins. I wiped the liquor out of my face and looked up just in time to see Shy flying toward us. Rah didn't have a chance to stop her open hand from slamming into Kenisha's face.

Shorty stumbled back and Shy was on her like ugly on Precious. She slung lil' mama around and landed a couple more punches. I stepped in and pulled her off of shorty before she did some real damage.

I looked up and saw Jada at the door being restrained by security. Rah had ahold of Kenisha now, she was kicking and cussing.

Shy snatched a bottle of champagne off of a nearby table. "Let that bitch go I'll crack her muthafuckin' head open," she hissed.

"Girl, sit your feisty ass down and enjoy your birthday party," I chuckled.

"You better teach your hos how to play their positions or they're going to get fucked up," huffed Shy, looking sexy as hell with that scowl on her face.

I pulled her to me and kissed her. "Happy birthday baby. Hood style!" I proclaimed. "It's all about you ma."

Kenisha was still fighting Rah. At the door she broke away from him and headed back our way. I was gonna have to tap that head myself this time. "Chill," I said tersely when I felt Shy tense up. I got this lil' bitch."

But Kenisha hadn't come back to rumble. She stopped a foot away from us and glared at me like she wanted to shoot me between the eyes. "I fucking hate you," she spat as Raheem tried to pull her away. "I hope your black ass die in the streets." She was breathing fire.

I shot her a smile and shooed her away.

Ca$h

FORTY

RAHEEM

As I pulled Kenisha away from VIP, she was cursing and yelling at CJ still. I was hurting for her; she was a good girl who had just gotten caught up with the proverbial bad boy. She had tears streaming and sweat running down her face.

I tried to get Kenisha and Jada to leave but neither one of them would listen to my advice. Finally I was able to prevail upon Jada to at least take her to the restroom to get herself together.

When they returned to where I waited at the bar Kenisha looked to be better. I returned back to VIP but kept a watchful eye on Kenisha.

I watched her throwback drink after drink while she stared bullets over CJ's way. Some thirsty looking dude pushed up on her, then I saw them go to the dance floor. Lil' Mama started dancing like she was on the stage at a strip club. Ol' dude was behind her grinding on her ass and reaching around, feeling her breasts. Jada was dancing beside her. Her head was thrown back and she was laughing.

"I'll be right back, yo," I told Legend. He hopped up and moved step by step with me.

I went over to where Jada was in full ho mode all up on some nigga'z dick. I walked right up on the dance floor and stepped in between her and son.

"Yo, you need to take lil' mama home," I shouted over the loud music.

"She grown. She can get home," Jada shot back and turned back to her dance partner.

"I'm not asking you I'm telling you," I said, trying to keep my composure.

"Telling me?" She turned in full hood rat mode. "I don't have to listen to you. These niggaz may have to do what you say but I am my own bitch. And like I said she grown, she can find her way home. I'm trying to get some dick in my life since you're not coming off of none."

I looked at her and for the first time in my life I almost put my hands on a woman. I could see she was on a *rat come up* mission and was not going to submit. I had to make a decision. I didn't want to leave my crew without the only sober eye but I damn sure was not going to put this little girl in a cab drunk and filled with hateful emotion.

I quickly gave my orders to Legend and led lil' mama outside.

Kenisha didn't want to go to home. She asked me to take her to her father's house. Knowing who her Pops was, I didn't think it was a good idea but she said it would be worse if she went to her mother's.

With a slur to her words, she managed to give me her father's address. I put it in my GPS and looked at her with tight lips. Then my expression softened. I had wanted to scold her for acting out of her character but she was already hurting. Besides she was too intoxicated to take my words to heart.

As we got ready to drive off, Legend came up to my door. I let the window down and asked him what was up.

"Hit the locks, bruh bruh, I'm not letting you roll alone," he demanded.

"I'm good, son. I'ma drop lil' mama off and come back. Go on back inside and enjoy yourself. You've been going hard for months, go cool your heels," I insisted but Legend wouldn't go.

We would've sat there debating all night so I just put the whip in gear and pulled off. I hadn't driven a mile when I had to pull over and help Kenisha out of the car so that she wouldn't throw up all over the seats.

"Shorty, this isn't a good look, you can't let a man get you all twisted like this," I told her as I helped her back inside the car and strapped on her seat belt.

"I can't help it," she cried.

"Yes, you can."

"No, I can't," she slurred. It's more than you think." She broke out in sobs.

I didn't know what she was trying to say but my heart ached for her. "We'll talk another day. Lay your head against the window and close your eyes. I'll wake you up when we get there. Man, your father isn't going to like this. I just hope he don't think I had anything to do with it."

By the time we reached Kenisha's father's house, she was passed out. I tried to shake her awake but she was gone. Spittles of vomit had dried around the corners of her mouth.

I looked at her and took a deep breath. I damn sure wasn't looking forward to knocking on Minster David X's door at one o'clock in the morning with his daughter slung over my shoulder. "This is some shit," I said out loud.

I took my strap off my waist and slid it under my seat because I didn't want to go in the Minister's house packing heat. I got out of the car, walked around to the passenger side, and lifted shorty out.

There was no telling what flashed through the man's mind when he opened the door and saw me half-carrying, half holding Kenisha up. But I know what flashed in his eyes.

I quickly set his mind at ease.

"As-Sailum Alaikum," I greeted.

He returned the salutation though hesitantly.

"She's okay and nobody has done anything to her. She has been drinking though and she got into a little scuffle at a nightclub that with all due respect she had no business at."

"I would think not," he replied strongly, sounding like a daddy instead of a minister.

He took Kenisha out of my arms and carried her inside, inviting me in with her.

"You can have a seat on the sofa," he politely offered.

While he helped Kenisha back to a bedroom I looked around the living room. The Muslim flag, the star and crescent, donned the wall along with a picture of Master Fard Muhammad and The Honorable Elijah Muhammad. There was a Holy Qur'an sitting high on a wooden stand as the centerpiece on a mahogany polished shelf decorated with framed pictures of sisters and brothers in full uniform.

Minister David X returned.

I stood and greeted him properly. When I told him my name he studied my face hard. "Raheem where are you from, young brother?" he asked, continuing to stare at me.

"I'm from The Bricks. If I look familiar it's probably because I attended service at Temple 7 a couple of months ago. I set up front while you were teaching class."

He smiled as if he recognized me now. Then he excused himself. "I think I heard Kenisha in there moving around. Please stay for a moment longer brother. I want to properly thank you for seeing that Kenisha got home safely. I keep telling her that Jada is a bad influence." He shook a stern finger.

I couldn't disagree with that.

When Minister X returned this time he indeed thanked me, and then we sat and discussed Islam for almost an hour.

By the time I stood up to leave I was more determined than ever to get back on my Deen.

FORTY-ONE

NARD

For the past month or so things had cooled down because those alphabet boys were rumored to be all over The Bricks. Nobody wanted to play themselves into a long sentence in the feds so the body count leveled off for the time being, but I still wanted CJ's ass worse than a dope fiend wants that first hit in the morning.

Papaya hadn't been able to lure CJ's new bitch, Shy, anywhere or trick her into telling where they rested at. I give the ho credit, she had dummied all the way up. Not even the threat of Papaya exposing her betrayal and her past life as a call girl to CJ could get Shy to meet with her. Had she slipped I would have followed her back home, snatched her up, and laid for CJ to return. Now she had changed her number so that was out the window.

I still kept Papaya on standby as convenient head but that's as close I would allow her to get. The last thing I wanted to do was let another snake bitch penetrate the wall I had put up after the foul shit the *original* serpent had done.

Just thinking about it caused my lips to quiver with anger. I wanted to go dig Tamika up and shoot her a few more times! Really the ho hadn't deserved no funeral or no grave. She hadn't given my seed either one. She had let that nigga talk her into having my child scraped and suctioned out of her ratchet ass womb, and probably thrown in a trash can.

She had killed my seed to be with CJ. Well, before it was all said and done I was gonna R.I.P that nigga so that they could be reunited.

I dreamed about the most viscous way to murk him. I had it all planned out in my head, I just had to have patience. In the meantime I kept my mind on my money and tried to come up with ways to expand my territories.

We was sitting over Man Dog's discussing whether or not we should fuck with Lil' City. It was a lot of money coming up out of that spot but it was Blood's turf and that presented a whole set of problems by itself, Man Dog pointed out.

"I don't give a fuck about no color but green. And I don't need their little turf, all of the city is gonna belong to us before it's over with. Right now we'll just supply them. If they come with some cruddy shit we'll turn their red bandanas crimson," I said.

"Fuck them niggaz," added Zakee. He lit up a blunt and put it to his lips.

I gave him a hard look and he put that shit out.

"Our spots are booming and the connect is real pleased with how we're putting it down. I told y'all we was gonna do this shit," I boasted.

"You're the reason we're feasting on these muhfuckaz," added Big Nasty.

I nodded my head, letting him know that I appreciated the acknowledgement.

I looked at Quent who was playing a game on the X box. He must've felt my gaze on his neck because he looked up and smirked.

"You in this discussion yo?" I hardened my stare.

I was about to get in Quent's ass when my cell phone lit up. It was almost two o'clock in the morning so I was surprised when I picked my phone up and saw that it was my connect calling. I put a hand up and silenced my people.

"What's good? You got something for me?" I asked. He had been expecting a shipment of guns.

"Yeah, but it's not what we talked about the other day. It's much sweeter."

After a pause, he said, "You'll never believe who's sitting in my living room."

"Who?"

When he told me, I got quiet. I couldn't wrap my mind around it. "You're fucking with me right?" I said.

"No, I'm not. Hurry up, get some people over here fast. I'm going to keep his mind occupied until you get here but you can't kill him in my house, my daughter is here. I would do it for you but it's an unforgivable sin for a Muslim to kill another Muslim."

"It don't even matter," I chuckled as adrenaline shot through my body like a surge of electricity. "Just don't let that muhfucka leave!"

I hung up the phone and looked at my niggaz with a maniacal smile on my face. They all looked at me with puzzled expressions on their faces.

"Let's move," I said wearing a wicked grin as I grabbed my banger off of the coffee table. "CJ is about to hurt. We got his boy."

CJ

I awoke with a mad headache and an unsettled feeling in my gut and neither was because of the amount of liquor I had drank last night. Next to me Shy was sleeping like a baby; I had did it up big for her birthday and topped it all off with some boss sex.

I sat up on the side of the bed and looked around the suite that I had rented at the Hyatt Regency in New Brunswick. My team had the whole sixth floor. The digital clock on the nightstand read 7:34 A.M. We hadn't gone to bed until 4:30 A.M. so I hadn't slept long.

I grabbed my cell phone and checked to see if Rah had called or texted. "Fuck you at, dawg?" I said with deep concern when I saw that he hadn't called.

I dialed his number but was sent straight to voice mail. As alarm rose up from my gut to my chest I tried to convince myself that his battery had died or he had turned his phone off. I had never known either to have happened but I didn't want to think the worst.

I waited five minutes then tried to call again. "Answer your phone son." I tried to will it to happen.

When it didn't, I got the same feeling in my heart that I had gotten as I drove out to Tamika's house the day I found her dead. I ran a hand over my head and let out a long worried sigh. I had begun to worry when he didn't return to the party but I'd told myself that everything was gucci. Now I wasn't so sure.

I walked over to the wet bar and poured myself a drink. I tossed it back, and then poured another. When that one vanished too, I slammed the glass down on the counter and went in the bathroom to take a piss. When I returned Shy was sitting up in bed.

"What's wrong, baby?" she asked.

"I don't know where my nigga at. He still hasn't called and that's not like him."

"Why don't you call, Kenisha? He's probably over her house all between her *virgin* thighs."

I caught myself before I slapped a new hairstyle on her muhfuckin' head. I looked at her and gritted, "Do I look like I'm in the mood to play?"

"Sorry." Her eyes dropped to the floor.

"Lay yo ass back down, before you make me act the fuck up."

I sat in the lounge chair and tried Rah again but got the same result. I scrolled through my phone until I found Kenisha's number. I called her hoping she could tell me something. The phone rung three or four times then went to voice mail. I waited twenty minutes then called again.

As I heard her voice mail pick up for the second time, my mind began wondering all types of shit. I sent her a text, sat the phone down and walked across the room and stared out of the window into the cold winter skyline. Snow was fluttering down in huge flakes. The streets were quiet down below but if something had happened to my mans, my gun was about to make a whole lot of noise.

Shy came up behind me and put her arms around my waist. "Baby, do you want me to call the hospitals and the jails?"

"Yeah, do that," I said.

While Shy handled that, I summoned my team to my room.

Hours later, we still hadn't heard from Rah and the calls to the jails and the hospitals had been fruitless. Kenisha had finally answered her phone. Of course she had an attitude until I told her my concern. She said that she could remember getting in Rah's car and telling him to take her to her father's house, where she was still at, but she couldn't remember anything beyond that.

Frustrated, I questioned her relentlessly. Fed up with her stupid ass, I demanded to speak to her father. He could only tell me what time Rah left there from dropping Kenisha off.

"Would you mind looking outside to see if his truck is still out there?" I asked him.

"No problem," he said then put me on hold. A minute later he came back to the phone and told me that Rah's truck was not out there.

I didn't even thank him, I just hung up the phone and looked around at my team. Everyone had disturbed looks on their faces. Legend was outside on the balcony with no coat on. I didn't go out and say anything else to him because I understood his desire to be left alone.

The mood inside my suite was somber. We all suspected the worst. I put a call in to Cujo and asked him to find out if an unidentified body had turned up at the city morgue this morning. He promised to check into it and get back with me ASAP.

Just when I was getting ready to go on a mad hunt for my nigga, my phone rung with his number flashing on the screen. "This Rah calling now," I announced to my squad.

A relieved smile came on my face as I answered the phone. "Nigga where you been?" I asked.

"I been chilling, looking for your pussy ass," he said, but the voice didn't belong to Rah. "I got your boy here. He ain't in no condition to talk right now though."

"Nigga, if you touch him, I'm killing everything you love."

"You already did that. Now I'ma kill who you love the most. I'ma fuck with you when I figure out where I'ma put his body. Be easy yo."

The screen on my phone faded to black.

FORTY-TWO

NARD

I hung up on CJ feeling victorious. I could hear the strain in his voice. I looked over at Raheem with a high measure of respect, but no sympathy. He was in the corner, on the floor, with his hands duct taped behind his back and his ankles bound together by a thick chain that I had tightened with every hour that passed.

From the moment we snatched him up leaving out of David X's house, I had been torturing him, tryna get him to call CJ and set him up or tell me where the nigga lived.

"Just do that and I'ma let you go. I don't have no beef with you my dude," I'd told him when we got him to Big Nasty's crib.

Not only would he not sell his man out, he wouldn't even respond. He'd been beaten, mauled by Lil' Nasty, and he still refused to utter a single word.

I walked over and looked down at him, he had bite marks in his face, his hair was matted with blood and one of his eyes was swollen. I pulled my dick out and took a leak right in his face. When I was finished I zipped myself up and yawned.

"We can do this shit for days, yo," I said, shaking my head as Big Nasty led his pit over to us.

Lil' Nasty growled low and menacingly.

"I tell you what," I said, staring down at Raheem. "Just say anything, just one word and I'll ease up on you. 'Cause like I said, this ain't about you. Right now I just want the satisfaction of seeing you break."

I waited, but not a sound came from his lips, he just glared up at me out of his one eye that wasn't swollen shut. "C'mon dawg, you can't be that hard," I appealed.

Still nothing.

I looked at Big Nasty and nodded my head. He gave the command and Lil' Nasty lunged forward and locked his teeth in Raheem's leg. I waited to hear him howl or wince or something, but he just gritted his teeth and endured the pain.

Have it your way, I said as I took a seat and watched the show.

RAHEEM

The dog had a death lock on my calf and he was shaking my leg like a piece of raw meat. An excruciating pain shot through my entire body. I gritted my teeth but refused to utter a sound. My face was coated with blood, sweat, and urine that ran down in my eyes, one of which I could not see out of.

I squeezed my eye shut as they began to burn terribly. My head felt as big as a basketball and I was certain that one of my ribs was broken; every breath I took was laborious and painful.

The dog locked tighter and drug me across the floor. "Break," I heard Big Nasty command.

I gnashed my teeth together tighter and prepared to feel my leg snap but the dog released its grip and went and kneeled at Big Nasty's side.

"That's enough for now," Nard said from the seat he had taken.

Through my blurred vision I saw them huddle up, talking in whispers. I didn't know how long it would be before they put a bullet in my head and ended my suffering but if they planned on leaving me alive until I folded, I was going to live forever.

There was no way the last breath I took was going to be through the lungs of a broken man.

Me, set up CJ? The world would end before I'd do that. I had already accepted that I was gonna die, Nard may have controlled when and how but I controlled how I would *not*.

The murmurings suddenly stopped and Nard walked back over to where I lay and looked down at me. "You 'bout this life. I respect that, but I'ma kill you anyway, he declared."

He pulled out and slammed a bullet in the chamber of his ratchet.

"CJ wouldn't have died for you," he said, and leveled the gun down at my head.

Ca$h

FORTY-THREE

CJ

I stood amongst my mans in the center of the warehouse; this had been headquarters for the past 48 hours, ever since I had gotten the call from Nard. As I prepared to send them on bloody missions with instructions to spare no one—man, woman nor child—another picture message popped up on my phone. I didn't want to open it because I knew what it would be. Nard had been sending them every few hours.

In spite of what I knew I would see, I opened up the message anyway. Rah looked in worse shape as each picture arrived. His whole face was bloody and swollen, his clothes were ripped and torn, and he was curled up on the floor. My nostrils flared in and out, and my eyes burned with regret. I should have never allowed him to come back home and involve himself in this beef of mine!

Fuck I do that for?

I looked at the picture closely. "He's not dead yet," I said optimistically as I passed my phone around for everyone's opinion. By the time it got back to me we were all in agreement.

"Those pussy muthafuckaz are torturing my nigga," I said bitterly as part of his pain coursed through my veins. "We gotta find them. Or snatch up somebody Nard loves." I looked into the eyes of my crew in search for answers.

"We been looking. I found somebody that knew where he moved his mother to in Philly. I sent a team of five down there to bring the bitch back in the trunk but she's ghost," reported Eric.

"What about his spots? Did y'all hit them? Snatch up some of them niggaz and kill anyone that don't have the information we want." I was seething. I looked from man to man wondering why the fuck nobody was doing anything.

Reluctantly, Snoop said, "We sent teams to every one of his traps that we know about, I went by three of them myself, they're all closed down and nobody has seen any of his runners. I think he anticipated us and pulled his people off the streets."

"Fuck!" I kicked over some boxes and slammed a chair against the wall. "I don't wanna hear none of that shit!" I growled. "I want some muthafuckaz laying out in the streets. Y'all better bring me some goddamn bodies." I snatched my banger off of my waist and glared around the circle. "This muthafucka shittin' on us! He killing our best. That nigga got our brother. Y'all gotta make them muthafuckaz suffer!" I yelled and my voice hit the walls and bounced back hard into the ears of my men.

All eyes held mine and no one flinched or bitched up, which reminded me that these were my niggaz and they were ready to ride for my number one.

I put my tool back in my waist and let out an exasperated sigh. My mind was all the way fucked up. I would've rather it had been me than Rah, that's how strong my love for him was.

"Tell us who to kill and we're on it," said Premo.

His words settled in my ears but nothing came back. I leaned up against my desk with desperate eyes staring back at me and for the first time, I felt helpless. I didn't know what to do, I had let Nard outsmart me and that shit was about to cost Rah his life. He had tried to talk me out of throwing Shy a birthday party but I had allowed my arrogance to rule over sound judgment once again. *"Fuck Nard, I'm not letting that nigga force me in a hole,"* I had said. Hearing my words replay in my mind made me sick to my stomach.

I had thrown the party to placate Shy. I shook my head at my own stupid ass mistake.

I looked up and my mans were standing there waiting for my word. "Everybody just fall back for a minute and let me think this shit out. They haven't killed Rah yet so there's gotta be a reason," I surmised.

Eric, Snoop and Premo took seats on crates and talked amongst themselves. Legend walked outside to clear his head. I went to the office to strategize alone and to call Shy and make sure shit was good with her because it was real bad with me.

Inside the office, I rested my head on the desk and tried to come up with the best move. Cujo had called earlier and asked if I wanted him to put out a Missing Person report. "Fuck no," I had flat out rejected his offer. What he was asking me to do was snitch because Rah wasn't missing, we knew who had him.

Another picture messaged popped up on my phone. This time I didn't open it. A few minutes later a text came.

Ya boy got mad luv 4 u. Do u got luv 4 him?

Nard was tryna toy with me but I wasn't about to let him play with me like that. I texted him back.

Suck my dick!

I waited to see how he would respond but he didn't reply at all. That made me fear that he had killed my nigga. I closed my eyes and tried to fight back the tears of deep remorse that pushed to come out. We had come up from the cradle together. There wasn't a more loyal nigga on the planet. *Damn I should've listened to him! Fuck I have that party for?*

It was ironic that Shy called at the very moment the thought ran through my mind. "Hello," I answered in a real hostile tone.

"Have y'all heard anything?" she inquired.

"Nah."

"Well, okay. I know you're really worried and have a lot going on but I was just checking on you. Have you eaten anything?" she asked timidly.

I hadn't and since she was still at the Hyatt in New Brunswick, I told her to bring food for the crew. They probably hadn't eaten either.

Two hours later Shy arrived with bags of White Castle. We sat in the warehouse with my mans as they attacked the food. I couldn't eat, I only had an appetite for destruction.

I looked around the room to make sure that every man was straight and accounted for and noticed Legend was missing. When I asked where he had gone, nobody knew.

I was pissed the fuck off. Nobody was supposed to move alone. "Why didn't one of y'all ride with him? Nard snatching muthafuckaz up and y'all letting him leave this bitch dolo?" I railed.

I got up, walked back to my office and slammed the door. I angrily swept everything off of my desk and onto to floor. Then, I walked over to the door that led out back and kicked it with my foot. I told myself that the next time I lifted it, it was gonna be to kick some ass.

Breathing hard, I walked behind my desk and flopped down heavily in the chair. Seconds later there was a knock at the door. "Fuck you knocking for? Bring your ass on in," I snapped, figuring it was Shy.

The door opened with a squeak.

Legend stepped in with a psychopathic look on his face. His mouth was twisted and his eyes were like red hot coals. He held a tennis bag in one hand and a bloody machete in the other.

He took three steps and was standing in front of my desk. I looked down and noticed blood seeping through the bag. He dropped the machete on the floor and dumped the contents on my desk.

"This shit happened through this muthafucka'z hands so I brought them to you," he snarled.

A pair of hands that had been chopped off at the wrists lay in front of me leaking blood all over the desk. My eyes moved from the pair of black and bloody hands to Legend's cold black eyes.

"Those belonged to Jamaican Black, he don't need 'em no more," said Legend calmly. "On my life I will not rest until you have a trophy of each of them niggas at your feet." He turned and walked out.

"This is how you turn up," I exhorted the rest of my squad as I walked around my desk with one of Jamaican Black's hands, waving it as I talked. Everyone stood in my office staring. "We gotta go ham around this muhfucka. I don't give a fuck about the consequences. Any fuckin' body can get it." Heat was pumping through my body causing my trigger finger to jump, I was ready to kill.

A light knock on the door interrupted me. "Come in," I said.

Shy stuck her head in.

"Sup?" I asked.

"Baby, if it's okay with you I'm going to go home."

I walked from behind the desk and hugged her. "Yeah, you good," I said, holding her tightly.

"Okay, baby, I hope things work out."

"Thanks." I kissed her lips then pulled back looking in her eyes.

She turned to leave and my tool came out in a blur. Boc! Boc! Brains, blood, and bits of skull flew out of her wig, her body lurched forward and she crashed to the floor on her pretty ass face.

I looked back at my mans who was all looking at me with gapping mouths and confused expressions on their faces. I pointed my gun in her direction ready to fill her with something else lethal. "I told y'all anybody can get it. If it wouldn't been her birthday I never would've had that party for her and my nigga would still be safe. Fuck that bitch, he never trusted her anyway."

I looked at Snoop and said, "Dispose of that rat before it starts stinking."

NARD

"You hungry, homie?" I held the sub out to Raheem. We had lifted him up on the couch.

He didn't respond. I had given up on making him talk. I took the sandwich and mashed it in his face. "You might really be hard but hard muhfuckaz die too, they just die slower," I taunted.

I looked at Big Nasty. "Take him out to the van, I'm tired of playing this game. It ain't even fun no more."

I put on my coat and prepared to leave. The plan was to take him to a location that we had picked, douse him with kerosene, and burn him alive. I had already told him exactly what awaited him but he still hadn't folded. I couldn't do nothing but respect that nigga'z gangsta and hope that if I was ever in his shoes I could stand that strong.

Really I hated to kill him but he had chosen the wrong team. I was convinced that CJ didn't have the same love for Raheem as Raheem had for him. But he would never know because his time was shorter than a mosquito's dick.

I watched Big Nasty lift him up like it was nothing. As he carried him toward the stairs a thought suddenly came to mind. There was only one way to find out if CJ was a real nigga. I would call and offer him a life for a life.

His life for his mans'.

CJ

I listened without saying a word as Nard made his offer. When I hung up the phone my squad wanted to know what he had said. "That pussy nigga didn't want nothin', he was just talking noise," I downplayed.

"Is Rah still alive?" asked Legend.

"I think so," I answered truthfully because I honestly didn't know.

After I sidestepped most of their questions I got up and walked from behind my desk and gave them each a gangsta hug. "I love y'all niggaz until the death of me. Believe that."

They all looked at me with wonderment in their eyes but probably attributed the sudden declaration to what was going on with Rah. I grabbed Eric and locked fists with him for a long time.

"Lil' bruh, I love you. I taught you the best I could. If I taught you anything wrong, blame it on my mind not my heart. Nah mean?" I said.

"Say dat," he agreed.

"Know dat," I reaffirmed. "Now y'all niggaz get out of my office, I need to think."

They filed out one by one. Eric was the last to leave. He got to the door and turned to ask, "You gucci?"

"Yeah, I'm good. I'm just mentally drained yo."

When they were all gone out front, I locked the office door and slipped out the back.

FORTY-FOUR

NARD

I stood inside a gutted out apartment in Little Bricks looking out the window. The projects were closed down and tall fences surrounded them. But that hadn't kept us from entering. Raheem was in a corner being watched over by Man Dog. The rest of my team along with two dozen souljahs were posted up outside on the sides of buildings with mad artillery ready to air the block out if CJ didn't arrive alone.

I glanced at my watch, CJ had five more minutes to show up or Rah was gonna leave this muhfucka unceremoniously. I didn't expect CJ to show up because I didn't respect his G. He was way too selfish to sacrifice his life for his mans.

CJ

As I turned into Little Bricks where Nard told me he would be, I had already prepared myself to die. That's the sacrifice I would make for my nigga because I was the one that had put him in this fucked up position. I knew that there was no guarantee that they would let him go after they killed me but that was a chance I was willing to take because they were gonna kill him for sure had I refused to come.

The way I saw it was if they killed Rah I might as well be dead too. Tamika was already gone and now my nigga? Fuck I had to live for? All of the money in the world couldn't take their place. Eric would be a'ight, I had taught him well, and I knew that Nard would die in these streets soon after me because my niggaz would never rest until his blood was on their shoes.

Ca$h

As I turned into the street where Nard was supposed to be, I saw niggaz posted up with AK-47s everywhere. I parked my car and got out without fear. Snow came down from the sky and melted at my feet. I looked around but didn't see Nard.

I stood next to the car and took a few deep breaths. I placed two fingers at my chest then kissed them before I shot them up to the heavens. I gave my baby the last of my tenderness. "Tamika, I'll see you soon," I said aloud before I faced my executioners.

I put a cupped hand to my mouth and yelled, "I'm here! Where you at, pussy boy?"

NARD

My eyes lit up with disbelief. CJ had shown up! I walked over and looked down at Raheem. "I guess he do got love for you," I said.

His expression didn't change.

"Stand him up," I told Man Dog.

Raheem was weak and his leg was swollen so we had to half walk/half carry him. Man Dog stopped at the doorway and posted up, I continued outside using Raheem as a shield though I had on a bulletproof vest.

CJ stood in the middle of the street about twenty feet away from where I stopped. The street was deserted except for the two of us and my goons. I saw the tool down by his side but if he lifted his arm to shoot, my gunners were gonna Swiss cheese his ass. Besides, he would have to blow a hole through his man to shoot me.

I looked over Rah's shoulder and smiled mockingly at CJ.

"Let him go," he sneered.

"Nah it ain't gonna be that easy, blood. I'ma find out how low your nuts hang." I slid my strap out and held it down at my side.

268

"They hang to the muhfuckin' ground nigga, you see I'm here. I ain't scared to die."

"We'll see," I said.

CJ

"You'll see? Nigga, you can see right now." I ripped my shirt off and pounded my chest with my fist. "I'm the muhfuckin' best that ever did it."

"You can't be the best when there's only one of me," he slung back.

"Young boy, you a Cam'ron wannabe. Fuck you saying? How are you the best hiding behind the next nigga? Let him go and let's play with these tools. Just you and me. Show me how low your little ass nuts hang," I tested his manhood in front of his whole bitch ass crew.

He placed his gun against Rah's leg and shot him. My gun came up automatically but I hesitated because he had pulled Rah back up and was ducked behind him.

I eased off of the trigger.

Out the corner of my eye I saw several assault rifles trained on me.

"Don't shoot him!" Nard yelled and they lowered their aim.

"Fuck you wanna do? Stand here all day tryna build up the courage to kill me?" I spat.

He smirked. "I'm not gon' kill you, I'ma make you murk yourself. If you love your man and want me to let him go, eat your gun, bitch ass nigga. Take yourself out of the game."

"What? Young, little ass boy you must think I'm pussy?" I unzipped my pants and pulled my wood out. "It's all hard dick over here." I took a piss in his direction. "This is what I think about you and your bitch ass crew."

"You think I'm playin' with you?" He yelled out and then shot Rah again. Blood ran from his body into the fresh white snow. I saw the pain all over Raheem's face. I raised my gun preparing to kill then be killed.

"Kill this nigga, yo," I heard Raheem mumble.

"Him or you? Eat that gun nigga before I release all your man's brains over *here*," he capped, pressing his heat at Rah's head.

"Let him go. He served his purpose. This shit is between me and you."

"Do it. Pull the trigga," he yelled back, ducking behind Raheem.

Visions of how dirty Nard did Tamika ran through my mind, he had taken my heart and the last thing I was going to do was watch as he stole my soul. Just when I had decided to run up on this nigga and try to kill him, Raheem's words flashed in my mind. *We gonna die side by side.*

"You think you're saying something? Huh? Huh?" I flailed my arms and began a light bounce on my feet as if I was amped for something to jump off. "You ain't saying shit! I'm G'd up 'til my feet up. I'll die for my nigga, can you say that? Pussy ass boy." Spit flew out of my mouth and my voice echoed off the abandoned buildings. I stuck my Nine in my mouth, way up to the roof, and showed him that my nuts really did hang to the ground.

NARD

The single gunshot sounded as loud as a clap of thunder. Blood and brain matter sprayed out the top of CJ's head and his body crumpled to the ground. Rah tried to fight but his hands were tied behind his back, his ankles were shackled, his head was cracked open to the skull, and he had two slugs in him. He slipped out of my hands and fell to the cold ground.

Man Dog came out and stood over CJ.

Blocka! Blocka!

He pumped two shots in CJ's body. Zakee, Quent and Big Nasty stood in line waiting their turn. When they each had pumped bullets in his corpse I delivered the coup de grace. I walked over to where he lay dead and drug his body over to a dumpster. Big Nasty came over and helped me hoist him up and throw him in the garbage can just like him and Tamika had done to my unborn.

"It's over dawg. You're the new king." Big Nasty raised my arm in victory.

I looked up and down the street at my people standing in the middle of the projects that had bred us. They were closed down now but we represented their legacy. I had proven that our team was the strongest. "We own The Bricks!" I declared boisterously.

My niggaz applauded.

When the applause died down, I rounded them up and we prepared to go.

"What do you wanna do with Raheem?" Man Dog asked, breathing heavy smoke into the cold air.

I walked over to where Raheem laid in the streets. I stood over him with my gun pointed down at his head. Tears ran down his face but I felt no pity.

"Do that nigga, bruh," urged Man Dog.

My trigger finger itched but I didn't wanna just blow a hole in his head, I wanted my signature on this kill. I contemplated a way to make a statement. It hit me instantaneously.

"He thinks he hard, let him lay here and die in the same streets he couldn't leave alone. Or maybe he can crawl over there and climb in the dumpster and die with his man."

Man Dog laughed. "You a cold muthafucka," he acknowledged as my whole team moved out, leaving Rah to die slowly.

RAHEEM

When the whistling of the winds and screeching tires were the only sounds I heard, I knew that Nard was gone. I also knew that if I made it out alive, Nard would learn the price of making such a grave mistake. There was no way I would allow us both to breathe. If I had to ascend to the top of the drug game in order to crush Nard and everyone associated with him, that's what I would do. But first I had to make it. I was determined not to die. I had to live to avenge my brotha's death but the cold that evaded my body was more than that of winter's relentless chills.

Death was on its way to claim me but I was determined not to go. I took a deep breath and willed myself to crawl but my legs wouldn't cooperate and everything went dark.

To Be Continued...
. Thugs Cry 3
Coming Soon

About The Author:

Cash was born and raised in Cleveland, Ohio, but lived most of his life in Atlanta, Georgia. He decided to start writing fiction while incarcerated at a state prison in Georgia. His style is street, raw and uncut. He has an imagination that's in overdrive. Cash is presently in his 24th year of incarceration, but he remains strong and strives to teach through the power of his pen.

"I write what has been termed 'fictional realism'. I give it to my readers just like it goes down in everyday life. I feel a responsibility to keep it one hundred. There is nothing glamorous about the streets. I don't write fairy-tales. I write with a message. Therefore, sometimes you'll need a box of tissue when you read my novels," he says without apology.

"Other times, I'll make you rejoice over the way certain characters persevere. But you'll never be left feeling indifferent toward my books," he promises.

From within his cell, he writes to change his legacy to one that his loved ones can be proud of. "I want them to know that my desire to rise above the present circumstances cannot be suffocated."

"A shout-out to my readers: You keep me motivated. I look forward to the day I can meet you all in person. Much love"

BOOKS BY LDP'S CEO, CA$H

TRUST NO MAN

TRUST NO MAN 2

TRUST NO MAN 3

BONDED BY BLOOD

SHORTY GOT A THUG

A DIRTY SOUTH LOVE

THUGS CRY

THUGS CRY 2

TRUST NO BITCH

TRUST NO BITCH 2

TRUST NO BITCH 3

TIL MY CASKET DROPS

Coming Soon

TRUST NO BITCH (KIAM EYEZ' STORY)

THUGS CRY 3

BONDED BY BLOOD 2

RESTRANING ORDER

Thugs Cry 2

275

Ca$h

By **Aryanna**

Available Now

LOVE KNOWS NO BOUNDARIES **I II & III**

By **Coffee**

SILVER PLATTER HOE **I & II**

HONEY DIPP **I & II**

CLOSED LEGS DON'T GET FED **I & II**

A BITCH NAMED KARMA

By **Reds Johnson**

A DANGEROUS LOVE **I, II, III, IV, V, VI**

By **J Peach**

CUM FOR ME

An **LDP Erotica Collaboration**

THE KING CARTEL **I & II**

By **Frank Gresham**

BLOOD OF A BOSS **I & II**

By **Askari**

THE DEVIL WEARS TIMBS

BURY ME A G **I II & III**

By **Tranay Adams**

THESE NIGGAS AIN'T LOYAL **I & II**

By **Nikki Tee**

THE STREETS BLEED MURDER

By **Jerry Jackson**

Thugs Cry 2

DIRTY LICKS
By **Peter Mack**
THE ULTIMATE BETRAYAL
By **Phoenix**
BROOKLYN ON LOCK
By **Sonovia Alexander**
SLEEPING IN HEAVEN, WAKING IN HELL **I, II & III**
By **Forever Redd**
THE DEVIL WEARS TIMBS **I, II & III**
By **Tranay Adams**
DON'T FU#K WITH MY HEART **I & II**
By **Linnea**
BOSS'N UP **I & II**
By **Royal Nicole**
LOYALTY IS BLIND
By **Kenneth Chisholm**

Ca$h

Thugs Cry 2

Ca$h